Galileo Galilei, Mary Allan-Olney, Maria Celeste Galilei

The Private Life of Galileo

Galileo Galilei, Mary Allan-Olney, Maria Celeste Galilei

The Private Life of Galileo

ISBN/EAN: 9783337332532

Printed in Europe, USA, Canada, Australia, Japan

Cover: Foto ©Andreas Hilbeck / pixelio.de

More available books at **www.hansebooks.com**

THE PRIVATE

LIFE OF GALILEO.

COMPILED PRINCIPALLY FROM HIS CORRESPONDENCE
AND THAT OF HIS ELDEST DAUGHTER,

SISTER MARIA CELESTE,

NUN IN THE FRANCISCAN CONVENT OF ST. MATTHEW, IN ARCETRI.

BOSTON:
NICHOLS AND NOYES.
1870.

PREFACE.

THE authorities which have been principally relied on in compiling the following work are: "Le Opere complete di Galileo Galilei," edited (1842–56) by Professor Eugo Albèri, from the Galileian manuscripts and correspondence preserved in the Palatine Library at Florence; "La Primogenita di Galileo Galilei (1864)," by Professor Carlo Arduini, containing one hundred and twenty-one letters (also preserved in the Palatine Library) addressed to Galileo by his eldest daughter, the Franciscan nun Maria Celeste, eighty-seven of which were first edited by Professor Arduini; and "Galilée, son Procès, sa Condamnation," published by M. Henri de l'Epinois in the "Revue des Questions Historiques (1867)." This last-named work supplies, what had hitherto been wanting, a mass of details concerning Galileo's trial, all of the highest interest, extracted by M. de l'Epinois from the original trial papers now in the archives of the Vatican. It has been the endeavor of the compiler to place before the reader a plain, ungarbled statement of facts; and as a means to this end, to allow Galileo, his friends, and his judges to speak for themselves as far as possible.

October 31st, 1869.

CONTENTS.

CHAPTER IV.

CHAPTER V.

CHAPTER VI.

CHAPTER VII.

CHAPTER VIII.

CHAPTER IX.

PRIVATE LIFE OF GALILEO.

CHAPTER I.

Galileo's Birth. — Family. — Early Education. — Studies at Pisa. — Opposition. — Hydrostatic Balance. — Lecturer at Pisa. — Departure to Padua. — Correspondence with Kepler. — Early Writings. — Geometrical and Military Compass. — Distinguished Friends and Pupils. — Sagredo. — Augmentation of Stipend.

GALILEO, eldest son of Vincenzio de' Bonajuti de' Galilei, a Florentine noble, and his wife Giulia Ammannati, was born at Pisa on the 18th of *Galileo's birth and parentage.* February, 1564. The original family surname of Bonajuti had been changed to that of Galilei at the end of the fourteenth or beginning of the fifteenth century, for the purpose, it would appear, of perpetuating the name of a member of the family, Galileo, a son of Tommaso de' Bonajuti, who was one of the Twelve in 1343. A grandson of Tommaso, also named Galileo, was a celebrated physician in 1438, at which period the Republic sent him to Piombino to undertake the cure of its ward, the young Giovanni d' Appiano, Lord of Piombino. He was for some time lecturer on medicine at the University of Florence, was twice elected member of the Priori, and in 1445 filled the office of gonfalonier. He was buried honorably in the church of Santa Croce, where his tomb, a slab of marble with a full-length figure in bas-relief, may yet be seen in the nave near the en-trance.   His great-grand-nephew, Vincenzio

Galileo's father.

Galilei, was a man of considerable talent, well versed in mathematics, and the author of several works on counterpoint, of which some have been published, while others are preserved in the Palatine Library among the manuscripts of authors anterior to Galileo.[1]   A passage in his " Dialogue on Ancient and Modern Music "[2] deserves to be noted, as affording a clew to the manner in which he directed his son's education.   " It appears to me," says one of the speakers in the " Dialogue," " that they who in proof of any assertion rely simply on the weight of authority, without adducing any argument in support of it, act very absurdly.   I, on the contrary, wish to be allowed freely to question and freely to answer you without any sort of adulation, as well becomes those who are truly in search of truth."   Sentiments such as these are clearly expressed in Galileo's writings, particularly in his famous letter to the Grand Duchess Christina on the Copernican System, and in the no less famous " Dialogue on the Two Systems of the World."

Though of an ancient and noble stock, Vincenzio Galilei appears to have been always in straitened circumstances.   Gherardini says that he had intended

---

[1] In one of these, entitled *Della Pratica del Moderno Contrappunto*, is inserted a short letter of Galileo's, written while he was professor of mathematics at Pisa, in 1590, and the blank side of which Vincenzio Galilei used to continue his manuscript. (See page 10.)

[2] Published in 1581.

his son to become a trader in wool, and was only deterred from this purpose by the hope that *Early indications of talent.* the talent evinced by Galileo at an early age would, in the long run, fit him for higher pursuits. For some time, however, Vincenzio was unable to provide the boy with such instruction as appeared in those days most desirable. There were no teachers of repute at Florence, and he could not afford to maintain Galileo at Pisa, where the best professors in Tuscany were to be found. Such instruction as could be had Galileo was eager to profit by. From his father, who was an exquisite performer on the lute, he learnt both the theory and practice of music with such success that he is said to have excelled him in charm of style and delicacy of touch. He was taught by his father to play on the organ and on other instruments ; but the lute was his favorite instrument. He found it a pleasure in youth, and a solace in the last days of his life, when blindness was added to his other sorrows.

In the sister art his talent was equally great. He used in later life to tell his friends that, had circumstances permitted him to choose his own profession, he would without hesitation have elected to *Love of painting.* become a painter. So well known was his talent both as a draughtsman and colorist, that such painters as Cigoli, Bronzino, Passignano, and Jacopo da Empoli, did not think it derogatory to their dignity to invite his criticism and abide by his judgment. Cigoli in particular, who was considered by Galileo to be the greatest painter of his time, was wont to say that Galileo alone had been his instructor in the art of perspective, and that whatever eminence he enjoyed as a painter was owing to him.

From a letter of Diego Franchi, a Benedictine of Vallombrosa, we learn that Galileo was an inmate of this monastery during his early youth, that he was taught logic by one of the monks, and that his father took him away before the termination of his novitiate, alleging, as a reason, that the boy was suffering from ophthalmia.

At the age of seventeen and a half, Galileo, already well versed in Latin and Greek, an excellent artist, *Studies medicine at Pisa.* and an accomplished musician, was sent to study medicine at the University of Pisa. Even then the step was not taken without difficulty, in consequence of his father's extreme poverty. But seeing that his own musical taste and erudition had been of no pecuniary advantage to him, Vincenzio Galilei thought that probably his son would be more likely to make a fortune in the practice of medicine than in that of either of the fine arts. Young Galileo was therefore placed as a boarder in the house of a relative who was settled in trade, and for three or four years followed the usual course in medicine and philosophy ; in the latter, we are told, not to the satisfaction of his teachers, owing to that habit already learned from his father of examining an assertion to see what it was worth, instead of relying on the weight of authority for authority's sake. In consequence of this habit he gained the unfortunate reputation among the professors of being imbued with the spirit of contradiction. His eager and constant study of Aristotle, Plato, and other ancient authors found no favor in their eyes. To their narrow ideas, a philosopher only needed to know Aristotle by heart; to understand him was a secondary consideration ; to contradict, a blasphemy.[1]

[1] As an example of the strong spirit of conservatism which

Galileo both understood and contradicted; and thus arose a feeling of hostility toward him, which at length passed into what may be termed a traditionary dislike, scarcely extinguished after a long lapse of years, nor even then so spent but that it again became active as soon as Galileo was assailed by adverse fortune.

The connection of the great bronze lamp in the nave of the cathedral at Pisa with Galileo's earliest mechanical discovery is well known. Viviani says that having observed the unerring regularity of the oscillations of this lamp and of other swing- *Discovery of the pendulum.* ing bodies, the idea occurred to him that an instrument might be constructed on this principle, which should mark with accuracy the rate and variation of the pulse. Such an instrument he constructed, after a long series of careful experiments. This invention, though imperfect, was hailed with wonder and delight by the physicians of the day, and was soon taken into general use, under the name of *Pulsilogia.* *pulsilogia.*

At the time of which we are speaking, the study of mathematics was completely neglected in Italy. In vain had Comandino and Mau- *Mathematics neglected in Italy.* rolico endeavored to rescue the despised science from its unworthy obscurity; the names of Euclid and Archimedes were but empty sound to the mass of students who daily thronged the academical halls

reigned at Pisa, a passage in Castelli's letter to Galileo, written in November, 1613, may be cited: "Of our controversies (on Galileo's opinion in favor of the earth's motion) *nec verbum quidem*, a thing which astonishes me. Your marvelous discoveries are scarcely known here even by name."

of Bologna, the ancient and the free, of Pisa, and even of learned Padua. Galileo's father, undervaluing a science in which we are assured he was well versed, considered that the time spent in the study of mathematics would be so much time wasted in the case of one who was destined to the medical profession. He not only abstained from teaching Galileo what he himself knew, but endeavored to prevent his obtaining knowledge from other sources, assuring him that it would be time enough to enter upon such a new pursuit when his medical studies were finished. But Galileo was not to be thus put off. A certain Messer Ostilio Ricci, who occupied the post of tutor to the pages of the Grand Ducal Court, was in the *Galileo's se-* habit of daily frequenting his father's house. *cret studies.* Unknown to his father, Galileo appplied to him for instruction. Ricci, pleased at the youth's anxiety to learn, spoke to Vincenzio Galilei, advising him not to combat what was evidently the natural bent of his son's mind. His advice so far took effect, that Vincenzio consented ; but Ricci was required to give his instruction clandestinely, lest Galileo should consider the paternal acquiescence an excuse for neglecting his medical studies. Finding, however, that his fears were soon verified, Vincenzio, after remonstrating in vain with his son, desired Ricci to discontinue his lessons. This was accordingly done ; but by this time Galileo was able to dispense with a teacher. With Ricci, he had not advanced so far as the end of the first book of Euclid. He proceeded secretly, wishing to attain at least as far as the forty-seventh proposition, then considered a famous one. So much being reached, he continued to study Euclid until he had got to the end of the sixth book, when he entreated his father to cease from prohibiting a pursuit which gave him such infinite delight. Convinced at length, not only by the fact of the boy's secret studies, but by the rare facility with which he invented various new problems, that in truth his son was a born mathematician, Vincenzio Galilei withdrew his opposition, and from that time abandoned all hope of Galileo making his fortune in the practice of medicine.

It was in 1586, while studying the works of Archimedes, that Galileo composed his first essay, *Galileo's first essay.* on the Hydrostatic Balance.[1] He also made some observations on the combination of metals, which, as well as the essay, were distributed in manuscript amongst his friends. He had already the reputation of being a bold and fearless inquirer. Some of his geometrical and mechanical speculations had been communicated to the Marquis Guidubaldo di Montebaroccio, a celebrated mathematician,[2] a member of the noble family of Del Monte, then residing at Pesaro. Struck by the marks of genius displayed in these speculations, Guidubaldo commenced *Correspondence with Guidubaldo.* a scientific correspondence with their author, which laid the foundation of a close friendship. At the suggestion of the Marquis, Galileo, then in his twenty-fourth year, applied himself to consider the position of the centre of gravity in solid bodies, a subject on which Comandino had already written. His observations were embodied in an essay,[3] *Essay on th. centre of gravity.* which, though full of merit, was not printed

---

[1] First published in 1615.

[2] He was a disciple of Comandino.

[3] *Theoremata circa Centrum Gravitatis Solidarum.* It was

till fifty years later. During the writing of this essay, Galileo, with that modesty which ever accompanies true genius, more than once submitted his manuscript to the Marquis for correction. He also corresponded on the subject with Clavio, a learned Jesuit,[1] whose acquaintance he had made on his first visit to Rome, in or about the year 1587. The earliest letter of Galileo which is known to be extant is one in which he frankly states a difficulty which had arisen respecting the demonstration of a certain lemma; those to whom he had already submitted it were not *Correspondence with Father Clavio.* satisfied, therefore he himself could not feel satisfied, though he had diligently sought for some better method of demonstrating the lemma, but in vain. In this dilemma, he earnestly asks the Father's opinion, declaring that, if it was unfavorable, he should not rest till he had found such a demonstration as would be satisfactory to him.[2]

Viviani says that Guidubaldo, to show his satisfaction at the manner in which Galileo had treated the subject he had suggested, took an early opportunity of introducing him to the notice of Ferdinand I., the

published as an appendix to the fourth conversation in the *Dialogues on Motion*, or *delle Nuova Scienze*, in 1638. It is said that Galileo proposed to Luca Valerio to publish it along with the work of the latter, *De Centro Gravitatis Solidarum;* which, however, was not done.

[1] Cristoforo Clavio was one of the most learned mathematicians of his time. The reform of the calendar was mainly due to him. He wrote various works on mathematics; died at Rome in 1612.

[2] Luca Valerio, with whom Galileo began a correspondence about 1609, declared that Galileo's genius was not inferior to that of Archimedes. This was indeed no slight praise from a man so justly celebrated as Valerio.

reigning Grand Duke, and Don Giovanni, natural
son of Cosmo de' Medici. He adds that Galileo was
soon admitted to the intimacy of both these illustrious
personages, and that the Grand Duke, to mark his
sense of Galileo's merit, appointed him, unsolicited,[1]
to the mathematical chair at Pisa as soon as a vacancy
occurred. Had the Grand Duke done so, it would
have been as great an honor to himself as to Galileo.
That the professorship was only obtained *Difficulty in*
after much solicitation, is evident on a peru- *obtaining
his profes-*
sal of Galileo's letter of the 16th of July, *sorship.*
1588, in which he begs the Marquis Guidubaldo to intercede in his favor with the Grand Duke, to obtain,
if possible, the revival of the mathematical professorship of Florence, as he despaired of ever getting that
of Pisa.[2] By the joint representations of the Marquis
and his brother, Cardinal Francesco Maria del Monte,
the professorship at Pisa was awarded to him the year
after, though with no better stipend than sixty crowns[3]

[1] *Di proprio moto.*

[2] "My wish regarding Pisa, about which I wrote your lordship, will not be carried out; for I hear that a certain monk,
who lectured there formerly, and then, on being made general
of his order, gave it up, has resigned the generalship, and has
taken to lecturing again; and that his Highness has already
appointed him to be lecturer. But as here in Florence there
was in times past a professorship of mathematics, instituted by
Grand Duke Cosmo, which many among the nobles would willingly see revived, I have petitioned for it, and hope to obtain
it through your illustrious brother's interest, to whom I have
intrusted my petition. As there have been foreigners here with
whom his Highness has been engaged, I have not been able to
speak on the subject myself, and therefore beg you to write again
and mention my name."

[3] Sixty crowns, or *scudi* Tuscan, per annum is about 10*d.* per
diem.

yearly, which was probably thought sufficient for a mathematician of barely twenty-six years of age.[1] Galileo was at this period already a member of the *Baccio Valori, President of the Accademia della Crusca.* Academy of Florence. In 1587 or 1588 he had been chosen by the President, Baccio Valori, to lecture on the" Inferno" of Dante, a fact which shows that even at that early age his reputation as a literary connoisseur must have at least equaled, if not exceeded, his reputation as a bold mathematician ; since Baccio Valori was an ardent admirer of Dante,[2] and would naturally make choice of the most competent member of the society to discourse on a poem which for grandeur and difficulty of elucidation knows no equal.

During the time Galileo remained at Pisa, the only friend he had among the professors was Jacopo Mazzoni, a man of vast erudition and enlightened views, who had been appointed to the chair of philosophy the year before Galileo's own appointment took place. With this notable exception, the whole body of professors was hostile to him. They, as well as the heads of the University, were stanch Aristotelians. They had not forgotten the boy's refusal to be silenced by

---

[1] It is asserted, on the faith of a short letter from Galileo to his father, written November 15th, 1590, that he endeavored to eke out his scanty stipend by practicing as a physician. This letter refers to the works of Galen, of which he says he only requires seven volumes. It exists in Vincenzio Galilei's unpublished MS. *Della Pratica del Moderno Contrappunto ;* he having used the blank side of his son's letter to continue his MS.

[2] These lectures are two in number. The manuscript was, till within the last few years, in the Valori Library, the owner of which was unconscious of possessing such a treasure. They are entitled *On the Site and Measure of the Inferno of Dante.*

a text of Aristotle; they could not forgive the man who, daring to see and think for himself, sacrilegiously put Aristotle to the test and found him wanting. It is true that this had been done before by Nizzoli, Benedetto, and Leonardo da Vinci;[1] but Galileo was the first who taught the contrary opinion publicly and persistently. These men had written, had said their say, and had satisfied their consciences. Galileo, not content with seeing and knowing himself, would have all Pisa see and know too. From the top of the Leaning Tower of Pisa a blow was struck at the Aristotelian philosophy from which it never recovered. Galileo might have written and lectured against Aristotle's theory of motion with impunity, but that he should provide the city with ocular demonstration of the falsity of the ancient theory, and the truth of the new, was an innovation as dangerous as it was powerful.

Experiments on the velocity of falling bodies.

The cabal, formed by the followers of the old school, was before long strengthened by the adherence of Don Giovanni de' Medici, then governor of the port of Leghorn. This personage, having taken offense at the freedom with which Galileo had expressed his opinion on a hydraulic machine by which he had proposed to empty the wet dock at Leghorn, resolved to do all in his power to

Cabal formed by the Peripatetics.

---

[1] In his *Lives of the Painters*, Vasari thus disposes, in a few contemptuous lines, of Leonardo's claims to the title of philosopher : "So many were his caprices, that he would e'en philosophize on the phenomena of nature, claiming to understand their secret properties, and observing the motions of the heavens, and the body of the moon, and the going forth of the sun. And his soul being thus filled with heretical conceit, he esteemed it better to be styled philosopher than Christian."

ruin the young professor. That the complete failure of his invention illustrated the soundness of Galileo's judgment was but an additional blow to his pride, and an additional reason for hating the man who had dared to speak the truth. Fearing that the resentment of the mortified governor would result in Galileo's disgrace, Guidubaldo advised him to resign the professorship of Pisa while he had it in his power to do so. Galileo had had some thought of soliciting a professorship at Bologna, but Guidubaldo dissuaded him from this idea, and not only proposed but obtained for him the mathematical professorship of Padua, whither he removed in the autumn of 1592.

Galileo resigns the Pisan professorship.

The terms of the diploma, preserved among Galileo's manuscripts in the Palatine Library, are sufficient to show in what esteem he was held in Italy, at the time when he was thus forced to expatriate himself from his beloved Tuscany. After a recitation of the names and titles of the members of the Senate, it continues : " Owing to the death of Moleti, who formerly lectured on mathematics at Padua, the chair has been for a long period vacant : which being a most important one, it was thought proper to defer electing any to fill it, till such time as a fit and capable candidate should appear. Now there has been found Domine Galileo Galilei, who lectures at Pisa with very great honor and success, and who may be styled the first in his profession ; who, being content to come at once to our said university, and there to give the said lectures, it is proper to receive him. Therefore the said Domine Galileo Galilei is to be appointed mathematical lecturer in our university

Enters the service of the Venetian Republic in the time of Pasquale Cicogna, 88th Doge.

His diploma.

for four years certain and two uncertain ; and the two last are to be at the will and pleasure of Our Serenity, with the stipend of one hundred and eighty florins [1] yearly."

It is not known in what house Galileo lived during his long residence at Padua.   On his first *Delivers his* arrival he was hospitably received by the *inaugural lecture, Dec.* celebrated Vincenzio Pinelli, a learned and *7th, 1592.* munificent nobleman of Genoese origin, of whom we are told that he possessed a library of 80,000 volumes. Pinelli, who seems to have divined Galileo's extraordinary genius at the very outset of their acquaintance, mentioned him to Tycho Brahe as a man whose friendship it would be well worth his while to cultivate.   But Tycho Brahe, then venerated as a living oracle of mathematical science, thought perhaps that his dignity might be compromised by his taking the initiative in a correspondence with a man whose fame was so recent as young Galileo's ; and deferred therefore making his acquaintance by letter till 1600, eight years after, and only one year before his own death.

Galileo's acquaintance with Kepler began probably by Kepler's making him a present of *Begins a correspondence* his book, the " Prodromus Dissertationum *with Kepler.* Cosmographicum."   In Galileo's letter of thanks,[2] he expresses his joy at meeting with so powerful an associate in the pursuit of truth, and deplores that the lovers of truth should be so few in number.   He goes on to say, " Many years ago I became a convert to the opinions of Copernicus, and by that theory have succeeded in fully explaining many phenomena which on

----

[1] About 144 crowns of Tuscan money, or 32*l.* English.
[2] Galileo to Kepler, 4th of August, 1597.

the contrary hypothesis are altogether inexplicable. I have drawn up many arguments and confutations of the opposite opinions, which, however, I have not hitherto dared to publish, fearful of meeting the same fate as our master Copernicus, who, although he has earned for himself immortal fame amongst a few, yet amongst the greater number appears as only worthy of hooting and derision; so great is the number of fools. I should indeed dare to bring forward my speculations if there were many like you; but since there are not, I shrink from a subject of this description."

Kepler, in his answer to this letter,[1] advised Galileo to continue his speculations, and to publish what he might have written in defense of the Copernican theory in Germany, if he were not allowed to do so in Italy. This, however, Galileo did not do. Although he discussed the Copernican theory privately, and succeeded in convincing many of his friends of its superiority to the Ptolemaic theory, yet he continued to teach the Ptolemaic system up to the year 1600, the approximate date of his treatise on the sphere. But at length the truth prevailed, and the inglorious shield *Self-distrust.* of prudential motives was cast away. It is to be observed that this fearfulness of giving offense, this lingering self-distrust, is a marked trait in Galileo's youthful character. He was always willing to think that older men were in the right, and that he himself might be in the wrong. Of Aristotle he was wont to say that his method of reasoning appeared to him unsatisfactory and erroneous, but no stronger terms of depreciation than these did he use in speaking of the great philosopher; and such of his works as

----

[1] Kepler to Galileo, 13th of October, 1597.

he did admire, he admired frankly and openly, particularly those on Ethics and Rhetoric.

The whole period of Galileo's residence at Padua was one of unceasing industry. His lecture-room was filled to overflowing, and he had a large house full of private pupils. Among the many treatises *Treatises on Fortification and on Mechanics, written 1593, which is also the approximate date of the treatise on Gnomonics.* which he composed during the first few years of his professorship may be mentioned the treatise on Fortification, that on Mechanics, on Gnomonics, besides many others, all written for, and circulated in manuscript among, his disciples, by whom copies were scattered through almost every country in Europe. From his carelessness in not attaching his name to many of these writings, a carelessness which probably arose from his slight opinion of their value, it happened in more than one instance that all which was most precious in them was adopted by some impudent plagiarist, and put forth as his own invention. As an example of this, *Baldassare Capra's plagiarism punished.* it may be sufficient to mention the case of Baldassare Capra, who, after having pirated Galileo's geometrical and military compass, now called the sector, wrote a book in which he endeavored to prove that Galileo, who had invented this compass about the year 1597, was the plagiarist. Galileo, who had dedicated his treatise on the use of the compass to Prince Cosmo, took some pains in this instance to prove his claim to the invention, and so far succeeded that Baldassare Capra's book was burnt by order of the Senate.

From the year 1597 Galileo seems to have turned his attention particularly to the manufacture and improvement of various scientific instruments. From his memorandum-book we find that, from the 5th of July, 1599, he took a workman of the name of Mazzoleni, *Marcanto- nio Mazzo- leni.* with his family, to lodge in his house, in order that the manufacture of instruments might proceed under his personal direction, and that his own inventions and improvements might be less *Geometrical and mili- tary com- pass.* liable to piracy. Viviani says that he not only wrote pamphlets to explain the use of his compass and other instruments, but made them the subject of public lectures, besides privately explaining their use to many foreigners of distinction. Among these are named John Frederick, Prince of Alsace ; Philip, Landgrave of Hesse ; the Archduke Ferdinand of Austria, and Vincenzo Gonzaga, Duke of Mantua. At a later period, this Duke,[1] finding that the Venetian. Senate had made great use of Galileo's knowledge of engineering in its measures of defense and offense, endeavored to attach Galileo to his person. But Galileo, feeling that his convenience and liberty were both best secured at Padua, excused himself courteously from accepting the Duke's offer.

Tiraboschi asserts, on the authority of a letter of Galileo to Renieri, now proved to be apocryphal, *Gustavus Adolphus.* that the famous Gustavus Adolphus was at one time his pupil. It does indeed appear probable that a Swedish prince of the name of Gustavus was for a time at Padua ; but if this were the case, it was a son of Henry XIV. of Sweden, born in 1568, the year of his father's deposition. The literati of the North deny the existence of any document proving

---

[1] Vincenzo Gonzaga, Duke of Mantua, to Galileo, May 26th, 1604.

that Gustavus Adolphus was ever in Italy. As he was born at the end of the year 1594, he would have been but fifteen in 1610, the year in which Galileo quitted Padua. It may be added that in a memorandum-book of Galileo's, now preserved in the Palatine Library, there is a long list of names of his pupils, and of such persons as were in the habit of attending his lectures, and that the name of the Swedish prince nowhere occurs.

Among the crowd of noble and learned men who felt themselves honored by the friendship of the Paduan professor may be named, besides Pinelli, already mentioned, Fra Paolo Sarpi, called the Machiavel of Venice ; Fra Fulgenzio Micanzio, Sarpi's friend and colleague ; Fabricio da Acquapendente, the famous surgeon [1] who directed the studies of the great Harvey ; Don Antonio de' Medici, a man of grave and studious tastes ; [2] and Gioan Francesco Sagredo, a witty and eccentric patrician, whose *Sagredo.* house at Venice resembled Noah's ark, having in it, as he tells us, all manner of beasts. Sagredo's friendship for Galileo was so strong, that he even ran the risk of offending some members of the Senate, in his strenuous endeavors to procure an augmentation of his friend's stipend in 1599. Contarini, who would seem to have ignored altogether the honor as well as the profit likely to accrue to the Republic by keeping in her service a man of such genius as Galileo, complained

---

[1] He wrote, amongst other things, a treatise *De Ostiolis Venarum*, from which it may be deduced that he was acquainted with the circulation of the blood before Fra Paolo Sarpi ; but this is a disputed point among Italian literati.

[2] Illegitimate son of Francesco I. and Bianca Cappello.

bitterly that he was pestered on the subject not only by Sagredo, but by his own nephews; and that if Galileo was not content with his stipend, he could resign. Moleti, he said, had never had more than 300 ducats; and it was a presupposed thing that the professors should eke out their income by their private lessons.[1]

In the deliberation of the Senate on the subject, on the 29th of October, the sum of 320 ducats was at length agreed upon instead of 350, which the procurator Donati had wished to concede. Sagredo was bidden to warn Galileo, if he were his friend, that he need expect no further augmentation whatever, for that the Senate did not choose to make his case a precedent for every learned and needy foreigner who might think fit to press his claims, and that the usage of Bologna with regard to her professors was not to be set up as an example (which Sagredo had seemed inclined to do), as Bologna had a larger amount of money at the disposal of her university than the Venetian Senate had. Sagredo's mortification was extreme at being unable to serve his friend as completely as he wished. It was not till seven years later, in 1606, that Galileo's stipend was further augmented, and this probably due to the good offices of Prince

Leonardo Donati, or Donà, 90th Doge. Cosmo,[2] in his behalf with Donati, who was at that time Doge. It was not till he had lectured in Padua for seventeen years that the Senate, roused at last to enthusiasm by his invention of the telescope, voted him the professorship for life, with the stipend of a thousand florins.[3]

---

[1] Sagredo to Galileo, September 1, 1599.

[2] Afterwards Grand Duke.

[3] August 25, 1609. The decree runs thus : " Domine Galilee

Galilei, having been mathematical lecturer in Padua for seventeen years, to the gain of the University and to the satisfaction of all ; and having during his professorship made known to the world divers discoveries and inventions, to his own renown, and to the common weal ; but in particular having lately invented an instrument whereby (knowing the secrets of perspective) those things which are visible but most distant are brought within our vision, and which may be made to serve in many occasions, . . . it is proper that this Council do gratefully and munificently recognize the labors of those who are employed for the public benefit. Therefore," etc.

CHAPTER II.

BY the death of his father in 1591 Galileo had become the head of his family. This position, *Vincenzio Galilei died July 2d, 1591.* always attaching a grave responsibility to its possessor, was at the time we are speaking of, and in Galileo's case in particular, fraught with care and heavy anxiety. Not only was he expected to provide money for the household requirements of the family, but it was his duty to see to his brother's setting out in life. A still more sacred duty was that of finding a suitable husband for his sister. That a girl's marrying was to be left to chance was a doctrine which would have been considered in those days at least as heretical and pernicious as that of the earth's motion. Such a spectacle as a house full of daughters, all grown up, the comfort of a mother's old age, was never seen. The girl's education finished, two paths were open, not for her to choose always, but to be chosen for her. One led to the cloister, the other to the house of a husband. The cloister was the refuge of such as possessed not dowries equal to the requirements of their birth. Brides of Heaven, they thus escaped two evils, the degradation of a *mésalliance*, and the disgrace of old-maidism.

It had been the family intention for Livia, the only unmarried daughter at the time of Vincenzio's death, to take the veil, but so great was her aversion to a monastic life that her brother did not insist on her doing what would have saved him much trouble and expense. Though his sister Virginia had married before his father's death, the burden of providing the dowry had in great measure fallen upon Galileo. Pressed on all sides for money, he had been unable to satisfy his brother-in-law's demands. At length, not choosing to wait any longer, and not caring who went without as long as he got his own, Benedetto Landucci resolved to proceed to harsh measures. Madonna Giulia, hearing of his intention, wrote [1] to warn Galileo, who was then just recovering from a serious illness, the first of the long series which was henceforward to form no small addition to the troubles of his life.

After thanking God for her son's recovery, Madonna Giulia goes on to say : " Now I must not fail to tell you how things go on here from day to day. If you carry into effect your intention of coming here next month, I shall be rejoiced. Only you must not come unprovided with funds, for I see that Benedetto is determined to have his own, that is to say, what you promised him ; and he menaces loudly that he will have you arrested the instant you arrive here. And as I hear you bound yourself (to pay), he would have the power to arrest you, and he is just the man to do it. So I warn you,

Letter from Madonna Giulia.

---

[1] This letter bears the following curious address : *Al Molto Magnifico e Fidelissimo Signore Galileo Galilei mio sempre Osservand: in Padova,* and is dated May 29, 1593.

for it would grieve me much if anything of the kind were to happen."

From a short letter from Livia Galilei to her brother, *Letter of Livia Gali-lei.* it would seem that there was actually no provision for the family beyond what Galileo gained by his stipend and his private lessons. She says : —

"Dearest Brother, — As our Lena[1] was here, I could not help writing these few lines to tell you about myself; and though your lordship may not care to hear about me, I care to hear about you, for I have none in the world except you. So please be so kind as to answer me, that I may have this little bit of pleasure ; for though your lordship writes to our mother, she never brings me the letter; she only says, 'Your brother sends his love.' She told me your lordship was going to send Michelangelo to Poland. I was extremely grieved at hearing this at first, but then I comforted myself, saying, 'If Galileo thought it was a dangerous place, he would not send him ;' for I know that you love him dearly. Besides that I heard that you were soon coming back, and it seems a thousand years[2] till you come. And please do remember to bring me some stuff to make a dress, for I am in great want of one."

At this time Galileo had only been settled at Padua seven months ; so that, although his prospects were very fair, his purse could not have been very heavy. He had had to pay a duty of $2\frac{1}{2}$ per cent. on his

[1] This Lena is supposed to have been an elder sister. A person of the same name was married and settled at Padua when Galileo first went there, and is also styled "our Lena" in his mother's letter.

[2] A common Tuscan expression.

stipend, namely, 25 lire 12 soldi in Venetian money, and 3½ lire for the bolla, or stamp.

Galileo found some difficulty in giving his brother his first start in life. He had wished him to *His brother.* have some post at the Grand Ducal Court, but there seemed no opening, though his musical talent and elegant manners had gained him many influential friends. Neither did any opening present itself for the exercise of his talents in Padua. The plan of going to Poland was for some time in abeyance, apparently from the indecision of the Polish prince — name unknown — for whose favor Michelangelo was a candidate. At last a distinct offer was made, and *Michelangelo goes to Poland.* Michelangelo set out, without further loss of time, well provided with clothes and money by Galileo. This was in August, 1600. Livia was getting heartily tired of convent life, and was plaguing her mother to find her a husband. Since the girl was not to be coerced into taking the veil, Madonna Giulia had no alternative but to search herself and set her friends to search ; it being understood that the *sposo* must be of birth equal to the Galilei. Upon Galileo, as it has been already said, lay the burden of providing the dowry. His correspondence with his mother shows how calmly and readily he accepted this burden, and all others relating to the providing of the family with money. Writing from Padua on the 7th of August, 1600, he says : —

" From your letter, and that of Messer Piero Sali, I hear of the proposed match for our Livia. *Letter to his mother.* With regard to it, I do not see how I am to act ; for though, from what Messer Piero says, I esteem it desirable, yet it is impossible for me to consent to it

just at present. The reason is, that this Polish nobleman (or prince) to whom Michelangelo had already
applied, has at last written for him to come instantly,
offering him very good terms, namely, his table, a
dress similar to that worn by the gentlemen of his household, two servants, a coach-and-four, and a salary of
two hundred Hungarian ducats, which make about
three hundred crowns of our money, besides perqui-
sites.   Michelangelo has decided on going, and is only
waiting in hopes of good company for the journey. I
think he will go within this fortnight. I, of course, must
provide him with money ; and besides that, this prince
wishes him to bring certain things, so that what with
the said articles, and what with what he requires for
himself, I cannot spend less than two hundred crowns.
Now you know what expenses I have had this last year,
so that I cannot do as I willingly would. On the other
hand, Sister Contessa 1 writes, telling me that on all
acounts I ought to take Livia away from the convent
(S. Giuliano), for she hates remaining there. Now, as
she has waited so long, I should like her to be well and
comfortably settled. If I am to believe Messer Piero,
this Pompeo Baldi is a good sort of man ; yet hearing
that, including his private income and what he gets besides, he has not one hundred ducats yearly, I do not
see how a household is to be maintained for that sum ;
therefore I would, if possible, have the matter delayed :
for Michelangelo will, without fail, send me a good
sum of money as soon as he gets to his destination, and
with this, joined to what I can get together, we may
take measures for establishing the child, since she too
is determined to come out and prove the miseries of this

1 The Superior of the Convent of S. Giuliano.

world. But I wish you would see about taking her away from S. Giuliano, and placing her in some other convent till her turn comes ; and persuade her that she will lose nothing by waiting. Tell her that there have been queens and great ladies who have not married till they were old enough to be her mother. Therefore pray see her as soon as you possibly can, and give the inclosed letter to Sister Contessa. She has been asking me to pay what is due for Livia's board ; find out how much it amounts to, and I will send it at once."

Galileo's hopes of his brother's assistance were vain. Depending on him for help in paying his sister's dowry, he made up a match between her and a Pisan gentleman, promising a dowry of 1,800 ducats, of which 800 were paid down. But of this 800 he had to borrow 600, which he did without hesitation, expecting that his brother would without fail send money from Wilna. Livia had been married almost a year, and Michelangelo had neither sent back the money his brother had generously advanced on his setting out, nor the money which he ought to have contributed to the dowry. Writing on the 20th November, 1601, Galileo thus expresses his resentment at such unworthy behavior : —

"Though you have sent no answer whatever to either of the four letters which I have writ- *Galileo's* ten within the last ten months, I never- *letter to his brother.* theless write, and repeat what I have said before. And I would rather think that all my letters had missed you, or any other unlikely thing, than think that you meant to be wanting in your duty, not only in answering my letters, but in sending money to pay the debts which we owe to various persons, and in particular to Signor Taddeo Galletti, our brother-in-law, to whom, as I have already written several times, I married Livia, our sister, with a dowry of 1,800 ducats.[1] I paid 800 down, and of these I was forced to borrow 600, depending on you to send, if not all, at least a good part of the sum ; expecting also that you would contribute so much yearly till the whole was paid, in conformity with the terms of the contract. If I had imagined things were going to turn out in this manner, I would not have given the child in marriage, or else I would have given her only such a dowry as I was able to pay myself without assistance, since I seem to be fated to bear every burden alone. I beg that you will without delay have a deed drawn out and witnessed by a public notary, in which there shall be an acknowledgment of your being bound to pay the said dowry to Signor Taddeo jointly with me. I insist on this being done without delay. And, above all, I desire that you will write and give me some news of yourself ; for every one is feeling anxious about you, there having been no word of your whereabouts since you left Cracow."

Michelangelo never paid his brother a farthing. In *Michelangelo returns penniless to Padua.* 1605 he was back again at Padua, living at Galileo's expense, till the latter succeeded in procuring him a post in the court of the Duke of Bavaria. That he should spend his money on himself while he had any, and, having spent all, fall back upon his brother, seemed to him a matter of course. Singularly egotistical by nature, never from first to last could he be brought to see that, being able to gain his own bread, the helping of others became

<hr>

[1] A ducat is equal to 4*s*. 2*d*.

at once a sacred obligation. In this the brothers stood apart, with a great gulf between them. A fragment of a letter remains to show how even during his father's life-time Galileo helped to provide his sister Virginia with such bravery as beseemed a young married lady of ancient birth : —

" The present I am going to make Virginia consists of a set of silken bed-hangings. I bought the silk[1] at Lucca, and have had it woven, so that, though the stuff is a wide width, it will only cost me about three carlini the braccio. It is a striped stuff, and I think you will be much pleased with it. I have ordered silk fringes to match, and could very easily get the bedstead made too. But do not say a word to any one, that it may come to her quite unexpectedly. I will bring it when I come home for the Carnival holidays ; and, as I said before, if you like I will bring her worked velvet and damask stuff enough to make four or five handsome dresses." *Galileo's present to his sister Virginia.*

Though Madonna Virginia could have done without silken bed-hangings and velvet dresses, yet it is impossible not to admire the generosity of the brother who thus provided out of his scanty stipend such bravery as should enable the 'bride to hold up her head among her new relations.[2]

More generous still was his behavior to Livia, as the following extract from his memorandum-book shows : — *Livia Galilei's trousseau.*

---

[1] Lucca *l'Industriosa* at one period enjoyed a monopoly in the production of silk, which, however, was extinct in the seventeenth century, though its manufactures were long considered the best in Tuscany.

[2] Benedetto Landucci was the son of Luca Landucci, who was ambassador at the Court of Rome, during the pontificate of Leo X.

"Note of the sums laid out for Livia's dress on her marriage : —

	lire	*soldi*
Gold bracelets	191	00
Woolen cloth for a train petticoat, braccia 4¾	71	15
Furniture for the said petticoat	9	00
High shoes	8	00
Light blue damask, braccia 13½	121	10
Gold trimmings	90	00
Silver trimmings	65	00
Black Naples velvet, braccia 21½	425	00
Linings and other things for the dresses	18	00
Tailor's bill	20	00."

This memorandum of money actually paid by Galileo in order to keep up such appearance as was commensurate with the family dignity, may be compared with a letter of Michelangelo's, in which the family money matters are discussed : —

"I was glad to get your letter, and though it was full of complaints, still I am pleased to find that you do not despise me quite so much as I had imagined. Now, then, I will answer you about the claims of our brothers-in-law. My dear brother, if I have not been able to pay them, as I certainly should have liked to do, I do not see that you can blame me so much. You complain of my having spent such a large sum of money in one feast. I do not deny that the sum was large, but just consider that it was on the occasion of my wedding. There were more than eighty persons present, among whom were many gentlemen of importance, and among these there were no less than four ambassadors ; and had I not followed the custom of the country, I should have been put to shame ; so that I was forced to spend what I did, and indeed could not possibly have managed with less.   You cannot accuse me of ever having spent such sums of money simply for my own gratification ; never, indeed, have I thrown money away on anything, but, on the contrary, have often denied myself what I wanted, in order to save.   You say that it does not serve your turn for me to write and tell you that ' God will not be pleased if you keep up a feeling of rancor against me.'   Of course, I know it will not serve your turn.   I did not write it supposing that it would help you to get rid of the debt to our two brothers-in-law. As to that matter, I tell you shortly that I will do what I can, and, indeed, will put myself to every inconvenience, rather than not satisfy their claim in part ; but as to my finding 1,400 crowns, which is the sum still remaining to be paid, I know that I cannot do it, and never shall, for I find it scarcely possible to pay the interest.   You should have given our sisters a dowry, not merely in conformity with your own ideas of what was right and fitting, but in conformity with the size of my purse.   God knows that if I had not paid off my share, it was because I could not.   When I sent you those fifty crowns, Signor Cosimo lent me thirty of them, and I have not yet repaid him, though I must soon, as he writes saying he wants one of my lutes.   By and by I will borrow another fifty crowns and send you.   I cannot promise more, for these last few months I have been obliged to spend a great deal for my house.   I know that you will say that I should have waited, and thought of our sisters before taking a wife.   But, good heavens !   The idea of toiling all one's life just to put by a few farthings to give one's sisters !   This yoke would be indeed too heavy and bitter ; for I am more than certain that in thirty years

I should not have saved enough to cover this debt.
God help me ! I would do more than that if I could.
Have a little pity on me, and consider that you cannot
say I ever had the heart to gratify my own liking without caring about others.   You may say that my having
married is a proof that I care not for paying my debts
as long as I can gratify my own liking.   To this I shall
make no answer.   God knows I am thankful to have
my wife, and I hope He will enable me to carry out
my desire in satisfying this debt.   I shall say no more,
but I trust that you will consider me a good brother ;
for I will do all I can to send you some assistance, as
you say it is all my fault that you are in such distress.
But excuse me ; if I failed, it was because I could not
help it.   I understand that you are going to send the
case of lutes shortly.   I have been expecting its arrival with some impatience ; for during this Lent I am
in great want of the lutes for playing concerted music ;
and to have them quicker, I would not mind paying
something more for carriage." [1]

Galileo must have been more than human not to
feel some resentment at such selfish conduct ; his
resentment, however, was but short-lived.   In 1610
the brothers had again resumed their correspondence,
and from that time Michelangelo never failed to write
to Galileo whenever he was in want of assistance.

[1] Michelangelo Galilei to Galileo, March 4, 1608.

CHAPTER III.

IT is not quite certain at what period Galileo invented the thermometer, but, from the testimony of Benedetto Castelli, we may fix it *Invention of the thermometer.* about the year 1602.[1] It was at first believed that Santorio was the inventor of this instrument. Sagredo, writing to Galileo in 1612, says: " Signor Mula was at Padua for the feast of St. Antony, and told me he had seen an instrument made by Signor Santorio, with which heat and cold were meas-

[1] Castelli to Monsignor Ferdinando Cesarini, September 20, 1638 : " About this time I remembered an experiment which our Signor Galileo had shown me more than thirty-five years ago. He took a glass bottle about the size of a hen's egg, the neck of which was two palms long, and as narrow as a straw. Having well heated the bulb in his hands, he placed its mouth in a vessel containing a little water, and withdrawing the heat of his hand from the bulb, instantly the water rose in the neck more than a palm above the level of the water in the vessel," etc.

ured ; and at last he told me that it was a large glass

Sagredo's letters on the thermome-ter or ther-moscope. bulb with a long neck. I began at once to make vessels of this description, and have succeeded in making some very handsome ones." Sagredo goes on to say that he inclosed a drawing of the best he had made ; but, as unfortunately there is no trace of this drawing, it is impossible to say precisely what the instrument was of which Santorio was the inventor. In another letter of Sagredo, of the 9th of May, 1613, he distinctly ascribes the invention of the thermometer to Galileo ; thus, " The instrument which you invented for measuring heat I have brought into various convenient and perfect forms, so that the difference of temperature between two rooms is seen as far as 100 degrees." It would appear, then, that Sagredo had been ignorant of Galileo's discovery,[1] and that the latter, on hearing his

Santorio. description of Santorio's instrument, had proved that he had forestalled Santorio. It is also possible, though by no means certain, that both Santorio and Galileo invented this instrument about the same time. Venturi observes that some

---

[1] Another letter of Sagredo's confirms this supposition : "I am daily making alterations and additions to the instrument for measuring the temperature. . . . But as you write me, and as I certainly believe, that you are the first author and inventor of the instrument, I think that those which you and your exceedingly clever workman have made must be far superior to mine. Pray write and let me know how you make yours, and I will in return inform you how I make mine. . . . The man who gives himself out as the inventor, is quite incapable of making such a thermometer as I wish to have ; and I have vainly endeavored to make him understand," etc. — *Sagredo to Galileo,* March 15, 1615.

ascribe the priority of the invention to Drebbel; but it is not said that he published it as his till 1620, when he was in England, which would *Drebbel.* be seventeen years after Galileo had brought it before his friend's notice. Fludd wrote a description of the thermometer in 1617 or there- *Fludd.* abouts, and Santorio in 1626. These three authors, as well as Galileo, fabricated their instruments in precisely the same manner, and it appears from their description that this heat-measurer was thermoscope and baroscope in one. It is evident that the first instruments of this sort were extremely rude. At a later period, Ferdinand II. of Tuscany introduced various notable improvements in its construction. Galileo pursued his experiments with it only so far as to use spirits of wine instead of water. Mercury was not employed till 1670.

By the Grand Duke's desire, Galileo began in 1601 to give instruction in mathematics to the *Prince Cosmo Gali-* young Prince Cosmo, a bright boy of *leo's pupil.* twelve, described by the physician Mercuriale as a *curioso cervello*, wanting to know the wherefore of everything. It seems that there was no one considered capable of carrying on this branch of the Prince's education during Galileo's absence at Padua, so that the progress of the pupil must have been but slow. But though Galileo was fully sensible of the honor done him by the Grand Duke in confiding to him alone the mathematical instruction of the heir to the grand-ducal crown, he was too sensible of what was due to himself to appear at the Court of Tuscany except by the Grand Duke's express invitation; not choosing, as he plainly wrote to Belisario Vinta, to be a mere hanger-on at court, or a crouching suppliant for the Serene favor.[1] This independent attitude was so far from displeasing, that it brought forth the grand-ducal testimony that Galileo was the greatest mathematician in all Christendom, and that he should find he had no reason to repent coming to Florence. Her Highness Christina was such a firm believer in his talent, that she applied to him to correct her husband's horoscope, during what proved to be the Grand Duke's last illness. Galileo of course did not *Galileo a horoscope caster.* refuse, but made the desired correction, according to which Ferdinand I. had still many years to live.[2] He died twenty-two days after, in spite of this happy prognostic, which Galileo himself had no more believed when he wrote it, than he did when he drew the horoscope of Margherita Picchena, of Sagredo, or of any of his other friends.

In the year 1607 Galileo made various observations *Observations on the loadstone.* on the loadstone, suggested to him at first, it may be, by a perusal of the work of William Gilbert, of Colchester, "De Magnete," etc.[3] These observations he imparted to his friend Secretary Picchena, who in his turn imparted them to Prince

[1] Galileo to Belisario Vinta, May 30, 1608.

[2] Galileo to the Grand Duchess Christina, January 16, 1609.

[3] " . . . Essendosi da grandissimo filosofo diffusamenta scritto, e con evidenti dimostrazioni confirmato, altro non esser questo nostro mondo in suo primario e universal sustanza, che un gran globo di calamita." — *Galileo to the Grand Duchess Christina*, 1606. In the *Dialogue*, he acknowledges Gilbert's merit in still warmer terms, declaring that his marvelous conception (that of the earth being a great loadstone) was to him a subject of praise, admiration, and envy. But Galileo's envy was not the envy of a mean mind.

Cosmo. The young Prince sent to say he would like to possess such a loadstone as the one Galileo had, weighing about half a pound Tuscan. The hint was plain enough. Galileo wrote back to say that the loadstone and all else belonging to him was at the Prince's disposal, but that a friend of his possessed a loadstone infinitely more worthy of the Serene notice, which might probably be parted with for a consideration. From the correspondence which ensued we learn that the Grand Duke was no more above bargaining than any peddler in Tuscany. It is with pain that we see Galileo, the man to whom the secrets of the heavens were so shortly to be revealed, actually lending himself to small subterfuges for the sake of saving his Serene pupil's father a few crowns. At the same time it is fair to state that this is the sole instance of the tortuous, higgling spirit, which we feel to be more fitting to a dealer at the rag-fair in Piazza San Giovanni than *Bargaining for the loadstone.* to the father of experimental philosophy.

The friend to whom this unique loadstone belonged was Sagredo. Galileo concealed his name, for what reason we are unable to guess, merely affirming that he (Sagredo) had been offered 200 gold crowns by a German jeweler, who had wished to buy the loadstone for the Emperor, but that he had declared he would only part with it for as much gold as it would carry fastened to the end of an iron wire, namely, more than 800 crowns ; or, in plain Tuscan, its price (*prezzo ristretto*) was 400 crowns. Galileo had invented a story about a Polish gentleman to account for his curiosity respecting Sagredo's loadstone.[1] To account for the delay in Picchena's answer, he found it necessary to state that

---

[1] Galileo to Picchena, February 8, 1608.

this Polish gentleman, his pupil, was staying at Florence for a time. It is probable that Sagredo did not wish to part with the loadstone, and therefore put a fancy price upon it. Galileo found to his mortification that the negotiation would have been expedited by his telling the truth at once, as Sagredo would have felt himself honored by Prince Cosmo's acceptance of the loadstone as a free gift. The bargain was concluded after four months' haggling over the price. Galileo, fearing that his friend Sagredo would feel that his interests had been quite lost sight of when he came to know who the Polish gentleman was, begged Picchena to ask his Serene Highness to give 100 doubloons instead of 100 gold crowns, which was the price agreed upon.

The year 1609 is memorable as the date of Galileo's *Invention of the telescope.* invention of the telescope. The honor both of this invention and the discoveries it directly led to, became a matter for fierce dispute. Not only was it claimed by the Dutch, but Galileo's own countrymen were eager to ascribe it to any rather than to him ; old authors were consulted and brought forward to prove that, if indeed Galileo had made the telescope, it was only because he had put into practice certain theories, or made experiments on certain phe- *Baptista Porta, Gerolamo Fracastoro, and De Dominis.* nomena described in their works. Thus, Baptista Porta, Gerolamo Fracastoro, a writer of the sixteenth century, and De Dominis, Archbishop of Spalatro, were named successively as the first discoverers of the telescope. Borelli endeavored fifty years later to prove that a Dutchman named Jansen was the first discoverer, and it would indeed appear that the priority of the discovery rests with him, though its only use was to serve as a toy for a prince, and scarcely as much value was attached to it as to the giant magnet which had delighted Prince Cosmo.[1]

Galileo thus describes his discovery in a letter to his brother-in-law Landucci:[2] "I write now because I have a piece of news for you, though whether you will be glad or sorry to hear it I cannot say, for I have now no hope *Letter to Landucci on the discovery of the telescope.* of returning to my own country, though the occurrence which has destroyed that hope has had results both useful and honorable. You must know, then, that about two months ago there was a report spread here that in Flanders some one had presented to Count Maurice (of Nassau) a glass,[8] manufactured in such a way as to *The occhiale, or cannocchiale, soon named telescope by Prince Federigo Cesi.* make distant objects appear very near, so that a man at the distance of two miles could be clearly seen. This seemed to me so marvelous that I began to think about it: as it appeared to me to have a foundation in the science of perspective, I set about thinking how to make it, and at length I found out, and have succeeded so well that the one I have made is far superior to the Dutch telescope.[4] It was reported in Venice that I had made one, and a week since I was

---

[1] This magnet, about which there was such a lengthy correspondence between Galileo and Secretary Picchena, was lost in 1698 (and perhaps before that time). Leibnitz deplores its loss in two letters written in 1698 to Magliabechi.

[2] Galileo to Benedetto Landucci, August 29, 1609.

[8] *Occhiale*, eye-glass ; spectacles in the plural.

[4] Daniel Antonini, writing from Brussels to Galileo, in April, 1611, complains that in Flanders no telescopes were to be procured capable of magnifying objects more than five times, and

commanded to show it to his Serenity and to all the members of the Senate, to their infinite amazement. Many gentlemen and senators, even the oldest, have ascended at various times the highest bell-towers in Venice, to spy out ships at sea making sail for the mouth of the harbor, and have seen them clearly, though without my telescope they would have been invisible for more than two hours.   The effect of this instrument is to show an object at a distance of, say fifty miles, as if it were but five miles off.

" Perceiving of what great utility such an instrument would prove in naval and military operations, and seeing that his Serenity greatly desired to possess

Il Collegio.   it, I resolved four days ago to go to the palace and present it to the Doge as a free gift. And on quitting the presence-chamber I was com-

The hall of Pregadi.   manded to bide a while in the hall of the Senate, whereunto, after a little, the Illustrissimo Prioli, who is Procurator and one of the Riformatori of the University, came forth to me from the presence-chamber, and, taking me by the hand, said that the Senate, knowing the manner in which I had served it for seventeen years at Padua, and being sensible of my courtesy in making it a present of my

Galileo elected to the mathematical professorship for life, Aug. 25, 1609.   telescope, had immediately ordered the Illustrious Riformatori to elect me (with my goodwill) to the professorship for life, with a stipend of 1,000 florins yearly ; and as there remained to me yet a year to terminate the period of my last reëlection, they willed that the in-

that he had endeavored to make a telescope himself, which had succeeded so far as to show the inequality of the moon's surface, and the satellites of Jupiter, or Medicean Planets, as they were then called.

crease òf stipend should date from that same day. I, knowing that Fortune's wings are swift, but that those of Hope are drooping,[1] said that I was content to abide his Serenity's pleasure.   Then the illustrious Prioli, embracing me, said, ' As I command *Leonardo Donati,* here, and can order what I please, it being *Doge.* my turn this week, I will that after dinner the Senate assemble, and that your reëlection be put to the ballot; ' which was done, without one dissentient vote. So that I am bound here for life, and can only hope to enjoy a sight of my own country during the Paduan recess."

Galileo himself seems at first to have been unconscious of the immense importance of his discovery. Writing, in the December of 1609, to Michelangelo Buonarotti the younger, he mentions casually that he had introduced some improvements into the manufacture of telescopes, and that perhaps he might make some further discovery.   He had used the telescope to make observations on the moon, subver- *Observa-* sive of the crystalline theory then in vogue, *tions on the moon, De-* but the discovery of Jupiter's satellites took *cember,1609.* him quite as much by surprise as it did the rest of the world.   His correspondence shows how that which might have easily been to him an occasion for vainglory excited on the contrary a feeling of deep humility, and a sense of his own unworthiness and insignificance.   Writing to Belisario Vinta, on the 30th of January, 1610, after thanking him for his kindness in helping one Alessandro Piersanti, his servant, to recover a sum of money which he was in danger of

---

[1] In allusion to the negotiations in which his friends were engaged relative to his return to Tuscany.

losing altogether, he goes on to say: "I am at present staying at Venice for the purpose of getting printed some observations which I have been making on the celestial bodies by means of a telescope which I have (*col mezzo di un mio occhiale*), and being infinitely amazed thereat, so do I give infinite thanks to God, who has been pleased to make me the first observer of marvelous things, unrevealed to by-gone ages. I had already ascertained that the moon was a body most similar to the earth, and had shown our Most Serene master as much, but imperfectly, not having such an excellent telescope as I now possess, which, besides showing me the moon, has revealed to me a multitude of fixed stars never yet seen ; being more than ten times the number of those that can be seen with the unassisted eye. Moreover, I have ascertained what has always been a matter of controversy among *The Milky*   philosophers ; namely, the nature of the *Way.*   Milky Way. But the greatest marvel of all is the discovery I have made of four new planets : I *Discovery of* have observed their proper motions in rela-*Jupiter's* *satellites,* tion to themselves and to each other, and *January,* *1610.* wherein they differ from all the other motions of the other stars. And these new planets move round another very great star, in the same way as Venus and Mercury, and peradventure the other known planets, move round the Sun. As soon as my tract is printed, which, as an advertisement, I intend sending to all philosophers and mathematicians, I shall send a copy to the Most Serene Grand Duke, together with an excellent telescope, which will enable him to judge for himself of the truth of these novelties."

A few stars more or less in the heavens, a few

spots more or less on the sun, so long as the sun of
Medicean favor shone on him, were but trifles to
Vinta, absorbed in the duties of his secretaryship.
Knowing, however, that his Highness was as eager to
hear new things as any Athenian of old, he, courtier-
like, took Galileo's letter immediately to the Grand
Duke, who directed him to write without delay to express his Serene admiration of Galileo's almost super-
natural genius, and his desire to possess a telescope
with all the latest improvements.

Jupiter's satellites, however, were not long in assum-
ing importance in the eyes of Secretary Vinta. Galileo, pleased at the Grand Duke's interest in the discovery, conceived the idea of naming the new planets,
as they were then called, after him. But he was in
doubt whether to call them *Cosmici*, in allusion to the
Grand Duke's name, or whether to dedicate them to
the four brothers,[1] under the name of *Medicea Sidera*.
This, to Vinta, was a matter for deep con- *The Medicea*
sideration. It was decided by him that the *Sidera.*
latter title would be most pleasing to their Highnesses,
and his decision was accepted by Galileo.[2]

During the Easter recess Galileo visited the Court
of Tuscany, for the express purpose of show- *Galileo visits*
ing the Grand Duke the new satellites.[3] *the Grand Ducal Court,*
His Highness asked for and obtained the *April, 1610.*
gift of the telescope with which the discovery had been

---

[1] Cosmo II. had three brothers living, namely, Francesco,
Carlo, and Lorenzo.

[2] Vinta to Galileo, February 20, 1610.

[3] Vinta, in his letter containing the Grand Duke's invitation,
qualifies Galileo's discovery of the satellites as a most ingenious
invention, *ingegnosissima invenzione*.

made, though Galileo ultimately, as it appears, kept it in his own hands ; and it did not become the property of the Grand Duke, who died in Galileo's life-time, but of his successor. It may well be believed that Galileo could not make up his mind to part with his " old discoverer," as he affectionately calls this telescope, even to gratify the Grand Duke's whim.

We learn from Galileo's correspondence with Vinta, that the second edition of his " Nuncius Sidereus," or " Messenger of the Stars," was put into press in less than two months after the appearance of the first edition, which, by an after-thought, was dedicated to the Grand Duke. At the same time, he tells us, he reprinted his treatise on the " Use of the Geometric and Military Compass," of which there was not a single copy left. Besides this, he was continually occupied in the manufacture of these compasses, of which, since 1596, more than three hundred had passed through his hands. Of the telescopes he had manufactured above a hundred, with great cost and labor ; and of these, but ten were capable of showing the satellites and the fixed stars. Three of these he designed for the Duke of Bavaria, the Elector of Cologne, and Cardinal del Monte, who had all begged for one. The rest he intended, with the Grand Duke's permission, to send to the great princes and reigning monarchs of Spain, France, Poland, and Austria, and to the Duke of Urbino. The Cardinal, in return for Galileo's present, sent him a small picture to which an indulgence was attached. The Duke of Bavaria was not behindhand : let us hope that his present was a more substantial one than the cardinal's.[1] The Elector of Cologne considered that the " Nuncius Sidereus " was incomplete, since it contained no receipt for the making of telescopes. He desired Galileo to make him a participator in his secret, promising to recompense him after his own princely fash- *Letter of* ion. " See if you can gratify the Elector by *Michel-* showing him how to manufacture the instru- *angelo* *Galilei.* ment ; and if not, write him a letter in your own way," says Michelangelo Galilei,[2] not choosing to bear the brunt of the electoral anger in case of Galileo's refusal. " You say not a word about the telescope I asked you for," he continues, much in the tone of a spoilt child who wonders at being denied a new toy. " And if I am not a prince able to remunerate you, at any rate I am your brother, and it seems very strange to me that you do not care to gratify me with this thing. Pray send me the cords[3] without fail ; and above all, do not forget, when you go to Florence, to procure me letters of recommendation from the Grand Duke to my mas- ter ; but mind you, let them be good ones, such as you know how to get easily enough. I have nothing more to say, except that I beg you not to forget what I have asked for."

Throughout Florence the excitement was immense. Every one desired to possess a Venetian *Excitement* glass. Alessandro Sertini, a clever advocate *in Florence.* and old friend of Galileo, writes an amusing letter[4] de-

---

[1] Maximilian, Duke of Bavaria, to Galileo, July 8, 1610. The " picciolo dono " was perhaps a sum of money.

[2] Michelangelo Galilei to Galileo, April 14, 1610.

[3] For the lutes.

[4] Alessandro Sertini to Galileo, March 27, 1610.

scribing the irrepressible curiosity of some of his friends
on hearing that the Venetian courier had brought him
a small box from Galileo. There must surely be a telescope in it. The box must be opened then and there.
When it was found to contain no telescope, but only the
" Nuncius Sidereus," still the curiosity did not abate.
Sertini was forced to read that portion of the " Nuncius "
relating to the new planets aloud to a circle assembled
at a friend's house. Sertini, too, asks for a telescope,
but prefers the request in rather more courteous terms
than had been used by Galileo's brother.

Michelangelo Buonarotti[1] wrote a sonnet in his
Michelangelo friend's praise. Thomas Segheti, a learned
Buonarotti,
called Il Englishman at Prague, whose name is
Giovane. scarcely discoverable in its Italian dress —
perhaps it was Segget — wrote Latin epigrams, which
were printed by Kepler's desire along with his treatise on the " Nuncius Sidereus." Galileo grateful tó
Kepler's Kepler for his adherence and approbation,
adherence. wrote sadly to Vinta, contrasting Kepler's
reception of his discovery with the violent opposition with which it had been met by some of his countrymen. " The Emperor's mathematician has sent
me a treatise in eight folios, in the form of a letter,
written in approbation of my book, of which he neither
doubts nor contradicts one word. And your lordship
may believe that Italian literati would have done as
much from the beginning, if I had been living in Germany or in some country still more distant." [2]

The whole University crowded to hear his three lec-

---

[1] Nephew of the great Michelangelo.
[2] Galileo to Belisario Vinta, May 7, 1610.

tures on the satellites. Most were convinced ; a few merely pretended to be convinced ; and a small minority declared that even if they were forced to look through the telescope and see the satellites, they would not believe them to be in the sky, "*because the heavens were unchangeable.*" The force of this argument is obvious : the satellites were not there before Galileo saw them. On hearing the first news of the discovery, Kepler, with that readiness to receive correction which so truly marks a great mind, had written off to Galileo, "that if he were right, which he was inclined to believe, then his own book on Cosmography must be entirely wrong." Galileo believed that his lectures had silenced, if they had not convinced, all his opponents. But three men still remained, whose stolidity was proof against all reason and experience ; namely, Martin Horky, a Bohemian, Cesare Cremonino of Cento, and Francesco Sizi, a Florentine. The latter wrote a foolish book entitled " Dianoia Astronomica," intended to disprove the existence of these obtrusive satellites. The only answer Galileo deigned to make, after a perusal of it, was by scribbling a verse of Ariosto[1] on the back of the title-page of his copy, intimating that it was not worth his while to do battle with such an adversary.

It was after Galileo's Easter visit to the Court of Tuscany, that Vinta began, by the Grand Duke's order, to sound him on the conditions under which his services might be se-

Lectures at Padua on the new satellites, April, 1610.

Opposition of Martin Horky, Cesare Cremonino, and Francesco Sizi.

Galileo's desire to return to Tuscany.

---

[1] " Soggiunse il duca : Non sarebbe onesto
    Che io volessi la battaglia torre
    Di quel che m'offerisco manifesto,
    Quando vi piaccia, innanzi agli occhi porre."
    Orlando Furioso, v. 40.

cured to his Highness alone. Some time before this Galileo had experienced that weariness of his life at Padua, that longing to return to Tuscany, which had its root in homesickness, quite as much as in desire of greater leisure for study. Yet his life at Padua was a life such as most men would have envied. Hard work he had, but it was voluntary, not forced labor. The houses of the witty and learned were open to him ; the most illustrious patricians of Venice sought after his society, and felt themselves favored by his friendship. Had he desired, he might have amassed almost as large a fortune as his friend Acquapendente ; he might have retired, like him, to a villa on the Brenta, to end in peace a laborious and useful life. But Galileo was not *Italianissimo.* His life at Padua was to him but an honorable exile. His thoughts turned constantly to his beloved and beautiful Florence ; his country, *la patria*, was little Tuscany. From the attachment of his pupil, Prince Cosmo, he had hoped much, and on the accession of this Prince he had imparted his hopes of a speedy recall to his friends Eneas and Silvio Piccolomini, the latter of whom had been Prince Cosmo's tutor. This desire of Galileo's was naturally kept very secret ; partly because he knew that the Senate valued his services too highly to bear the loss of them with equanimity, but also be-

Cosmo II. succeeded his father, Ferdinand I. Feb. 7, 1609. cause his friends felt that it was necessary to prepare the mind of the new Grand Duke to receive the idea in such a manner as that his Highness should believe that he himself had originated it. It appears certain that in this scheme the two Piccolomini and one other gentleman, Signor Vespuccio, were Galileo's only confidants.

Vinta knew nothing of it, nor did Galileo wish him to know, as may be gathered from the following letter.[1]

"It becomes my duty, as a sign of my lively sense of the good offices of yourself and Signor Eneas Piccolomini, to unfold to your lordships my thoughts respecting that state of life in which I would desire to pass the years that yet remain, so that, on any other occasion which may present itself to the illustrious Signor Eneas, he, with that prudence and dexterity which belongs to him, may answer our Serene master *Galileo's wish to return to Florence, and in what manner, explained in his letter to Signor Vespuccio.* more determinately; to whose Highness, besides the reverent service and humble obedience which every faithful vassal owes him, I feel myself drawn with a devotion which I may call by the name of love (for God himself asks us no more than love), so that, setting aside my own interests, I would without hesitation change my fortune, to do his Highness a pleasure. So that this answer alone may suffice to bring his Highness to a decision in his intention respecting me.

"But if his Highness, with that courtesy and humanity which distinguish him above all other men, would deign to take me into his service, thereby rendering me satisfied to overflowing, I would say without hesitation that, having now labored for twenty years, and these the best years of my life, in dealing out, so to speak, by retail, to all who chose to ask, that small portion of talent which, through God and my own labor, I have gained in my profession, my desire would be to possess so much rest and leisure

[1] Galileo to a Florentine gentleman, whom he addresses as *Sig. Vesp. : mio gentilissimo*, in the spring of 1609.

as to be able to conclude three great [1] works which I
have in hand, and to publish them before I die. This
might possibly bring some credit to me, and also to
those who had favored my undertaking ; and peradventure it may be of greater and more lasting utility
to the studious in my profession than in the rest of
my life I could afford them. I do not think that I
could meet with greater leisure anywhere than at this
place, so long as I find it necessary to depend on my
public and private lectures for the support of my family ; nor would I willingly teach in any other city than
this, for many reasons which it would be too long to
state. Nevertheless, even the liberty which I have
here is not enough, where the best hours of my day
are at the disposal of this man or the other.

"It is impossible to obtain from a republic, however splendid and generous, a stipend without duties
attached to it ; for to have anything from the public
one must work for the public, and as long as I am
capable of lecturing and writing, the Republic cannot
hold me exempt from duty, while I enjoy the emolu-
ment. In short, I have no hope of enjoying such
ease and leisure as are necessary to me, except in
the service of an absolute prince.

"But I would not that, from what I have said, your
lordships should think that I have unreasonable pretensions, as that I desire a stipend without merit and
without service, for such is not my thought. As to
my merit, I have various inventions, of which one
alone, should a great prince take a delight in it, might
suffice to place me above want for the rest of my life.

[1] The Dialogues on Motion, on the Two Great Systems, and
the treatise *De Incessu Animalium*, which is lost.

For experience shows me that many discoveries of far less value have brought honor and riches to their discoverers.[1] And it has always been my intention to offer my inventions to my prince and natural master, that he might do with both the invention and the inventor according to his good pleasure.

"Daily I discover new things, and if I had more leisure, and were able to employ more workmen, I should do much more in the way of experiment and invention. And since you ask for some details respecting my gains here, I will say that my lectureship is worth 520 florins, which I feel assured will be increased to as many crowns on my reëlection, and these I can easily put by, as I am greatly helped in the maintenance of my household by taking pupils, and by giving private lessons, of which I can give as many as I choose. I say this because I refrain from giving many, desiring to have leisure much rather than gold; for it would be easier to me to gain renown by my studies, than by working for such a sum of money as might render me conspicuous amongst men.

"Thus succinctly, most gentle Signor Vespuccio, have I laid before you my thoughts. Whenever you see a fit opportunity for doing so, I would beg you to make the illustrious Signori Eneas and Silvio acquainted with the same. I know that I can thoroughly depend on the friendship of these two, and I shall have recourse to none besides. I therefore beg your lordship not to communicate the contents of this letter to any but these gentlemen."

---

[1] This discovery or invention is not further specified. The telescope was not invented till the June of the same year in which this letter was written (1609).

But in less than a year after this letter was written, Galileo was in a position to dictate his own terms to the Grand Duke. "I desire greatly," he wrote to Secretary Vinta,[1] "to have my mind set at rest on that business which we discussed lately at Pisa. For, seeing that every day is one more day gone, I am entirely resolved to fix once for all on the mode in which the rest of my life is to be passed, and turn all my energies to bring to a termination the labors of all my past life, from which I hope to gain some renown." After mentioning his income and prospects at Padua, he continues: " And, in short, I should wish to gain my bread by my writings, which I would always dedicate to my Serene master. Of useful and curious secrets I possess so many, that their very abundance does me harm; for if I had but one, I should have esteemed it greatly, and perhaps, through it, I might have found that fortune which as yet I have not met with, nor have I sought it: *magna, longeque admirabilia apud me habeo:* but they are no good to me, or rather they can be no good except to princes; for they alone make war, erect fortresses, and for their royal pleasure spend such sums of money as private gentlemen cannot, any more than I can. The works which I wish to finish are principally these: two books on the system of the universe; an immense work (idea, *concetto*), full of philosophy, astronomy, and geometry: three books on local motion, a science entirely new; no one, either ancient or modern, having discovered any of the marvelous accidents which I demonstrate in natural and violent motions; so that I may with very great reason call it a new science,

----

[1] Galileo to Belisario Vinta, May 7, 1610.

discovered by me from its very first principles : three books on mechanics, two on the demonstration of its first principles, and one of problems ; and though this is a subject which has already been treated by various writers, yet all which has been written hitherto, neither in quantity nor otherwise, is the quarter of what I am writing on it. I have also various treatises on natural subjects, on sound and speech, on sight and colors, on the tide, on the composition of continuous quantity, on the motions of animals, and others ; besides, I have also an idea of writing some books on the military art, giving not only a model of a soldier, but teaching, with very exact rules, all which it is his duty to know that depends on mathematics ; as, for instance, the knowledge of encampment, drawing up battalions, fortifications, assaults, planning, surveying, the knowledge of artillery, the use of various instruments, etc. Besides this, I wish to reprint the ' Use ' of my geometrical compass, dedicated to his Highness, which is entirely out of print. In fact, this instrument has met with such favor from the public, that no others of the kind are ever made ; and I know that up to this period some thousands of mine have been made. I will not say what an amount of labor will be required to fix the periods of the four new planets ; a task the more laborious the more one thinks of it, as they are separated from one another only by very brief intervals, and are very similar to one another in size and color.

" So that, Illustrissimo Signore, I must begin to think in what way I may free myself from those employments which only retard my studies ; particularly from those which another might fill quite as well as I can : therefore I pray you to propound these considerations to their Highnesses and to yourself, and acquaint me with their decision. As to stipend, I should be content with the sum you named to me at Pisa,[1] feeling it to be an honor to be his Highness's servant. I say nothing on the amount, being sure that, as I have to give up what I get here, the graciousness of his Highness will not allow me to be deprived of any of those comforts which others enjoy who are less in want of them than I ; therefore I say no more on this point. Finally, as to the title and pretext by which I take service, I would desire that to the title of Mathematician his Highness would be pleased to add that of Philosopher, as I profess to have studied a greater number of years in philosophy than months in pure mathematics. And how I have profited, and if I can and ought to merit this title, I may show their Highnesses as often as it is their pleasure to give me an opportunity of discussing such subjects in their presence with those whose knowledge is most esteemed."

Their Highnesses were not long in coming to a decision. Galileo was presented with a gold chain as a badge of merit ; the title of Philosopher was gladly conceded to him, and endowed with a gratification of two hundred crowns. The first step taken *Galileo pays his brother's debt to Taddeo Galletti and Benedetto Landucci.* by Galileo, after his appointment was fairly settled, was to ask for an advancement of the two first years' salary, for the purpose of paying off his brother Michelangelo's debt to his sisters' husbands.

Galileo finally quitted Padua in the beginning of the autumn. It seems from a letter he wrote to Vincenzo

---

[1] 1,000 Tuscan scudi per ann. A scudo is 10 pauls = 4*s.* 3*d.*

Giugni in the June preceding his departure, that his enemies had been endeavoring to discredit him with the Grand Duke; for he says:[1] *Quits Padua.* "Tell his Highness that the discoverer of the new planets is none other than Galileo Galilei, *Letter to Giugni, the Grand Duke's private secretary.* his faithful vassal, to whom the observation of three nights only was enough to assure him of the truth of the discovery, and not the observation of five months, which I have devoted to it; and let him lay aside all hesitation or shadow of doubt, for these planets will leave off being true planets when the sun leaves off being the *Secret enemies at the Court of Tuscany.* sun. Assure his Highness that these rumors owe their existence to malignity and envy, of which I find no lack; and let not his Highness hope to be exempt from it either.

"But I trust to have found means to stop the mouths of the envious and ignorant. The clearest argument against them is that they prate in corners, and speak vain words, but avoid establishing their conceits with pen and ink. But the fruits of this malignity will be contrary to its authors' intention; for so far from annulling this great discovery by crying out on it as false, impossible, contrary to all the ordinances of nature, it will only shine out the more sublime, the more to be wondered at, and worthy of more esteem than hath ever been accorded to any heroic greatness. And how this discovery is esteemed, and what an honor is thought to be connected with it, let the following letter prove, which was written to me by a valued servant of his late Majesty of France. It was written on the 20th of last April; I need hold it secret no longer, since

---

[1] Galileo to Vincenzo Giugni, June 25, 1610.

5

the earthly grandeurs of this monarch are miserably passed away.[1]   The words are these : —

" ' The second request, and the most pressing I can make you, is, that when you discover some other beautiful star, you would call it by the name of the great Star of France, by far the brightest in all the earth, and rather by the name of Henry than by the appellation of Bourbon, if it so please you. By so doing, you will do a very just, right, and proper thing ; you will gain renown, and likewise lasting riches for yourself and your family. Of this I can assure you on my honor. Therefore, pray discover as soon as possible some heavenly body to which his Majesty's name may be fitly attached ; and send the intelligence of it by letter through Signor Vanlemens, so that we may have the very first advice ; and be assured, as if his Majesty himself were speaking to you, that you will gain infinite content and happiness therefrom.' "

Galileo concludes : " I pray you therefore to take a fitting opportunity to entreat his Highness not to retard the flight of fame by showing himself doubtful of a thing which he has seen so many times with his own eyes."

We are told how Marie de' Medici, in her eagerness *Marie de' Medici.* to see the moon through the telescope, would not wait for it to be adjusted, but went down upon her knees before the window, thereby greatly astonishing the Italian gentleman who had brought the telescope into the royal presence.[2]

From the letters of Martin Hasdale, an Englishman

---

[1] In allusion to Henry IV.'s assassination on the 14th of May, 1610.

[2] Matteo Botti to Galileo, August 18, 1611.

settled at Prague, we get an amusing account of the wordy war waged against Galileo.[1] Magini, a native of Padua, but professor at Bologna, had declared superciliously that Galileo had deceived himself or that his telescope had deceived him, just in the same way as he (Magini) had been for a moment deceived by the sight of three suns on the occasion of viewing a solar eclipse through some colored spectacles which he had made himself. It was utterly ridiculous to suppose that such a thing could exist as that four planets were constantly chasing each other round a larger planet! He would go to Venice soon and procure a telescope, in order to make more evident the truth of his words. Kepler had declared that Magini's opposition arose from mere envy that any Italian should by his discoveries gain greater renown than himself. Horky, Magini's secretary, had gone so far as to declare[2] that Galileo had been at Bologna, and had departed covered with confusion, having been triumphantly defeated in the presence of several people by Magini, who had written to Zugmesser, mathematician to the Elector of Cologne, and to the principal mathematicians in Europe, in the hope of inducing them to take his side of the question. Hasdale says that Magini wished to be the phœnix of his profession, and that besides the opposition to Galileo, prompted by his own envious feelings, he was suspected of being under the influence of the Jesuits, who, since their banishment from the Venetian territory in 1606, had nourished a deep hatred to the whole body

Martin Hasdale.

Magini, professor of astronomy at the University of Bologna.

Martin Hasdale's letter.

---

[1] Martin Hasdale to Galileo, April 28, 1610.
[2] *Ibid.*, May 31, 1610.

of lay professors in Padua. The Lucchese ambassador and others had behaved insultingly to Hasdale, calling him " Lutheran," because he had so warmly undertaken Galileo's defense ; and had declared they would rather go wrong by believing with Magini than go right by holding an opinion put forth by any one else. Kepler, however, was a stout champion for Galileo, and such as valued Kepler's good opinion did not *Martin Hor-* venture to oppose him openly. Horky had *ky.* imagined that Kepler was as much opposed to Galileo as his master was, but quickly found out his mistake. In a letter to Francesco Sizi he declares : " Per Deum vivum hoc tibi dico, quod in æternum vir hic Galileus novas quatuor planetas ostendere non poterit." During Galileo's short stay at Bologna, this worthy had taken advantage of his sleeping at Magini's house to commit an act of treachery, which he confided to Kepler in the expectation of obtaining great credit from the latter. " I have contrived," he wrote, " to obtain a mould of the glass in wax, and when I get home, I intend, please God, to make a telescope as good or *Martin* even better than Galileo's." In another let- *Horky's cor-* ter to Kepler[1] he declares that he will never . *respondence* concede to that Italian his four planets ; he *with Kepler.* will die first. " At Italo illo Patavino quatuor novas planetos in Nuncio suo, vel cum capitis mei periculo *His book,* non cedam." He was going to print a book *entitled* which should quickly dispose of Galileo and *"Martini* *Horky a* his pretensions. This book was published *Lodovic* *brevissima* before Horky had received any answer to the *peregrinatio* various letters he had written to Kepler on *contra* *Nuncium* various letters he had written to Kepler on *Sidereum* the subject. It was divided into four parts, *nuper*

[1] Martin Horky to Kepler, April 27, 1610.

in which the question of the existence of the new planets was successively treated, much to the satisfaction of the author, who never *emissum a Galileo Galileo, Mutinæ,"* 1610. doubted but that he was about to draw down on himself the applause of all the scientific world. Part the first was devoted to the examination of the proofs of the existence or non-existence of the new planets. The questions, What they are? What they are like? and Why they are? were successively treated. To this last question — which Horky imagined to be a proper termination to his book, since the obvious answer to it was that as astrologers had done very well without these new planets hitherto, there could be no reason for their thus starting into existence — Wedderburn, a Scotchman then studying at Padua, answered with the dry humor of his nation, that the evident use of the new planets was to torment and put to confusion Horky and all superstitious astrologers.

On receiving the last of Horky's diatribes, Kepler had written him an indignant letter, declaring that he would have no further dealings with *Kepler's indignation.* him, and advising him, if he valued his liberty, to leave Pavia, where Horky, under the protection of the Jesuits, was preparing another work in confutation of Galileo ; telling him that he had informed the authorities there of his being a Lutheran. This, whether true or false, would be enough to render a residence in Italy unsafe at that time. This letter missed Horky, who had no idea of Kepler's real feeling towards him, and shortly afterwards presented himself at Kepler's house, unconscious of the storm of indignation ready to burst upon him. On perceiving his mistake, Horky, wishing at all hazards to preserve Kepler's friendship, confessed his

folly, and excused himself by declaring that he was induced to write by people in authority, that is, by Magini.
Moved by the fellow's abject entreaties, Kepler at
length not only forgave him, but endeavored to obtain
Galileo's pardon also, on the condition, as he wrote to
Galileo, "that he should let him (Kepler) show him the
satellites, *and that he was to see them and own they
were there.*"

Roffeni, who was professor of philosophy at Bologna,
Gioan Antonio Roffeni's letter. endeavored to prove to Galileo that Magini
was in no way anwerable for Horky's inso-
lence ; and that on hearing that Horky had
ventured to print a book in confutation of the " Nuncius
Sidereus," he had instantly dismissed him from his service.   Roffeni took great pains to assure Galileo that,
if Horky brought out his book after what Magini had
said to him, it would be merely a proof of the obstinacy
natural to Germans, not of the complicity of Magini or
any other professor at Bologna. One of Roffeni's letters
on this affair of Horky is so characteristic of the times
that we venture to give an extract from it.[1] " Since
the day that Magini drove Horky from his house, I
have not seen the miserable wretch. However, I set
one to watch for him, and this person informed me that
he had seen and spoken to him. I desired to take care
and not lose sight of him, but to follow him till he got
beyond the Bolognese territory, and then take from him
all his books, and leave him instead thereof a good
Horky escapes a beating. reminder. But Horky evidently suspected
something, for he went off secretly, but with-
out his books, which he had left at Baldassere Capra's
house, where he lodged when he was at Pavia. He

---

[1] Gioan Antonio Roffeni to Galileo, July 6, 1610.

was heard to say that he knew that I and Magini intended to do him a mischief, but that he was going where he should fear nobody. Believe me, Signor Galileo, it was a piece of luck for Horky that he knew by sight certain honest fellows with whom he had seen me in conversation ; for finding himself followed by some of them, he managed to disappear."

Contrary to Roffeni's expectation, Galileo did not consider Horky even worth a beating. He had at one time intended to answer his book, but quickly gave up this intention on being assured by Kepler that it was a production totally unworthy of a reply. While Hasdale, Kepler, Roffeni, and the rest, were disputing with Clavio, Horky, and others of his opponents, Galileo wisely pursued his observations with the telescope. He was before long (in July) rewarded by the discovery of Saturn's ring, and a few months after (in October) by that of the phases of Venus. Both these discoveries were announced to his particular *Discovery of Saturn's ring, July 25, 1610, and the phases of Venus in October, 1610.* friends anagrammatically, and they were invited to give a solution. Galileo's reason for adopting such a puerility was that, by announcing his discoveries in this manner, he saw less risk of being robbed of his right to them. Kepler endeavored to read the anagram referring to the ring of Saturn, but read it wrong, presupposing it to have some reference to the planet Mars. At the request of the Emperor Rudolf, Galileo sent the true reading : "*Altissimum Planetam tergeminum observavi.*" The discovery of the phases of Venus was felt by Galileo to be highly important, as containing in it the solution of that vast problem, the truth or falsity of the Copernican system.

It was not till after this third great discovery, that

*Tardy rec-
ognition of
these dis-
coveries by
the Jesuits.* the Jesuits, with Father Clavio, Rector of the Roman College, at their head, at last deigned to confess the existence of the satellites of Jupiter. Clavio had declared so late as October, 1610, " that he laughed at the idea of these four new planets ; that to see them, they must first be put inside the telescope ; and that he should hold to his opinion, and let Galileo hold his too, and welcome."

By this time, however, Galileo had less anxiety for the adherence, and less desire for the good opinion, of such men. Speaking of the death of Libri, one of the professors at Pisa, whose opposition had been somewhat violent, he observes, with quiet irony : " Libri did not choose to see my celestial trifles while he was on earth ; perhaps he will now he is gone to heaven." [1]

Convinced of the treasure he possessed in Galileo, the Grand Duke not only offered him a choice of any of the grand-ducal villas in the neighborhood of Florence, in order to relieve him from the necessity of living in the city, where he never enjoyed a day's health, but he also gave him permission to go to Rome for the purpose of showing his discoveries. This

*Galileo goes
to Rome,
March,* 1611. journey, delayed for some months in consequence of Galileo's ill-health, was undertaken at length towards the end of March, 1611, at the Grand Duke's expense. Galileo was lodged first at the ambassador's residence, and then at the Palazzo Medici in the Trinità de' Monti, as the Grand Duke's guest. Here, and in the gardens of the Quirinal, did

---

[1] Galileo, in a letter of which the address is wanting, but bearing the date of December 17, 1610.

Galileo display his " celestial novelties," as they were styled, the satellites, Saturn's ring, and the phases of Venus, to a crowd of Cardinals and Monsignori, adding his latest discovery, that of the solar spots. The honor of this discovery was claimed by a Jesuit named Scheiner, Professor of Mathematics at the University of Ingolstadt, who published three letters to Welser, under the pseudonym of Apelles, exposing his theory, namely, that the spots were due to the passing of certain stars or planets across the face of the sun. Galileo's reply consisted of three letters to Welser, which, indeed, were brought forth by a request of the latter to know Galileo's real opinion of the theory held by a person calling himself Apelles. These answers were published at the expense of the Lyncean Academy, of which the president was Prince Cesi, and of which Galileo had become a member on this visit to Rome, " in order," as the report of the Academy set forth, " to mark their sense of the merit of the book, and the claim of Galileo to be regarded as the first discoverer." This, of course, did not lessen the animosity of Scheiner, and of the body to which he belonged, who could not brook aught that savored of public depreciation.

Discovery of the solar spots, March, 1611.

Father Scheiner, the Jesuit, claims the priority of the discovery of the solar spots.

In the summer and autumn of 1611, during intervals of severe indisposition, Galileo had written two pamphlets in the usual form of letters, to Griemberger and Gallanzoni, on the lunar appearances. These had been followed up by a " Discourse on Floating Bodies," which, when printed in the year following, aroused the most violent opposition. Viviani relates that the

" Lettere intorno le Apparenze Lunare," written July and Sept. 1611.

" Discourse on Floating Bodies, 1612

whole host of Peripatetics rose to do battle with the
theories advanced in this work, and that the
press teemed with refutations and apologies
by Colombe, Grazia, Palmerini, and others.   Galileo,
in reference to the controversy occasioned
by his book, declared that ignorance had
been the best master he had ever had ; for
that in order to demonstrate to his adversaries the truth of his conclusions, he had been forced
to prove them by such a variety of experiments as
made him doubly confident, though to satisfy his own
intellect alone, he had never felt it necessary to make
them.

CHAPTER IV.

GALILEO was never married. By his mistress, Marina Gamba, a Venetian of the lower class, he had three children : Polissena, born in 1601 ; Virginia, who is supposed to have been next in age ; and Vincenzio, born in August 1606.[1] It appears probable, though not certain, that when Galileo quitted Padua in the autumn of 1610, he took the two elder children with him. We may presume they were placed for the time under the care of their grandmother. Vincenzio was left with his mother till October, 1612, when Galileo had him brought to Florence. Shortly afterward Marina married a well-to-do man in her own station of life ; one Giovanni Bartoluzzi, who was employed in some way by the Delfino family. This step we may believe to have been taken with Galileo's entire concurrence, judging from the tone of respectful cordiality of the only letter of Giovanni

Marina Gamba. Polissena Galilei, born 1601 ; Virginia ; Vincenzio, born August, 1606.

Giovanni Bartoluzzi.

[1] This boy was legitimated by the Grand Duke of Tuscany in 1619.

Bartoluzzi found among the Galileian papers.[1]　The eldest daughter of Marina Gamba and Galileo is here mentioned in terms of warm affection.　It also appears from this letter, and from two others, written by Liceti[2] and Pignoria,[3] that Galileo behaved with great liberality both to Bartoluzzi and to Marina Gamba.

The year before Galileo's final departure from Padua, he had had an intention of placing his eldest daughter as a boarder in the Convent of La Nunziatina at Florence.　It is not known why this intention, of which all the preliminaries were settled, was not carried into effect.　For some time after his arrival at Florence, *Don Antonio, son of Francesco I. and Bianca Cappello.* Galileo was the guest of Don Antonio de' Medici at his villa at Marignolle.　Later he took up his abode at the Villa delle Selve, *Filippo Salviati, died at Barcelona, March 22, 1614.* near Signa, the property of his friend Filippo Salviati.　It was not till after Salviati's death in 1614 that he fixed his residence at Bellosguardo, at the Villa Segni (now Villa Albizzi), where he remained till 1631.[4]　It is possible that his mother's temper,[5] as well as her age and infirmities, may have had an influence in the decision

---

[1] Giovanni Bartoluzzi to Galileo, August 17, 1619.

[2] Fortunio Liceti to Galileo, December 31, 1610.

[3] Lorenzo Pignoria to Galileo, January 25, 1613.

[4] In Galileo's Book of *Ricordi*, there is the following memorandum : "*Laus Deo.*　Mem. : That in the year 1617, on the 15th day of August, I returned to the villa at Bellosguardo, which I have taken for five years of Signor Lorenzo Segni, paying 100 scudi *pr. ann.*"

[5] Michelangelo Galilei, writing to Galileo, October 10, 1619, says : "I hear with no small wonder that our mother is so terrible ; but as she is so much aged, it cannot last very long ; and then there will be an end to quarreling."

taken by Galileo in 1611 of placing both his daughters in a convent for life.

But he did not wish to separate the two sisters; and hence arose a great difficulty. Pope Leo XI. (Alessandro Ottaviano de' Medici), when Cardinal, had obtained a brief to prevent two sisters taking the veil in the same convent in Florence. Cardinal del Monte[1] offered to use his influence with the Congregation of Bishops and Regulars, or, if necessary, with the Pope (Paul V.), to obtain a dispensation for the admittance of both the children into one convent. There was another difficulty in the way, namely, that in case the number of nuns was already complete in the convent chosen by Galileo, the dowry must be doubled for both daughters. This difficulty was insurmountable or not, according to the length of Galileo's purse. But the third difficulty was insuperable. No grace could be obtained for the removal of the restriction of age; and Polissena, the eldest girl, was but ten years old. It appears from Cardinal del Monte's letter of *Cardinal* the 16th December, 1611, how strongly Gali- *del Monte.* leo desired to place his daughters in a convent. He says: "In answer to your letter concerning your daughters' claustration, I had fully understood that you did not wish them to take the veil immediately, but that you wished them to be received on the understanding that they were to assume the religious habit as soon as they reached the canonical age.[2] But as I have written to you before, even this is not allowed, for

---

[1] Cardinal del Monte to Galileo, November 11, 1611.

[2] The text of the Canon is as follows: Sess. xxv., cap. 15: "In quacumque religione, tam virorum, quam mulierum professio non fiat ante decimum sextum annum expletum; nec qui

many reasons; in particular, that it might give rise
to the exercise of undue influence by those
who wished the young persons to take the veil
for reasons of their own. This rule is never
broken, and never will be, by the Sacred
Congregation. When they have reached the
canonical age, they may be accepted with
the ordinary dowry, unless the sisterhood
already has the prescribed number; if such be the
case, it will be necessary to double the dowry. Vacan-
cies may not be filled up by anticipation under severe
penalties, that of deprivation for the Abbess in particular, as you may see in a Decretal of Pope Clement
of the year 1604."

The Council of Trent laid down the general rule that no one of either sex should take the vows until fully 16 years of age.

Del Monte finishes by assuring Galileo that if there
had been the slightest chance of success, he would
have used his influence to obtain a dispensation.
Whether he felt that his influence was not strong
enough, or did not choose to use it in Galileo's behalf, is not quite clear. Galileo sought
the aid of Cardinal Bandini, and having
through his good offices obtained a dispensation of age,
was enabled, in October, 1613, to place his
daughters in the Convent of St. Matthew at
Arcetri, with a view to their taking the veil.
At this time a sister of Secretary Vinta was
Abbess of St. Matthew. She seems to have
felt a kindly interest in these unfortunate children.

Galileo applies to Cardinal Bandini.

Polissena and Virginia Galilei enter the Convent of St. Matthew, at Arcetri, Oct. 1613.

They took the veil in the autumn of 1614, Pol-
lisena, the eldest, being but thirteen years of

They take the veil, 1614.

minore tempore, quam per annum post susceptum habitum pro-
batione steterit, ad professionem admittatur. Professio autem
antea facta, fit nulla; nullam que inducat obligationem ad alicujus
regulæ, vel religionis, vel ordinis observationem, aut ad alios
quoscunque effectus."

age. By Abbess Ludovica's suggestion, the feasting usual on such an occasion was dispensed with. It would be better in every way, she wrote to Galileo, for the ceremony to take place quietly ; and any money which he might have to spend would be far better employed in increasing his daughters' comfort than in regaling a host of friends and relatives.[1]

In 1613, Benedetto Castelli was nominated to the mathematical lectureship of Pisa. The echo of Galileo's two watchwords, Analysis, Investigation, still resounded in the ears of the University authorities ; for it was thought necessary to warn Castelli, before his inaugural lecture could take place, that the theory of the earth's motion (of which the probability had been whispered since Galileo's discovery of the satellites of Jupiter) was to be passed over in profound silence, as well as any theory or argument in any way appertaining thereto. Castelli was as sincerely Copernican at heart as his master Galileo ; but he knew the men with whom he had to deal, and framed his answer prudently, for Galileo's sake as well as for his own. "I answered Monsignor,"[2] he says, "in these exact words : 'What your lordship commands me (and I shall take care to observe) my master, Signor Galileo himself, has already advised, whose counsel will always be listened to respectfully by me, particularly as I know that during the four-and-twenty years he has been a professor he has never discussed such subjects as those you mention.' To which his lordship answered that I might perhaps have spoken on

---

[1] Abbess Ludovica Vinta to Galileo, July 2, 1614.

[2] Arturo d'Elci, Provveditore of the University.

the probability of the truth of the theory in my private capacity. I answered that I should have abstained from so doing even had he not warned me."[1]

During the winter sojourn of the Court at Pisa, Castelli was admitted to the Grand Ducal table, and invited to take part in discussing scientific matters with the Serene Highnesses. The Grand Duchess Christina would be learned, but would above all things be orthodox. Father Caccini had been preaching a *Fra Tommaso Caccini, Dominican, on the Book of Joshua.* course of Advent sermons at Santa Maria Novella, taking for his subject the Book of Joshua. On the Fourth Sunday in Advent, having to expound the tenth chapter, he had taken occasion to inveigh against the already eighty years old doctrine of Copernicus, now revived by Galileo and reëchoed by his followers, by this time so numerous as to be styled the "sect" of the Galileists. Against this sect a few of the most bigoted and ignorant of the monks in Florence had formed a league. The depth of their ignorance may be gauged from the fact that Lorini the *Fra Nicolò Lorini.* Dominican did not so much as know who or what Copernicus was, but styles him "this Ipernico, or whatever his name may be." Well might Galileo complain that such calumniators as these should have power to bring him under ecclesiastical censure ! But the monks, having possession of the bare fact that one "Ipernico" wished to make the earth move in opposition to the Bible, supplied their want of other necessary information by loud denunciation of "Ipernico," his books, which they had not read, the science of mathematics, which they knew not, and Galileo, whom they had not seen. It is barely possible that,

---

[1] Benedetto Castelli to Galileo, November 6, 1613.

had they known that Copernicus was a Canon of the Church, who had been called to Rome by Leo X. while the Council of the Lateran was sitting, for the express purpose of remodeling the ecclesiastical calendar, they might have proceeded with more caution. But hearsays were to them all-sufficient. The very fact of their being the first to raise the cry, "The Church is in danger," gave them an advantage over men who were sober inquirers after the truth of the so-called new doctrine.   Her belief in Galileo's *Archduchess Christina.* transcendent genius for a moment shaken by the violent denunciations of the Dominican monk, Christina explained her doubts to Castelli. Castelli, rejoiced to have an opportunity of defending his master's opinions, put forth his strength to convince her Highness of the truth of the Copernican doctrine in a discourse which must have been of the nature of an impromptu lecture, for we are told that the discussion, which was opened by her Highness at dinner, was continued by her desire after she had retired to her private apartment, and that Castelli spoke at great length, and to the satisfaction not of her Highness only, but of the Grand Duke and his consort, Magdalen of Austria, and of Don Antonio de' Medici, who was present.[1]   But though the Serene mind was

[1] Letter of Father Benedetto Castelli to Galileo, December 14, 1613 : —

"On Thursday I dined at their Highnesses' table. The Grand Duke asked me how my lectures were attended. I entered into various minute particulars, with which he appeared much pleased. He asked whether I had a telescope. I answered that I had; and with this I gave an account of my observation of the Medicean planets the preceding night ; and Madama Serenissima *

* Christina of Lorraine, widow of Ferdinand I. and mother of Cosmo II.

satisfied for the nonce, other doubts might arise which might not be so easily set at rest; and Castelli the inquired their position. And hereupon some began to say that indeed these must be realities, and not deceptions of the instrument; and their Highnesses began to question Dr. Boscaglia, the professor of physics, who answered that the existence of these planets could not be denied. I took occasion to add what I knew of your wonderful invention, and of your having fixed the periods of revolution of the said planets. Don Antonio was at table, who showed by his countenance how much pleased he felt with what I said. At length, after many solemn ceremonies, dinner came to an end, and I took leave; but scarcely had I quitted the palace when Madama Serenissima's porter came after me, and called me back. But before I narrate what followed, I ought to tell you that during dinner Boscaglia was talking privately to Madama for a while; and he said that, if it were conceded that the celestial novelties discovered by you were realities, then only the motion of the earth was incredible, and could not be, for the reason that Holy Scripture was manifestly contrary to it.

" To return : I entered her Highness's apartment, where were the Grand Duke, Madama the Archduchess,* Don Antonio, Don Paolo Giordano, and Dr. Boscaglia. Here Madama, after a few inquiries as to my condition in life, began to argue against me with the help of the Holy Scripture; and I, after making a proper protest, began a theological exposition in such a masterly manner that you would have been delighted to hear me. Don Antonio helped me, and so encouraged me that, though the majesty of their Highnesses was enough to appall me, I behaved like a paladin. The Grand Duke and the Archduchess were on my side, and Don Paolo Giordano brought forward a passage of Scripture very opportunely in my defense. So that at length Madama Serenissima was the only one who contradicted me, but it was in such a manner that I judged she only did it to draw me out. Signor Boscaglia said nothing either the one way or the other.

" All the particulars of this audience, which lasted two hours, shall be told your lordship by Signor Nicolò Arrighetti. But I ought to tell you that, as I was praising you, Don Antonio joined

* Magdalen of Austria, the wife of Cosmo II.

disciple needed strengthening and confirming at the hands of the master. Galileo, in his letter *Galileo's letter to* to him on the Copernican system,[1] declares *Castelli.*
in, in what way you may imagine; and when I had taken leave, he offered me his services in the most princely manner, and desired me to give you an account of what had taken place, and what he had said ; and said in these very words : ' Write thou to Signor Galileo that I have made thy acquaintance, and tell him what I said in her Highness's chamber.' "

Letter of Galileo to Father Benedetto Castelli, Professor of Mathematics at Pisa, 1613 : —

" It seems to me that it was well said by Madama Serenissima, and insisted on by your reverence, that the Holy Scriptures cannot err, and that the decrees therein contained are absolutely true and inviolable. But I should in your place have added that, though Scripture cannot err, its expounders and interpreters are liable to err in many ways ; and one error in particular would be most grave and most frequent, if we always stopped short at the literal signification of the words. For in this wise not only many contradictions would be apparent, but grave heresies and blasphemies. For then it would be necessary to give God hands and feet and ears, and human and bodily emotions, such as anger, repentance, hatred, and sometimes forgetfulness of things past, and ignorance of the future. And in Scripture there are found many propositions which, taking the bare sense of the words, appear contrary to the truth ; but they are placed there in such wise in order to accommodate themselves to the capacity of the vulgar ; so that for those few who merit to be separated from the plebeian crowd, it is necessary for wise expositors to produce the true meaning, and to explain the particular reasons for which they have been thus worded. It being laid down, therefore, that Scripture is not only capable of divers interpretations, but that in many places it requires an interpretation differing from the apparent meaning of the words, it seems to me that in mathematical disputes it must be interpreted according to the latter mode. Holy Scripture and nature are both emanations from the Divine word ; the former dictated by the Holy Spirit, the latter, the executrix of God's commands. Holy Scripture has to be accommodated to the common understanding in many things which

that Scripture does not even accord with the Ptolemaic system, and further insists that God gave us the holy

differ in reality from the terms used in speaking of them. But Nature being, on the contrary, inexorable and immutable, and caring not one jot whether her secret reasons and modes of operation be above or below the capacity of men's understanding, it appears that, as she never transgresses her own laws, those natural effects which the experience of the senses places before our eyes, or which we infer from adequate demonstration, are in no wise to be revoked because of certain passages of Scripture, which may be turned and twisted into a thousand different meanings. For Scripture is not bound to such severe laws as those by which nature is ruled. For this reason alone, that is, to accommodate itself to the capacities of rustic and undisciplined men, Scripture has not abstained from veiling in shadow its principal dogmas, attributing to God himself conditions differing from and contrary to the Divine essence. And who can assert or sustain that, in speaking incidentally of the sun, or of the earth, or of other created bodies, Scripture should have elected to restrain itself rigorously to the strict signification of the words used? May it not be, that, had the truth been represented to us bare and naked, its intention would have been annulled, from the vulgar being thereby rendered more contumacious and difficult of persuasion in the articles concerning their salvation? This, then, being conceded, and it being manifest that two truths cannot be contrary to each other, it becomes the office of wise expounders to labor till they find how to make these passages of Holy Writ concordant with those conclusions, of which either necessary demonstration or the evidence of our senses have made us sure and certain. . . . As we cannot be certain that the interpreters are all divinely inspired, I think it would be prudent if men were forbidden to employ passages of Scripture for the purpose of sustaining what our senses or demonstrated proof may manifest to be the contrary. Who can set bounds to the mind of man? Who dares assert that he already knows all that in this universe is knowable? And on this account, beyond the articles concerning salvation and the stability of the faith, against the unchangeableness of which there is no danger of any valid and efficacious innovation being introduced, it would perhaps be

Scriptures to teach us those things that are necessary to salvation, but not to teach us that which may be learnt by the proper exercise of our senses, also a gift from Him.

A copy of this letter to Castelli, written by Galileo, as he says, *currente calamo*, and merely with a view to his friend's private satisfaction, was obtained either by indiscretion or treachery, — by the latter Galileo himself believed, — and thus fell into the hands of the Dominicans of the Convent of St. Mark, whose horror at its contents could only be appeased by taking measures for the speedy burning of its author. Animated by this motive, the fathers of St. Mark held a chapter extraordinary over the heretical manuscript. To Lorini was formally delegated the task of denouncing it to the Holy Office, the most damnable passages being first carefully

Lorini denounces Galileo's letter to the Holy Office, Feb. 5, 1615.

best to counsel that none should be added unnecessarily ; and if it be so, how much greater the disorder to add to these articles at the demand of persons who, though they may be divinely inspired, yet we see clearly that they are destitute of the intelligence necessary, not merely to disprove, but to understand, those demonstrations by which scientific conclusions are confirmed.

"I believe that the intention of Holy Writ was to persuade men of the truths necessary to salvation ; such as neither science nor other means could render credible, but only the voice of the Holy Spirit. But I do not think it necessary to believe that the same God who gave us our senses, our speech, our intellect, would have us put aside the use of these, to teach us instead such things as with their help we could find out for ourselves, particularly in the case of these sciences, of which there is not the smallest mention in the Scripture ; and, above all, in astronomy, of which so little notice is taken that the names of all the planets are not mentioned. Surely if the intention of the sacred writers had been to teach the people astronomy, they would not have passed the subject over so completely."

underlined.   It is to be noticed that in Lorini's letter of denunciation he complains, not only that the Galileists expound Holy Writ after their own manner and not after the method approved by the Fathers, not only that they speak with scant reverence of the ancient Fathers and of St. Thomas, but also that they utterly impugn and condemn the whole philosophy of Aristotle, so much in use by the Schoolmen.   The controversy, begun from the pulpit of Santa Maria Novella, had spread and raged hotly throughout Florence.   The preacher at the cathedral of Santa Maria del Fiore, a Jesuit, had undertaken to show that Copernicus was right, that the Galileists and their master were good Catholics, and that Caccini and the Dominicans were *Caccini's* ignorant fools.   Nothing daunted, Caccini *invectives.* had continued his invectives from the pulpit of Santa Maria Novella, dividing his discourse on one occasion into two heads, — namely, that mathematics was a diabolical art, and that mathematicians, being authors of every heresy, ought to be exiled from all Christian states, and making use of the text, "Ye men of Galilee, why stand ye gazing up into heaven?" in order to attract the Florentines, always ready to enjoy the fun of a play upon words.

This last piece of insolence had made Galileo lose *Fra Luigi* patience for a moment, and he had written *Maraffi.* to Fra Luigi Maraffi, then general of the Dominicans, to complain of Caccini's unseemly conduct.   Maraffi, who greatly esteemed Galileo, had written back in reply that the sermon had been preached without his knowledge or consent, that he was greatly mortified that a Dominican should have committed such a piece of foolery, and felt it a deep disgrace to himself to be implicated in the ill-behavior of thirty or forty thousand monks. He declared that if it were possible he would make Caccini retract what he had ventured to say from the pulpit, and that at least he would express his own opinion of him both orally and by letter. " I will say no more," he concluded, " for fear of expressing myself too strongly, and therein will take example by your own modest and temperate note to me."[1]

But the harm was done, and Maraffi's good will and fair words could not undo it.

Caccini was called to Rome in the March following, and interrogated by the Holy Office. Not only was he required to give evidence on what Galileo had writen, but on what his followers had said; of whom it is more than probable that their zeal sometimes outran their discretion. Even the public report respecting Galileo's sayings and teachings was considered fit matter for the ears of this venerable and awful assembly ; on the principle, it may be supposed, of there being no smoke without fire. Thus, Caccini deposed that the reverend Father Ximenes, Chancellor of Santa Maria Novella, had once told him in conversation that he had heard some Galileists utter the following propositions : *God is not substance, but accident. God is a sensitive being. The miracles attributed to the saints are not true miracles.* Not only were Galileo's reputation, profession, and birthplace the subject of inquiry, but Caccini was required to state such hearsays as were current among the monks concerning his inti-

Caccini's examination, March 5, 1615.

The Congregation of the Index.

---

[1] Fra Luigi Maraffi to Galileo, January 10, 1615.

macy with suspected persons. Thus, Lorini had said,
Galileo ac-
cused of
being on
friendly
terms with
Fra Paolo
Sarpi. and Ximenes had corroborated it, that Galileo was in the habit of corresponding with Fra Paolo Sarpi, so famous in Venice for his impiety.[1]

The fact of the preacher of the cathedral having preached against Caccini's exposition of the Book of Joshua was naturally too important to be omitted; especially as Caccini was inwardly convinced (it is not clear why) that Galileo's disciples had persuaded him to it. In answer to the demand whether he had not some reason for being inimical to Galileo, he declared that not only he felt no ill-will against Galileo (whom he had never seen) or against his disciples, Attavanti and the rest, but on the contrary he prayed for them. Attavanti was the name of a young priest whom " he thought Ximenes had mentioned as having held the propositions relating to the nature and substance of God." It appeared, on Attavanti's examination, that Caccini had listened to his conversation with Ximenes through a wooden partition, and had heard imperfectly, as they were neither discussing Galileo nor his doctrines ! Neither was Attavanti a disciple, but only an acquaintance of Galileo.

In Lorini's letter of denunciation, and Caccini's
Lorini's
letter and
Caccini's
deposition. deposition, which followed it closely in date and substance, we see the first germs of the memorable trial of 1633. For false charity, for false humility, for cant, in a word, it is probable that these two documents stand unrivaled. Lorini had denounced Galileo on the 5th of February. On

[1] He was suspected (most unjustly) of a leaning towards Lutheranism.

the 26th, Cardinal Mellini ordered the Secretary of the Congregation of the Index to write to the Archbishop and Inquisitor of Pisa, to procure dexterously and forward to Rome the original letter of Galileo to Castelli on the Copernican system, of which Lorini had only handed in a copy. The Archbishop thereupon sent for Castelli, and requested to be favored with the original, alleging, as a reason for this request, curiosity and their common friendship for the writer. Castelli had returned the letter to Galileo, but wrote to ask for it, suspecting nothing. Galileo delayed in giving his friend an answer, and the Archbishop wrote to inquire of Mellini whether he wished him to explain himself more clearly to Castelli. The answer was in the negative. Meanwhile, Galileo's suspicions had been roused by the Archbishop's earnest desire to possess the original, and he sent a copy without signature to Castelli, desiring him not to let it out of his hands. This injunction Castelli took care to observe. He satisfied the *soi-disant* curiosity of the Archbishop and of some canons of the cathedral by reading the letter aloud, but, as he tells Galileo in his letter of the 9th of April, he was careful not to let it out of his own hands.

Mellini, Cardinal Inquisitor of Rome.

Francesco Bonciani, Archbishop of Pisa, endeavors to obtain the letter by false pretenses.

Galileo, being warned of the league formed against him, and of the use which was being made of his letter to Castelli, wrote in self-defense to Monsignor Dini, declaring that if his enemies charged him with heresy, it was because they had willfully misunderstood his letter, or, what was more likely, had only a spurious copy of it. He therefore sent him a true copy, begging him to take the opinion of Father Griemberger[1] on it, and also, if he should think fit, to submit it to Cardinal Bellarmine.

His correspondence with Dini is, if possible, more remarkable than the famous letter on the Copernican system addressed a year later to the Grand Duchess Christina. Though Galileo was at the time severely tried by illness, there is not a trace of carelessness in his style, nor a single argument omitted which might serve to support the Copernican theory. Determined to fight his adversaries with their own weapons, he adduced, in his letters to Dini and to the Grand Duchess, not only verses in the Psalms which supported his own views, but also various passages in the writings of St. Dionysius the Areopagite, St. Augustine, St. Jerome, Tertullian, and others. But so much learning availed not with those who had already prejudged him. The Grand Duke wrote a recommendatory letter with his own hand to Cardinal del Monte.[2] By the advice of his Highness and of Monsignor Dini, who warmly espoused his cause, Galileo went to Rome to plead for himself and for the Copernican doctrine. But[3] though he counted numerous friends among the cardinals and

Galileo's letters in defense of the Coperni- can theory.

Galileo goes to Rome to plead his cause and bear witness to the truth of the Copernican system, Dec. 1615.

---

[1] Professor of Mathematics at the Collegio Romano.

[2] Cosmo II. to Cardinal del Monte, November 28, 1615: —

"Galileo, a mathematician well known to your illustrious lordship, informs me that, having felt himself deeply aggrieved by the calumnies which have been spread by certain envious persons, to wit, that his writings contain erroneous opinions, he has of his own accord (*spontaneamente*) resolved to go to Rome, and has for this purpose asked my permission, having a mind to clear himself from such imputations."

[3] Monsignor Ciampoli to Galileo, March 21, 1615: —

"The great rumors which were supposed to be circulating here

learned ecclesiastics, not to speak of the host of lay-
men whose adherence he had gained, the Dominican's
ignorance eventually gained the day. It had at one
time appeared that Lorini, not Galileo, was *Evil reports*
to be put to confusion; therefore, in order *spread by*
the Domini-
to strengthen their cause, the Dominicans *cans con-*
cerning
spread reports that Galileo had fallen into *Galileo.*
disgrace with the Grand Duke, and that he had been
ordered to live at his villa and not appear in Florence.
It was also hinted that Galileo had been guilty of other
crimes besides heresy, and that the Grand Duke would
see him punished with much pleasure.

have, to the best of my belief, not gone farther than to the ears
of four or five people at the most. Monsignor Dini and I have
both been trying to find out whether there was much stir, but it
appears that the matter is not being talked of at all; and therefore the report that all Rome was talking about it must have
been invented by the first movers of this fuss (the Dominicans of
Florence).

"I and Monsignor Dini were with Cardinal del Monte this
morning. His Eminence has an extraordinary esteem and liking
for you. He said he had had a long discussion with Cardinal
Bellarmine about your affair. They had come to the conclusion
that no impediment could be offered to your treating of the Copernican theory, or offering demonstrations of its truth, as long
as you keep clear of Holy Scripture; as the interpretation of
Scripture must be reserved to such professors of theology as are
approved by public authority; but that there would be great
difficulty in admitting interpretations of passages of Scriptures,
however ingenious, which diverge so much from the common
opinion of the Fathers of the Church.

" All with whom I have spoken consider that it is extremely
impertinent that preachers should take advantage of the pulpit
to introduce such a grave and difficult subject as this to an
audience composed of women and of the lower orders, in which
scarcely a person is to be found with sufficient intelligence to
grasp such a subject."

Finding that, in spite of all their efforts, Galileo himself was held blameless, they endeavored to palliate their conduct. Caccini[1] sought an interview with Galileo, for the purpose of assuring him that he had not been the prime mover in the quarrel ; that what he had said and done had been by commandment of *Hypocritical* his superiors. Lorini made excuses which *excuses of* were still more contemptible ; declaring freely *Caccini and* *Lorini.* that he knew nothing, and wanted to know nothing, of the merits of the pending controversy, and that he had only spoken in the first instance "for the sake of saying something," lest men should think that the Dominican fathers were asleep or dead.

But Lorini and Caccini knew not the power they had evoked. The Congregation of the Index, once set to the task of scenting out heresy, was not to be quieted till a victim of some sort was given it. Failing Galileo's body to torture, they took the book of Copernicus, " De Revolutionibus Orbium Cœlestium," and placed it on the Index, unmindful of the fact that their so doing loudly proclaimed the fallibility of Paul III., to whom it was dedicated. Galileo's position at Rome at this time is painted in lively but somewhat exaggerated colors, in the ambassador's letter to the Grand Duke.[2]

" Galileo has chosen rather to follow his own opin- *Guicciar-* ion than that of his friends. Cardinal del *dini's letter* *to the Grand* Monte, and I as much as I could, besides *Duke.* many Cardinals of the Holy Office, have

---

[1] Galileo says of him : " I perceived not only his great ignorance, but that he has a mind void of charity, and full of poison." — *Letter to Secretary Picchena*, February 20, 1616.

[2] Piero Guicciardini to Cosmo II., March 4, 1616.

endeavored to persuade him to be quiet and make no more stir in this matter, but if he will hold this opinion, to hold it tacitly, without endeavoring to make others hold it too.   For we feared that his coming here would be both prejudicial and dangerous to him. . . . . . But he, ... after importuning many of the Cardinals, threw himself on the favor of Cardinal Orsini, and for this end procured from your Serene Highness a warm letter of recommendation to this Cardinal, who last Wednesday spoke in the Consistory to the Pope in favor of the said Galileo. The Pope an- *Paul V.* swered that he would do well to persuade *(Camillo Borghese.)* Galileo to give up this opinion.   Orsini made some answer which roused the Pope to opposition.   He cut the discussion short, saying he had referred the matter to the Congregation of the Holy Office.   As soon as Orsini was gone, his Holiness had Cardinal Bellarmine called, and after discussion they decided that Galileo's opinion was erroneous and heretical ; and the day before yesterday there was a Congregation to declare the same.   And Copernicus as well as other writers hold-ing his opinion are either to be corrected and altered, or else prohibited.   I do not suppose that Galileo's person will suffer, as of course he will see the pru-dence of hearing and willing what Holy Church doth will and hear.   But he fires up in defense of his opin-ions, and has small strength or prudence wherewith to control himself ; so that he renders this climate of Rome extremely dangerous to himself, particularly in these times, when we have a Pope who ab- *Guicciar-* hors *belles-lettres* and geniuses, and will not *dini's opinion of* hear of these novelties and subtleties. And *the Pope.* every one seeks to accommodate his own brain and nature to that of our lord' Pope ; so that even those who know something, and are curious to know more, if they have any wisdom, pretend to know nothing, in order to keep free from suspicion. There are monks *Guicciar-* and others here who hate Galileo and per- *dini's letter* *to Cosmo II.* secute him ; and, as I say, he is in a false position here, considering what Rome is ; and he may not only get into trouble himself, but get others into trouble too. I for my part do not see what reason he had for coming, nor what good he has got by being here. Your Serene Highness knows well what has been the attitude of your Serene House in times past towards the Church of God, and how you have deserved of her, in matters relating to the Holy Inquisition. I do not see why you should put yourself to such embarrassment, or undertake such risks, without weighty reason, seeing that no good can result from it, but only great injury to your Serene Highness's interests. . . . . This thing (the theory of the earth's motion) is abhorred at Court ; and if the Cardinal,[1] on his arrival here, does not, as becomes a good ecclesiastic, assent to the deliberations of the Church ; if he does not second the Pope's will, and that of a Congregation such as that of the Holy Office, which is the very base and corner-stone of religion, and the most important assembly in Rome,—he will lose much ground, and give great cause for displeasure. If he chooses to have in his antechamber or in his circle of acquaintance infatuated men who will make a parade of their opinions, and uphold them with strife (particularly these astrological or philosophical opinions), he will find himself avoided by everybody ; for, as I

---

[1] Carlo de' Medici, brother of the Grand Duke.

said, the Pope is so alienated from such opinions, that every man endeavors to feign a rustic ignorance. . . . . So that the less parade literary men make of their opinions here, the better. And if Galileo remains here for the coming of my lord Cardinal, and succeeds in mixing him up in this business, it will be to my lord's hurt. For Galileo is so vehement, so obstinate, and so infatuated, that it is impossible for any one who has him in his neighborhood to escape from his hands. And as this is no matter for mirth, but may become extremely prejudicial (if indeed it is not already become so), and as this man is in your Serene Highness's and my lord Cardinal's house,[1] and under your protection, I considered it my duty to represent to your Serene Highness what has passed, and what the common report is concerning this matter."

This dispatch of Guicciardini's is not only exaggerated, but incorrect ; for, as the dates affixed to the trial papers show, the last Congregation had been convened on the 24th of February, not the 2d of March. Galileo had been called and admonished (not censured) by Cardinal Bellarmine on the 26th ;[2] therefore, for the time at least, and at all

Guicciardini's inaccuracy.

---

[1] Galileo was residing at Villa Medici, in the gardens of Trinità de' Monti.

[2] The order for Galileo's admonition is dated *Die Jovis*, 25 *Februarii*, 1616 : . . . " Sanctissimus ordinavit Ill. D. Cardinali Bellarmino ut vocet coram se dictum Galileum, eumque moneat ad deserendam dictam opinionem, et si recusaverit parere, Pater commissarius coram notario et testibus faciat illi preceptum ut omnino abstineat hujusmodi doctrinam et opinionem docere aut defendere, seu de ea tractare ; si vero non acquieverit, carceretur."

The Pope's order was carried out on the following day, *Die*

events as far as it was then possible for any one to
foresee, the whole affair was at an end. We must remember that Galileo was a gentleman and a courtier,
and that his whole correspondence shows him to have
been a man of exquisite tact. It was hardly possible
that, in the face of the friendly admonition received
but a few days before from Cardinal Bellarmine, he
should have continued vehemently to assert and uphold the truth of the Copernican system, to all and
sundry, in season and out of season. Such a proceeding would have shortly resulted in his arrest by the
familiars of the Holy Office on the charge of contu-
macy. Guicciardini, while endeavoring to represent
Galileo as devoid not only of the commonest appreciation of fitness of time and place, but as devoid also of
common sense and prudence (two qualities peculiarly
Tuscan), does show very plainly that he disliked both

Veneris, 26 *ejusdem* : " In palatio solitæ habitationis D. Ill.
Cardinalis Bellarmini et in mansionibus D. supradicti Illustris-
simi : idem Ill. D. Cardinalis, vocato supradicto Galileo, ipsoque
coram D. S. Illustrissimæ existente in præsentia adm. R. fratris
Michaelis Angeli Seugnitii de Landa, ordinis predicatorum, com-
missarii generalis S. Officii, prædictum Galileum monuit de errore
supradictæ opinionis et ut illam deserat et successive ac inconti-
nenti in mei præsentia et testium et præsente etiam adhuc eodem
Ill. D. Cardinali supradictus Pater commissarius prædicto Galileo
adhuc ibidem præsenti et constituto præcepit et ordinavit pro
nomine S. D. N. Pape et totius Congregationis S. Officii, ut
supradictam opinionem quod sol sit centrum mundi et immobilis
et terra moveatur omnino relinquat, nec eam de cætero quovis
modo teneat, doceat, aut defendat, verbo aut scriptis ; alias contra
ipsum procedetur in S. Officio : cui præcepto idem Galileus
acquievit et parere promisit. Super quibus peractum Romæ ubi
supra, præsentibus ibidem ad. Badino Nores de Nicosia in regno
Cypri et Augustino Mongardo de Loco Abbatis Rottz diocesio
Politianeti, familiaribus dicti Ill. D. Cardinalis, testibus."

Galileo and his philosophy, and that, however ignorant the Pope may have been of all that appertained
to science, Guicciardini himself probably did not feign
more than his actual rustic ignorance of such matters,
since he evidently considers the words " astronomical,"
" astrological," and " philosophical," as synonymous,
whereas there was no need of feigning ignorance with
a master who loved science and esteemed scientific
men.

The decree of the Congregation was promulgated
on the 5th of March. A treatise of Father *Decree of the Congregation of the Index respecting books in favor of the Copernican system.*
Antonio Foscarini, a Carmelite monk, on
the Copernican system,[1] and an exposition
of the Book of Job by an Augustine monk
named Didacus or Diego of Stunica, containing a commentary on the passage " *qui commovet ter-
ram de loco suo,*" etc., which favored the new doctrine,
were included in the probihition of Copernicus' work,
" De Revolutionibus Orbium Cœlestium." This decree
was a great blow to Galileo, who had hoped for a far
different result. It was a small thing to him that he
escaped personal censure. Convinced of the truth of
the Copernican theory, and having convinced others
daily, in hall and antechamber, wherever he could find
listeners, the condemnation of that theory was not only
a proof of the willing subservience of the Congregation
to the views of an unscientific and perhaps prejudiced

---

[1] Benedetto Castelli to Galileo, April 9, 1615 : —

" I think that my Lord Archbishop (of Pisa), now he sees that
the monk has been writing in defense of this opinion (of the earth's
motion), is more astonished than he had been at any previous argument in its favor. His lordship no longer says that these are
follies, but begins to say that Copernicus was really a great man
and a great genius."

Pope, but seemed to him to be likely to damage the interests of the Catholic religion, and to bring into disrepute that Church of which he was a sincere and faithful member. Of all the calumnies raised by his enemies, the only one which affected him painfully, was that which accused him of being a bad Catholic. Suspecting that Guicciardini had insinuated into the Grand Duke's mind a suspicion that his behavior had been characterized by a violence unworthy of a philosopher, and compromising to the Government of Tuscany in its relations with the Court of Rome, Galileo wrote to Curzio Picchena, the Grand Duke's secretary and his intimate friend, to vindicate himself. " That *Galileo's defense of his conduct while at Rome.* which I have done," he says, " my writings will always show, and I keep them to the end that my calumniators' mouths may be stopped. They will show sufficiently what my behavior has been in this matter, and I assert that no saint could have acted with greater reverence or greater zeal for Holy Church. And I would say that it has not been thus with my enemies ; for in their endeavor to ruin me, they have left untried no calumny, or machination, or diabolical suggestion, as you and their Serene Highnesses shall hear at the proper time. And as it has appeared to me that certain persons, being ill-inclined towards me, might make one-sided reports to his Highness, I pray his Highness to keep his good opinion of me till I come back. . . . . Above all, I would have your lordship know how calmly and temperately I ruled myself, and how careful I was to say nothing which could damage the reputation of those who, on the contrary, had done their very worst to ruin mine. I believe your lordship will be much astonished at what I shall have to relate to you."

If Picchena was astonished at anything, we think that the particulars of Galileo's interview with the Pope must have contained more matter for astonishment than the recital of his enemies' machinations. For men of opposite parties to blacken each other's characters and to contrive each other's ruin was nothing new or strange ; on the contrary, it was considered a custom both ancient and honorable. But Galileo, in his interview with Pope Paul, thrust his head, so to speak, into the lion's mouth, and drew it out again unhurt. *Galileo's interview with Pope Paul V.* According to his own account,[1] the Pope was very gracious, and conversed with him, walking up and down, for three-quarters of an hour. Galileo mentioned some of the false reports which had been spread by his enemies, and complained of the causeless and rancorous persecution to which he had been subjected. The Pope desired him to take no heed of the evil reports which had been spread, but to keep a quiet mind ; for that he himself was assured of his orthodoxy, and Galileo might rest secure of not being troubled by the Congregation during his life-time at least. The Grand Duke had taken no further notice of Guicciardini's letter than to send a message to Galileo through Picchena, desiring him to take matters quietly. But Guicciardini, evidently disliking philosophical and " astrological " discussions even more than the Pope did, wrote again, insisting on the propriety and necessity of Galileo's leaving Rome.

" Galileo shall be paid," he says curtly,[2] " what he

---

[1] Letter to Picchena, March 12, 1616.
[2] Guicciardini to Picchena, May 13, 1616.

says he requires.   He is in a humor to try to vanquish even the monks' obstinacy ; and if he fights with them, of course the day will go against him.   So you may shortly expect to hear down there (in Florence) that he is utterly ruined and compromised.   However, the heat will probably drive him from Rome before long, and that will be the best thing that can happen to him."

The answer to this was a message to Galileo from the Grand Duke.   "You, who have tasted the monks' persecution," says Picchena,[1] *Picchena's warning.* "know what sort of flavor it has.   His Highness desires you not to rouse up sleeping dogs, but to come away from Rome without further delay ; for we have heard reports which are not pleasant, and we know that the monks are omnipotent : therefore take warning."

It is probable that the Grand Duke feared that his brother, who was friendly to Galileo, might be induced by the latter to express such opinions on the Copernican theory as might compromise the Court of Florence.   Bellarmine wrote a declaration of Galileo's innocence, which was made public, as, indeed, was its author's intention ; though if the Cardinal had known what a powerful weapon this document would be sixteen years later in the hands of Galileo's enemies, it is certain he would never have written it.[2]

[1] Picchena to Galileo, May 23, 1616.

[2] Cardinal Bellarmine's Declaration : —

"We, Robert Cardinal Bellarmine, having heard that it has been calumniously stated that Signor Galileo Galilei has abjured before us, and that he has been ordered to submit to salutary penances, and wishing that the truth may be known, declare that Signor Galileo has not abjured either before us or any one

Cardinal del Monte also furnished Galileo with a letter to the Grand Duke, desiring the latter to take no notice of the many false reports which had been spread with a view to disgracing Galileo with his Highness.

Before his departure from Rome Galileo recommenced a correspondence, begun some years before, with the Court of Spain, through the Count of Lemos, then Viceroy of Naples, on his method of discovering longitudes at sea. The Count's secretary, Argensola, who appears to have undertaken to make both Lemos and Di Castro understand Galileo's method before they arrived at Madrid, wrote to Galileo, saying, "that he thought he had done what was sufficient to set the matter a-going, which till now had been as silent as a watch which had lost its mainspring." As a contrast to the stately elegance which is so strong a characteristic of Galileo's style, comes the following rugged sentence at the close of Argensola's letter: "I have observed with what compliments your lordship honors me in your letter, but I pray you not to take it ill if I write according to our Spanish style, which is briefer and more familiar to me. Nevertheless, if your lordship chooses the contrary, I will e'en

Correspondence with the Court of Spain.

Argensola's letter.

else in Rome, nor in any other place that we know of; neither hath he received any salutary penances, but that merely hath been made known to him the declaration of our lord Pope, published by the Sacred Congregation of the Index, which adjudges the doctrine attributed to Copernicus, respecting the motion of the earth round the sun, to be contrary to Scripture, and therefore not to be held nor defended. In faith of this we have written and subscribed this with our own hand."

write as it shall best please you. And I pray God to
have you in his keeping." [1]

Galileo's attempts to improve the method for determining the longitude at sea.
Before the discovery of Jupiter's satellites, the
eclipses of the moon, whenever they occurred, had been made use of in determining the longitude at sea. But this method
was both inconvenient and inaccurate, though
it was not till Galileo had discovered the satellites of
Jupiter that the inconvenience was supposed to admit
of a remedy. Finding himself able to predict with
certainty the times of eclipse of each satellite, it immediately occurred to Galileo to what account their
discovery might be put; since by this means the longitude might be accurately determined, instead of its
being, as heretofore, determinable only to within about
four degrees. Galileo in his letters to Orso d'Elci, the
Tuscan ambassador at Madrid, declares that his invention was proportionate to the grandeur of the
Spanish Crown, whose dominion spread over the
whole terrestrial globe. But neither Galileo's courtly
flattery, nor the undoubted use which the possession
of his method would have been to the Spanish navy,
could rouse the Court of Madrid from its apathy.

Philip III.
His proposition was indeed discussed in
Council by the King's order, and a report
was made to his Majesty. From the ambassador's
letters, however, it appears that the members of the
Council had to be instructed, first, in the importance
of obtaining the correct longitude at sea; secondly, as
to the means whereby it was proposed to be obtained.
The ambassador himself professed to be much in the
dark, and craved explanation. But though Galileo

[1] Bartolommeo Leonardi d'Argensola to Galileo, May, 1616.

was willing to explain, and had even offered to go to any Spanish seaport and hold a public course of instruction in this new method, which would have combined instruction in the use of the telescope, the scheme was looked upon with coldness, and the King declined to spend money in an experiment which might prove as fallacious as many others which had been tried. Galileo's disappointment was *Disappointment of Galileo.* in some degree mitigated by the Grand Duke's taking up the discovery for the use of the Tuscan navy. But the application of it was found to be beset with so many difficulties that it was never made of general use. The negotiations with the Court of Spain were renewed from time to time, but never came to any definite conclusion.

CHAPTER V.

SINCE Galileo's return to Florence his health had
been extremely indifferent. Severe and painful mala-
dies, aggravated by fits of hypochondria, frequently
prevented him from corresponding even with his most
intimate friends. It is wonderful to note how, in
spite of such serious drawbacks, he pursued those
observations and experiments which had already made
Galileo's his name so prominent in the literary and
industry. scientific world. From 1611 to 1616 he had
published the treatise (in the form of a letter to Father
Griemberger, the Jesuit) " On the Inequalities of the
Moon's Surface ; " the " Discourse on Floating Bodies ; "
" On the Spots observed on the Body of the Sun ; " and
the " Discourse on the Tides." The famous letter to
the Grand Duchess Christina was written in 1615, as
well as two on the same subject to Monsignor Dini
and to Castelli. Besides this, he embodied various
observations on the inequalities of the surface of the
moon in his letters to Welser, Breugger, and Gallanzoni, and to the Duke Muti ; and in 1615, under the
name of Castelli, published an answer to the writings
of Colombe and Grazia against his " Discourse on
Sagredo's Floating Bodies." His friend Sagredo ad-
advice. vised him in vain to take his ease, and be

content with the laurels he had already won. "Philosophize comfortably in your bed, and let the stars alone. Let fools be fools ; let the ignorant plume themselves on their ignorance. Why should you court martyrdom for the sake of winning them from their folly ? It is not given to every one to be of the number of the elect. I believe the universe was made for my service, not I for the service of the universe. Live as I do, and you will enjoy life." This was the burden of Sagredo's letters from the time his friend quitted Padua till his own death in 1620.

But Galileo was no Epicurean. Speculation and experiment were as necessary to him as food and air. The appearance of the three comets in the *Appearance of the three* autumn of 1618, of which the most con- *comets, 1618.* spicuous was in the constellation Scorpio, excited the attention of every astronomer in Europe. Galileo's observations of them were greatly interrupted by a serious illness which confined him to his bed for nearly the whole time of their appearance. At the request of the Archduke Leopold of Austria, who condescended to visit him while confined to bed, he wrote down such reflections as appeared to him most pertinent, and confided them to his disciple Mario Guiducci, who based on them a discourse which Galileo revised and corrected with his own hand, and which was afterwards printed. In this discourse *Grassi the* some opinions of the Jesuit Grassi were con- *Jesuit.* tradicted [1] with a force which betrayed the master's hand. Grassi, offended that his position of Mathe-

---

[1] Ciampoli, writing July 12, 1619, regrets deeply that Grassi had not been let off with greater leniency, as now the whole Roman College was offended with Galileo.

matician to the Roman College had not secured greater respect for his opinions, shortly after published *Grassi's "Astronomical Balance."* a book called the "Astronomical Balance," under the pseudonym of Lotario Sarsi. Though it was considered by many of Galileo's friends that, taking into account the scurrilous language of the generality, the Jesuit had written temperately enough, *Stelluti's advice.* yet a reply appeared inevitable. Francesco Stelluti, a member of the Lyncean Academy, advised that, as Grassi under the alias of Sarsi pretended to be a learner, Galileo should let Guiducci bear the responsibility of the reply, since it scarcely suited his dignity as master to come to words with a student. Thus, Stelluti suggested, Galileo could express himself with greater freedom, and could desire Sarsi to give the name of his master, that he might present himself and carry on the controversy. Galileo, however, thought fit to reply to Grassi himself, and to this end laid aside the manuscript of his "Dialogue on the Two Great Systems," on which much of his time had been employed since he had quitted Padua. But though by no means wanting in diligence, and though his friends were constantly urging him to greater haste, *"Il Saggiatore."* the state of his health was such that the " Saggiatore " (the Assayer), as his answer to Grassi's book was called, was not ready for publication till the autumn of 1622. The printing and the obtaining of the license caused a delay of another *Death of Gregory XV. (Alessandro Ludovisi).* year, and during this interval important changes had taken place. The reign of Gregory XV. was over, and the Cardinals were debating on their choice of a head.

It was the first fortnight of August, and the heat

was suffocating. Many prelates and members of the Conclave fell ill ; some died. This, Stelluti says [1] was the means of bringing the Conclave to a decision much sooner than would otherwise have been possible. The tiara fell to the lot of Maffeo Barberini, *Maffeo Barberini elected Pope, Aug. 1623.* who took the name of Urban VIII. As Cardinal, Urban had been on such intimate terms with Galileo as to sign himself his " affectionate brother." He had not thought it beneath his dignity to write Latin sonnets in praise of Galileo and his discoveries. On his accession to the papal chair, his first step was to make Cesarini and Ciampoli — both, like himself, members of the Lyncean Academy — Chamberlain and secret *Cameriere* respectively. Another member of the Lyncean Academy, *The Pope's nephew, Cardinal Francesco Barberini.* Dal Pozzo, was attached to the service of the Pope's nephew. The Academicians trusted that under such auspices, science, on the basis of free inquiry, would receive such a favorable impulse as to shame the ignorant followers of the old school into silence. Galileo, who had at first intended to dedicate as well as to address the " Saggiatore " (which was written in the form of a letter) to Don Virginio Cesarini, was for a moment inclined to dedicate it to Father Griemberger, who was not personally ill disposed to him. But from this he was strongly dissuaded by Ciampoli, who was rightly of opinion that such a dedication would draw down on Griemberger the suspicion and ill-will of the whole company of Jesus. It was necessary, according to Ciampoli, to *Ciampoli's advice.* use the greatest discretion in order to avoid wounding the susceptibilities of this all-powerful body,

---

[1] Francesco Stelluti to Galileo, August 12, 1623.

and various alterations in the " Saggiatore " were suggested by him with a view to this. But Ciampoli's advice was disregarded. In courteous and knightly fashion, Galileo utterly demolished his adversary's arguments. The Jesuits had declared openly that the *Ill-will of the Jesuits.* author of the " Astronomical Balance " belonged to their Order, and that his arguments were unanswerable. Galileo's crushing reply was dedicated to the new Pope. This was an injury to their prestige which it was impossible for the Order to forgive. From that day they became Galileo's open enemies.

CHAPTER VI.

OUR first glimpse of Polissena Galilei was when the convent gate opened to receive her and her sister Virginia in 1614. In 1623 she appears as Sister Maria Celeste. All we know of her *Sister Maria Celeste.* from that time is told in her letters to her father. His letters to her, though we know that she kept them carefully, and was in the habit of perusing them during such leisure moments as her duties in the pharmacy and still-room left to her, have unfortunately disappeared ; nor was a trace of them to be found when the search for his writings and correspondence brought to light all that is now carefully preserved in the Pitti Library. It is probable that these letters, so treasured by his eldest daughter during her life, were destroyed by the Mother Abbess after her death, lest at some future time the convent should be compromised by their presence among its archives. Supposing this to be the case, it must be remembered, lest the reader should charge the Mother Abbess with cowardice and ingratitude towards Galileo, who was a kind friend and benefactor to the convent as far as in his power lay, that we are by no means sure that the Abbess in office at the time of Sister Maria Celeste's death was the same whom she mentions as having embraced her and wept for joy at the news of her father's release from the Inquisition in 1633. Unless this friendly Abbess had been reelected, there must have been a change between July, 1633, and April, 1634. The elections were held in the month of December, and the term of office in the convents belonging to the Franciscan Order was only for a year. Though Sister Maria Celeste had many friends among the nuns, it was not to be expected that all would love her in that large community. And though the whole of the inmates profited alike by Galileo's advice and his position at court, and his friendship with men in office and with various prelates at the Court of Rome, still we must not forget, what the Abbess of St. Matthew could not and dared not forget, that Galileo had been declared by the Holy Office to be vehemently suspected of heresy, and that his prison had only been transferred from the archiepiscopal palace at Siena to his own house at Arcetri, because the spies of the Holy Office had discovered that during his residence at the former place he had sown heretical opinions.

Let us, then, forgive the Abbess for destroying letters the possession of which might have exposed her to ecclesiastical censure.

It may be objected that Galileo himself may have requested these letters from the Abbess after his daughter's death. This is barely possible, but most unlikely. Everything which a nun possessed was, in theory, the property of the sisterhood; in practice, the property of the Abbess for the time being, as she it was who alone could order the disposal of a nun's possessions. At a nun's death everything belonging to her, from her breviary to the veil she wore, became the absolute property of the convent. The first act of the Abbess, as soon as the breath of a nun was out of her body, would be to enter the cell and make a list of the effects therein. Nay, she might not always wait till its inmate was actually dead, if she suspected the existence of anything that were best destroyed; · letters from a person " vehemently suspected," for instance.

We can sometimes guess the contents of these lost letters by the answers which, thanks to Galileo's loving care, and his disciples' reverence for that which their master had thought worthy of preservation, have come down to us. Sister Maria Celeste emerges from behind the convent grating. She lifts the veil which envelops her, and shows us, beneath the black serge which tells all that its wearer is dead to the world, a woman's heart; a heart beating fast, full of filial tenderness, full of self-abasement, full of interest in the things of that world she had renounced in her childhood. We see this heart of hers, often *Sister Maria Celeste's character.* pierced with sorrow, divided always between love and fear — love for her father and fear of impending evil. Tender and timorous, she yearns over him as a mother yearns over her only son. Besides the father-worship which breathes and glows in every page, these letters, one hundred and twenty in number, bear evidence throughout of sound sense and sober judgment, joined to a simple piety, rare, perhaps, at any time, but extremely rare in those days. There is not a trace of mysticism ; there is no mention of minute practices of devotion. She does not pass her nights in the church, kneeling on the cold stones, expecting a vision. She goes to bed like a sensible woman, and takes her seven hours' sleep. She regrets sometimes that her constitution should require so much sleep, but only because she would like better to sit up and write long letters to her dearest lord and father. Of our Heavenly Father she discourses much ; of the Madonna, though she calls her "Most Holy," scarcely ever. We hear of no patron saint. The nuns have each their patron, she says, their *Devoto*, to whom they tell all their joys and sorrows. A piteous picture this. Imagine a poor woman, whose heart is not quite dead, in spite of her vow and her black veil, flying to an image, a painting hung on the wall of her cell, for the sympathy which she dare not ask from her fellow-prisoners ! Imagine her talking to her saint's effigy, for want of father, or brother, or husband ![1] [Sister Maria Celeste tells us that she has her father to tell her joys and griefs to, and therefore wants no patron saint.]

Around this nun, who shows us her inmost heart, so that we feel as if she were known to us, — as if, having read her letters, we should recognize her here-

[1] It is well known that while the nuns' devotion was towards some particular saint of the male sex, the monks, on the other hand, chose female saints for their friends and confidantes.

after, — the sisters stand ; a group of shadows with a name attached to each. Some flit by, once mentioned : sisters these, — for were not all the nuns sisters ? — but not friends. One or two are more prominent, Sister Luisa Bocchineri in particular, who was Sister Maria Celeste's bosom friend. Her own sister, Virginia Galilei, Sister Arcangela in religion, appears as little more than a *Sister Arcangela (Virginia Galilei).* shadow, and what we are told of her inclines us to exceeding pity, but to little love. Her disposition would seem to have been decidedly selfish ; her sister was accustomed to give up a great deal to her for the sake of peace, or, as she puts it, " in order not to disturb the love we bear each other." We further learn that Sister Arcangela was subject to frequent fits of hypochondria, and that she was constantly an invalid. Ill-health was the rule, not the exception, at St. Matthew's. Sister Maria Celeste herself was scarcely ever well. Sometimes she, sometimes another sister, sometimes half the convent, were ill with fever. Rheumatism is frequently complained of. In winter the nuns were starved with the cold ; in summer they were melted with the heat. Of the convent discipline, though we learn but little, nevertheless we gather from the freedom with which Sister Maria Celeste expresses herself that it was by no means vexatious. No letters which were to pass *Discipline of the Convent of St. Matthew.* through the hands of the Mother Abbess before reaching Galileo would have been written in such a strain of complete confidence. What would Mother Abbess have said, for instance, to one of the sisterhood who wrote that convent life weighed heavily on her ? Yet Sister Maria Celeste confesses this more than once when her father is ill and unable to come as far as the convent to see her. We gather, therefore, that though neither of the sisters were happy in their prison, yet that it was not in consequence of any great severity of discipline. Their friends were allowed to visit them on all feast-days. During Lent, and before Advent, intercourse was not the rule, though it does not appear to have been strictly forbidden, in this convent at least. But it was no uncommon thing for those who wished to lead a religious life while living in the world to impose on themselves certain restrictions in their intercourse with friends during seasons of abstinence, so that, even had the retreat at St. Matthew been a strict one, it could not have been made a matter of complaint. What Sister Maria Celeste wanted was home life. She stands before us, eagerly striving to learn something of the dwelling which her father's presence renders sacred, but which she can never enter. Discreet Dame Piera, careless, unloving brother Vincenzio, good Signor Rondinelli, the gardener, the boy Geppo, may all go in and out, may all serve her *Devoto*, sit by him when he is ill, help to tend the vines, run the errands ; only *she* is debarred from the daily intercourse which would be her supreme delight. At least a third of the contents of her letters consists in anxious inquiries and tender entreaties that he will take

Sister Maria Celeste's love for her father. care of himself. " What should we two poor creatures do," she cries, " if you were taken from us ? " Again and again she begs him to say what he would like her to do for him. Does he like baked pears and quinces ? Shall she send him confectionery, or fragrant waters from the still-room stores ? Does he want his linen collars washed or mended?   So "sweet and serviceable" is she, that she cares not what she does, so long as the work is for her father's benefit and comfort.   She tells him often that he knows well she is never so entirely happy as when she is busy for his sake.

The Convent of St. Matthew belonged to the Order of St. Francis of Assisi.   Probably the extreme poverty of the sisterhood was the chief if not the sole reason of their freedom from Jesuitical influences.   Nevertheless there are evidences that the vow of poverty, stringent though it was, was unequally borne.   Those of the nuns who could afford to purchase comforts were allowed to do so; consequently one sister might be shivering in her bare, scantily furnished cell, while her next-door neighbor was enjoying the comfort of bed-curtains and door-hangings.   Of candied fruits and cinnamon-water the convent still-room contained a perennial supply; of solid food and good wine there was too often a scarcity.   Galileo was in the habit of sending all sorts of provisions to his daughters: often Sister Maria Celeste writes begging for a supply of wine, or fresh meat to make broth for herself when ill. If such presents arrive during a time when *Her unself-ishness.* she does not consider herself in need of delicacies, she keeps none for herself, and always, even when ailing, gives away the best flasks of wine to the sick and aged sisters. (For though, from her own admissions, we judge that she suffered at least as much as her sister or any other nun in the convent, or even as Galileo himself, she never seems to take much account of her own health.) If unusual suffering elicits a complaint, she instantly chides herself, and thanks God for having given her so many blessings already. "Doubtless," she says, submissively, "our Heavenly Father would give me health too if it were good for me."

The first of this long series of letters, which, un-learned and full of small housewifely detail though they were, the great astronomer thought well worth *Death of* preserving, was written on hearing of the *Galileo's* *sister,* death of her aunt, Virginia Landucci, in the *Virginia* *Landucci.* spring of 1623 :[1] —

"Very illustrious and most beloved lord and father, — We are very much grieved to hear of the death of your beloved sister, our dear aunt. And not for her loss alone do we mourn, but also for the affliction it must be to you, who, as one may say, possessed but her in this world, nor could scarcely lose aught more dear, so that we may imagine how severe this unex-pected shock must have been. And, as I said, we sympathize fully in your grief; though, indeed, the consideration of human misery should suffice to make us take comfort, seeing that here we are but pilgrims and strangers, and that soon we shall set out for our true country in heaven, where is perfect bliss, and where we may hope that this blessed soul is gone. For the love of God, then, we entreat your lordship to be comforted, and to put yourself into the Lord's hands, to whom you well know it would be displeasing were you to do otherwise ; also that it would injure both yourself and us. For, seeing that you are our only treasure in this world, how can we but grieve infinitely when we hear of your being sick and in trouble ?

"I will say no more, except that with our whole

[1] This letter is dated May 10, 1623.

hearts we entreat the Lord to bless you and be with you always.

"Your very affectionate daughter."

This letter is addressed to Galileo's house at Bellosguardo, now known as Villa Albizzi.

Remembering with what warmth Barberini had written to him shortly before his election, Galileo considered that the time spent in going to Rome to lay his homage at the feet of his Holiness would not be time wasted. He thought that he had reason to hope, from a Pontiff so enlightened as Urban had appeared to be, the recognition of the Copernican theory, now banned for nearly a century. He felt that, as far as he himself was concerned, he must gain permission to teach it as actual truth now or never; and according as his desire was fulfilled or not would his life be complete or incomplete.

Galileo hopes for the recognition of the Copernican theory.

Knowing her father to be the object of animosity in so many quarters, the accession of Urban VIII. was a source of great rejoicing to Sister Maria Celeste. Having been favored with a sight of the Pope's letters to her father when Cardinal, she writes, on returning the letters, in a strain of eagerness which indicates sufficiently the lively interest she took in all that concerned her father's welfare : —

"I cannot describe the pleasure with which I perused the letters of the illustrious Cardinal who is now our high priest, knowing as I do how greatly he loves and esteems you. I have read the letters several times, and now send them back as requested, having shown them to

Letter on the accession of Cardinal Barberini to the papal chair.

no one except Sister Arcangela, who, as well as myself, is much delighted to see how greatly you are favored by such an important personage.   May the Lord give you health to fulfill your desire of visiting his Holiness, so that you may enjoy a still greater measure of his favor.   Seeing how many promises he makes in his letters, we may hope that you will easily get something to help our brother.[1]

" Meanwhile we will not fail to entreat the Lord, from whom all grace proceeds, that your desire may be granted you, if indeed it be for the best.

" I imagine that by this time you will have written a most beautiful letter to his Holiness, to congratulate him on his having obtained the tiara.   As I feel rather curious about it, I should like extremely, if you do not object, to see a copy of what you may have written.

" I thank you infinitely for what you have sent, and also for the melons, which we were very glad to get. As I have written in very great haste, I must beg you to excuse the bad handwriting.   All join me in hearty greetings."

Devout Catholic as she was, Sister Maria Celeste had not perceived the immeasurable distance between her father, principal Philosopher and Mathematician-in-chief to his Serene Highness of Tuscany, and Maffeo Barberini, possessor of the papal tiara.   To the child Polissena, Galileo had doubtless appeared the greatest man on earth, and the nun Maria Celeste had not deposed him from his pinnacle.   Galileo, not the less man of the world because he happened to be a man of science, wrote instantly to enlighten his daugh-

---

[1] Vincenzio had not long before commenced his studies at Pisa.

ter as to the behavior fitting for an occasion such as this.   In her reply, dated the 13th of August, she confesses her ignorance with the most touching humility: —

"From your beloved letter I see fully how little knowledge of the world I must possess to *Letter confessing her ignorance of worldly etiquette.* have thought as I did that you would write immediately to such a personage, to one who is in fact the head of Christendom.   I therefore thank you for the hint you have given me, and feel sure that your love for me will induce you to excuse my ignorance as well as many other faults which I possess. I trust that, always being warned and reproved by you, I may gain in knowledge and discretion.

"Since we are not able to see you in consequence of your lingering indisposition, we must patiently resign ourselves to the Lord's will, who permits all things for our good.

"I put by carefully the letters you write me daily, and when not engaged with my duties I read them over and over again.   This is the greatest pleasure I have; and you may think how glad I am to read the letters you receive from persons who, besides being excellent in themselves, have you in esteem.

"Fearing you may think me tiresome, I conclude, with affectionate salutations from Sister Arcangela and those who belong to the same room."

A few days after, the convent steward, who had been sent with a message or a note to the villa at Bellosguardo, brought back the news that Galileo *Illness of Galileo.* was at Florence ill.   Fearing that the indisposition might be more serious than usual, and that her father had perhaps gone into the city for medical advice, Sister Maria Celeste sent the steward to Florence, to see Galileo and hear from himself what state his health was in. She says, in the affectionate little note of which the steward was bearer, " that she never regrets being a nun except when her father is ill, because then she would like to be with him. Yet," she adds submissively, " let our Lord God be praised for everything, for without his will not even a leaf may turn."

" I do not suppose," she continues, " that you are in want of anything ; but if you are, let us know, and we will supply it with the best we have. Meanwhile we will continue, as we are wont, to entreat our Lord to give you that measure of health so much to be desired, and also that He will give you his heavenly grace."

Galileo's illness would seem to have been more *Sister Maria* serious than usual, for four days after we *Celeste's* *anxiety.* find Sister Maria Celeste writing again, and sending, as an excuse for the steward's going so often to her father's house, a present of biscuits, baked in a mould representing a fish. The truth is, as she confesses in her little note, she wants the steward to see Galileo and learn how he is from his own mouth. Evidently she will place little reliance on messages given by those around Galileo, even though they be of his kindred. Galileo was at this time sojourning in the house of Messer Benedetto Landucci, his brother-in-law. One of Landucci's daughters was already a nun in the convent of St. Matthew. Her dowry had only been paid in part, and Galileo, always ready to accommodate his relatives in every possible way, had become security for the rest.

On the 28th of August, Sister Maria Celeste writes again : —

"We were much grieved to hear yesterday from Messer Benedetto that there was no improvement, but that you were still in bed, suffering, and without appetite. Nevertheless we firmly hope that the Lord in his mercy will shortly restore you to some measure of health. I do not say entirely, for this seems impossible, with so many complaints as are constantly troubling you ; but these, being borne with such patience as yours, will undoubtedly procure you greater merit and glory in the life which is to come.

" I have succeeded in procuring four plums, which I send, hoping that if they are not in as great perfection as I could have wished, you will take the will for the deed.

" Please remember that when you get an answer from those gentlemen at Rome, you have promised me a sight of it. I say nothing of the other letters you promised to send, as I suppose they are at the villa (at Bellosguardo). Fearing to be tiresome, I will only add that Sister Arcangela and the rest of our friends here join me in kindly greetings. May our Lord comfort and be with you always."

By the end of August, Galileo, though still ailing, was sufficiently restored to allow of his resuming his correspondence with his daughter. On his return to Bellosguardo, the letters she had wished to read were sent to her, as also the thread and other trifles which she had requested her father to procure. Before long, Galileo, feeling his strength unequal to the demands on it, bethought himself of making his *She is her father's secretary.* daughter secretary, when he wished copies taken of any particular letters or papers. It is not too much to suppose that her clear, delicate handwriting may first have suggested to him that she might be of use as a copyist.   In the letter in which she incloses one, of which Galileo had desired a copy, she expresses a hope that he will think it well done, as then, perhaps, he will let her copy some more.   She reminds him that to be occupied in his service is her great pleasure and contentment.

Galileo, finding that he had more wine than he required for his household, thought to do the Lady Abbess a good turn by offering it to the convent rather than to a neighbor.   But Madonna — as Sister Maria Celeste styles her — had no money to buy wine just then, and excused herself for not becoming a purchaser ; they must finish what they have already before they buy more, she ordered Sister Maria Celeste to say.   This is the first glimpse we get of the poverty of the convent.

The next letter, dated October 20th, is mostly on domestic matters : —

"I send back the rest of your shirts which we have *Domestic de-* been working at, also the apron, which I *tails.* have mended as well as I possibly could. I likewise return the letters you sent me to read ; they are so beautiful that my desire to see more of them is greatly increased.   I cannot begin working at the dinner napkins till you send the pieces to add on.   Please bear in mind that the said pieces must be long, owing to the dinner napkins being a trifle short.

"I have just placed Sister Arcangela under the *Sister* doctor's care, to see whether, with the Lord's *Arcangela's* *illness.* help, she may be relieved of her troublesome complaint, which gives me great anxiety.

"I hear from Salvadore (the servant) that you are coming to see us before very long. We wish to have you very much indeed ; but please remember that when you come, you must keep your promise of spending the evening with us. You will be able to sup in the parlor, since the excommunication is for the table-cloth, and not for the meats thereon."

The meaning of this phrase is, that although the rule of the Order forbade guests being received in the refectory under pain of excommunication, there was nothing to prevent their being asked to dine or sup in the parlor, nor was it considered a breach of discipline for any nun who might be invited to join in the meal. Sometimes indeed, by way of "dining out," a nun's friends might ask her to partake, in the convent parlor, of a meal which they had brought from their own abode.

It will be remembered, that though Galileo had, in 1619, taken steps to legitimize his son Vincenzio, his daughters carried the stain of illegitimacy with them to their graves. From the abject gratitude which Sister Maria Celeste's letters express for favors which most daughters would consider as their birthright, it would appear that she was fully, painfully conscious that she and her sister had no real — that is to say, no legal — claim on their father. She had sent him a list of things which she and her sister required. The following letter, dated October 29th, was written on receipt of the package : —

"If I should begin thanking you in words for the present you have sent us, besides not knowing how to quench our debt with words, I believe that you would not care for them, *Sister Maria Celeste's gratitude to Galileo.*

preferring, as you do, our gratitude to demonstrative phrases and ceremonies. It will be better, therefore, that in the best way we know of, that is, by praying for you, we endeavor to show our sense of gratitude, and to repay this and all other great benefits which we for such a length of time have received from you.

"When I asked for ten braccia [1] of stuff, I meant you to get me a narrow width, not this cloth, so wide and fine, and so expensive. This quantity will be more than sufficient for us.

" I leave you to imagine how pleased I am to read the letters you constantly send me. Only to see how your love for me prompts you to let me know fully what favors you receive from these gentlemen is enough to fill me with joy. Nevertheless I feel it a little hard to hear that you intend leaving home so soon, because I shall have to do without you, and for a long time too, if I am not mistaken. And your lordship may believe that I am speaking the truth when I say that except you there is not a creature who gives me any comfort. But I will not grieve at your departure because of this, for that would be to complain when you had cause for rejoicing. Therefore I too will rejoice, and continue to pray God to give you grace and health to make a prosperous journey, so that you may return satisfied, and live long and happily; all which I trust will come to pass by God's help.

" Though I know it is not necessary for me to do so, yet I recommend our poor brother to your kindness; and I entreat you to forgive him his fault in

---

[1] The braccio is equal to about twenty-three English inches.

consideration of his youth, and which, seeing it is the first, merits pardon.[1] I do beg and entreat *Sister Maria Celeste intercedes for her brother.* you to take him to Rome with you, where opportunities will not be wanting to give him that assistance which paternal duty and your natural kindness will prompt you to seek out.

"But fearing that you will find me tiresome, I forbear to write more, though I can never cease to recommend him to your favor. And please to remember that you have been owing us a visit for a very long time."

What the escapade was which had brought Vincenzio into disgrace with his father, we are not *Vincenzio's ill-conduct.* told. This was not the last time that his sister had to intercede to obtain a removal of Galileo's just displeasure. In disposition Vincenzio *His untoward disposition.* would seem to have resembled his uncle Michelangelo. Years brought him no discretion. Wayward, selfish, idle, with a great capacity for spending money he had not earned, and a no less capacity for sulkiness, this only son was a constant thorn in his father's side. Castelli, who looked after him with paternal solicitude, even to the buying of his shoes and stockings, complained bitterly to Galileo of his mulish obstinacy. A fault confessed was half atoned for, the good Father thought, and strove hard to bring him to confession, assuring him that no punishment should follow. "But he is as hard as a stone," he *Castelli's letter.* wrote, "and one would think he were struck dumb by enchantment. As for me, I am in utter despair."[2]

[1] Vincenzio was then seventeen years of age.
[2] Castelli to Galileo, December 5, 1623.

Galileo's intention of visiting Rome was not put into execution till the Easter of 1624. This delay was occasioned by the state of his health, which absolutely forbade his braving the fatigue of a journey to Rome during the winter. Meanwhile his friends at the Papal Court anxiously watched the temper of the new Pope, and kept him well informed of every favor- *Friendship of the new Pope for Galileo.* able indication. "Under the auspices of this most excellent, learned, and benignant Pontiff," wrote Prince Cesi, "science must flourish. . . . Your arrival will be welcome to his Holiness. He asked me if you were coming, and when ; and, in short, he seems to love and esteem you more than ever." Ciampoli wrote in the same strain. Yet a certain amount of caution was necessary ; and of this Galileo seems to have been as fully aware as Prince Cesi, to whom he had imparted his great desire to bring about the recognition of the Copernican theory. Writing in October to this nobleman, who was then residing on his estate of Acquasparta, near Todi, he says : —

"I have received the very courteous and prudent advice of your Excellency respecting the time and manner of my going to Rome, and shall act upon it. I shall pay you a visit at Acquasparta, that I may be fully informed of the present state of things at Rome."

Meanwhile Sister Maria Celeste was busy working *Sister Maria Celeste's preparations.* at the new set of dinner napkins which had been cut too short, and must therefore have pieces added. How her housewifely soul must have been vexed at those pieces !

" I cannot rest any longer without news," she wrote in the last week of November, "both for the infinite love I bear you, and also for fear lest this sudden cold, which in general disagrees so much with you, should have caused a return of your usual pains and other complaints. I therefore send the man who takes this letter purposely to hear how you are, and also when you expect to set out on your journey. I have been extremely busy at the dinner napkins. They are nearly finished, but now I come to putting on the fringe, I find that of the sort I send as a pattern, a piece is wanting for two dinner napkins : that will be four braccia. I should be glad if you could let me have it immediately, so that I may send you the napkins before you go ; as it was for this that I have been making such haste to get them finished.

"As I have no sleeping room of my own, Sister Diamanta kindly allows me to share hers, depriving herself of the company of her own sister for my sake. But the room is so bitterly cold, that with my *Privation* head in the state in which it is at present, I *and discom-* *fort.* do not know how I shall remain, unless you can help me by lending me a set of those white bed-hangings which you will not want now. I should be glad to know if you could do me this service. Moreover, I beg you to be so kind as to send me that book of yours which has just been published, ' Il Saggiatore,' so that I may read it, for I have a great desire to see it.

"These few cakes I send are some I made a few days ago, intending to give them to you when you came to bid us adieu. As your departure is not so near as we feared, I send them lest they should get dry. Sister Arcangela is still under medical treatment, and is much tried by the remedies. I am not well myself; but being so accustomed to ill health, I do not make much of it, seeing, too, that it is the Lord's will to send me continually some such little trial as this. I thank Him for everything, and pray that He will give you the highest and best felicity.

" P. S.   You can send us any collars that want getting up." [1]

Galileo had written to ask his daughter what service would be most acceptable to the convent. At Rome he would be in constant communication with Church dignitaries. In expectation of all sorts of proffers of favor and friendship, such as it was the fashion among the scientific or free-thinking party to hold out to learned men, philosophers, and poets, Galileo wished to have an answer ready. In Sister Maria Celeste's reply, besides evidences of her own good sense, we gain some insight into the habits of the clergy of the period.

" From your very kind letter, written some days ago, I had hoped to be able to give a *vivâ voce* answer to your question. But as the state of the weather prevents you coming, I have decided on telling you my thoughts in writing. I must begin by saying what pleasure your very kind offer of help to the convent gives me. I have spoken about it to Madonna and to some of the elder mothers, and all showed that amount of gratitude which the nature of the offer merited. But as they could not decide amongst themselves what it would be best to ask, Madonna wrote to our governor to ask his opinion. His answer was that, considering the extreme poverty of the convent, he thought it would be wisest to ask for alms rather than anything else. Meanwhile, I have been talking a good deal on

---

[1] Sister Maria Celeste to Galileo, November 21, 1623.

the subject with one of the nuns, who is a person of good judgment, and kinder and better than any of the sisterhood as far as I see ; and she, moved not by passion or interest, but by pure zeal for the well-being of the convent, has advised, and, indeed, begged me to ask for a thing which doubtless will be as useful to us as it will be easy for you to obtain, namely, that his Holiness would grant us the favor of choosing for our confessor a Regular or Brother of some Order, on condition of changing him every three years, as is the custom in other convents. We do not wish to be absolved from obedience to the Ordinary because of this, but we desire such a confessor for the administration of the most Holy Sacraments. I cannot tell you how neces-·sary such a confessor is to us ; some of the various reasons we have for wishing him to be a member of some Order, I have noted down in the inclosed sheet of paper.

"But as I know it would not do for you to act in this matter merely on a word from me, you might, besides asking the opinion of some person of experience, endeavor, when you come here, to find out Madonna's mind on the subject, as well as the opinion of some one of the elder mothers : only you must take care not to let them find out why you ask. And pray do not say a word about this to Messer Benedetto (Landucci), for he would instantly tell Sister Clara,[1] and she would tell all the nuns. In this way everything would be spoilt, for in so many heads there must needs be a variety of fancies. Consequently, any nun who might dislike the plan would throw some impediment in the way. And it seems to me that it would

---

[1] Benedetto Landucci's daughter.

not be right, that, for the sake of two or three sisters, the whole community should be deprived of what would be both a temporal and a spiritual benefit, if we could but obtain it.

"We mean to abide by your good judgment. It therefore only remains for you to examine whether or not our demand be a proper one; and if so, in what way it had best be made to be easiest granted. To me it seems a proper thing to ask, and there is no doubt at all of the great want of it.

"I have written to-day, for, seeing the weather so calm, I think you may be coming to see us before it breaks again; and I wanted to tell you how you must ·set to work with that old man.[1]

"Fearing to weary you beyond measure, I write no more, reserving many things till we meet. To-day we expect Monsignor the Vicar-General, who is coming on *Election of the new Abbess.* account of the election of the new Abbess. May it please God that the election fall on one who is most conformed to his will. And to your lordship may He vouchsafe abundantly of his heavenly grace."[2]

The paper inclosed in the preceding letter is as follows:—

"The first and principal reason for my making this *Sister Maria Celeste's remarks on monastic discipline.* request is that I see and know what scanty knowledge and experience these priests have of the rules and requirements of us nuns; and that in consequence they give us great occasion, or I might say permission, to lead a life [8]... which...,

---

[1] Not further specified. Probably the ordinary or governor of the Franciscan convents in that district.

[2] Sister Maria Celeste to Galileo, December 10, 1623.

[8] The concluding words of the sentence are illegible.

and with small attention to our rule. And who can doubt that, while we live without the fear of God, we must expect to be in perpetual misery regarding temporal matters? Thus we ought to begin by removing the cause of offense which I have already stated.

"The second reason is, that, owing to the poverty of the convent, we cannot satisfy the claims of the confessors, by paying them the salary owing at the expiration of the three years of office. I know that three of the former confessors have large sums still owing them; and they make this a pretense for coming here frequently to dine, and getting friendly with one or other of the nuns. And, what is worse, they make *Her opinion of the priests from the Casentino.* a common talk of us, and complain of us wherever they go, so that we are become the laughing-stock of the whole Casentino,[1] from whence these confessors come, who are more apt at chasing hares than at guiding souls. If I once began telling you all the absurdities committed by our present confessor, I should never have done; they are so numerous and so incredible.

"The third reason is, that a Regular cannot be so ignorant as not to know more, at any rate, that one of these Casentini. And even though he be as ignorant, at least he will not go asking advice at the Episcopal Palace or elsewhere, as to what his conduct and decision should be, in every trifling case that may arise in the convent, as these priests are constantly in the habit

---

[1] The upper valley of the Arno is thus named : —

> "Li ruscelletti, che de' verdi colle
> Del Casentin discendon giuso in Arno,
> Facendo i lor canali e freddi e molli."
>
> *Inferno,* canto xxx.

of doing; but on the contrary, he would ask the advice of some learned father belonging to his own Order.   In this way our affairs would be discussed in one convent only, and not in all Florence, as is the case now.   Besides this, a Regular, however great his want of experience, would know that he ought so to rule his behavior as to give no possible occasion for dispute among the nuns ; whereas a priest who comes here unacquainted with monastic life has finished his term of three years before he has learnt what are our rules and obligations.

"We do not desire our confessors to be of any one Order more than another ; that particular can be decided by the person who grants our request.   It is true, however, that the brethren of Santa Maria Maggiore, who have come here as confessors extraordinary, have given us great satisfaction ; and I should consider that the appointment of one of these would quite meet our case.   First, because they observe their own rule very strictly, and are greatly looked up to. Secondly, because they do not expect grand presents, nor do they care (being used to live poorly) for such dainty fare as is expected by the priests whom we have had for confessors, who, coming for three years only, seek nothing during that time but their own interests ; and the more they can squeeze out of us nuns, the better opinion they have of themselves.

"I might add other reasons to those already given, but instead of doing so, I would ask your lordship to inform yourself as to the state in which were formerly the convents of S. Jacopo, S. Monaca, and others, and also what their state is and has been since they have been governed by brethren who knew how to bring them into proper order."

The journey to Rome, so long contemplated, was at length undertaken.   Furnished with a letter *Galileo sets out for Rome.* of the Grand Duchess Christina recommend- ing him to the favor of her son, Cardinal de' Medici, Galileo set out in April (after Easter), going by way of Perugia, and stopping at Acquasparta to visit Prince Cesi.   From Acquasparta he wrote to his daughter. His reception at this place was most flattering, and he had the further satisfaction of learning that his presence at Rome was anxiously desired " by great personages."   On the other hand, he had the grief of learning the sudden death of Monsignor Cesar- *Death of Monsignor Virginio Cesarini.* ini,[1] whom he both loved and honored, and who, while President of the Lyncean Acad- emy during Prince Cesi's absence, had introduced his new book, " Il Saggiatore," to the notice of the Pope.

This event, Sister Maria Celeste reminds him in a letter written on the 26th April, "gives food for reflection on the fallacy and vanity of all earthly hopes," Then she adds timidly, " But I would not have you think that I wrote merely to sermonize you, therefore I will say no more."   Galileo remained at Rome about two months.   During this time he had no less than six long interviews with the Pope, who, on his *Urban's presents to Galileo.* departure, presented him with " a fine painting, two medals, one of gold and the other of silver, and a good quantity of *Agnus Dei*."[2]   Of these last we may suppose the nuns of St. Matthew to have had *Promise of a pension for Vincenzio.* the largest share.   Besides this there was a promise of a pension of sixty crowns to be settled on

[1] He was a member of the ancient ducal family of the same name.   He bequeathed his library to the Lyncean Academy.

[2] Galileo to Prince Cesi, June 8, 1623.

Vincenzio,[1] as an acknowledgment of his father's merits. Anxious to appear as Galileo's chief patron, the Pope took advantage of his return to Florence to write the *The Pope's letter recommending Galileo to the Grand Duke's favor, June 8, 1624.* young Grand Duke Ferdinand a letter, recommending Galileo to him as a person worthy of protection and favor, on account not only of his scientific attainments, but of his orthodoxy. "For," thus the papal brief runs, "we find in him not only literary distinction, but also the love of piety, and he is strong in those qualities by which pontifical good-will is easily obtained. And now, when he has been brought to this city to congratulate us on our elevation, we have very lovingly embraced him, nor can we suffer him to return to the country whither your liberality calls him without an ample provision of pontifical love. And-that you may know how dear he is to us, we have willed to give him this honorable testimonial of virtue and piety. And we further signify that every benefit which you shall confer upon him, imitating or even surpassing your father's liberality, will conduce to our gratification." [2]

The foundation of the great work of Galileo's life, *Galileo's reply to Ingoli's* "The Dialogue on the Two Great Systems," had long been laid. But, mindful of the

---

[1] This was an empty promise, as appears from Castelli's letter to Galileo of the 21st of August, 1626: "I told Don Taddeo Barberini what had been his Holiness's will as regards the pension, and implored his favor. . . . He promised to do everything he could towards the carrying out of the Pope's wishes. I also mentioned the thing to Monsignor Ciampoli, who will, without fail, take an opportunity of reminding his Holiness of the promise."

[2] Recommendatory letters were also written by Cardinal Francisco Barberini to the Grand Duchess Magdalen, of Austria, wife of the reigning Grand Duke, and to his mother Christina.

decree of 1616, he took measures to dis- *treatise on the Copernican system, written September, 1624, and circulated in manuscript.* cover the Pope's opinion by writing an essay or pamphlet in the form of a letter of reply to a certain Ingoli, who had some years before written a treatise on the Copernican system. This treatise, though a mere burlesque, had not damaged its author's reputation, since he was then at the head of the Propaganda College. Galileo distributed a few copies of his pamphlet among his friends and adherents, and sent one to Monsignor Ciampoli, the Pope's secretary, desiring him to choose a fitting moment to submit it to his Holiness. Ciampoli informed Galileo in a letter written on the 28th of December, 1625, that the Pope was greatly pleased with *The Pope's approval.* both the manner and the matter of the pamphlet. This announcement of Ciampoli's was all the more gratifying, as Galileo knew that the anti-Copernicans had endeavored to obtain the *Attempts to obtain the suppression of "Il Saggiatore."* suppression of "Il Saggiatore." It had been denounced by a "a pious person" to the Congregation of the Index, as a book of undoubted heretical tendency.[1] One of the members of the Congregation, a cardinal, not named, undertook to appoint a fit person to make a report on the book. By an apparently happy accident, the person appointed as examiner was Guevara, General of the Order *Guevara, General of the Theatines, appointed examiner of "Il Saggiatore."* of Theatines, a learned and enlightened man, attached to the service of Cardinal Francesco Barberini. Guevara examined the book diligently and returned it, with a

[1] In a letter of Tommaso Rinuccini to Galileo, December, 1623, he mentions that a severe order had been issued by the General of the Jesuits, forbidding members of the company to speak of *Il Saggiatore* among themselves.

high eulogium on its merits.[1] It is more than probable that the cardinal in question was perfectly aware that Urban's liking for the book was so great that he had it read to him at meal-times,[2] and that he was careful to choose an examiner whose report would be in favor of its orthodoxy : for it is certain that in one passage of the book, at least, there is a strong leaning to the Copernican, *i. e.* the unorthodox theory. Car-

Cardinal Zoller's opinion on the Copernican theory. dinal Zoller, who had sounded the Pope's mind on the subject, informed Galileo that he had represented to his Holiness, " that all the heretics considered the truth of the Copernican theory to be beyond doubt, and that therefore it would be necessary to be extremely circumspect in coming to

The Pope's reply. any resolution," to which the Pope had replied that the Church had not condemned it, nor was it to be condemned as heretical, but only as rash, adding, that there was no fear of any one under-

Riccardi's view of the matter. taking to prove that it must necessarily be true. Riccardi, whose intellect, as Galileo truly judged, was not capable of penetrating as deep as was necessary to understand and weigh the merits of the two world-systems, settled the matter in quite another way, and succeeded in satisfying his own mind if he satisfied that of no one else. " As to the truth or falsity of the theory," wrote Galileo to his friend Cesi,[3] " he adheres neither to Ptolemy nor to Copernicus, but quiets his doubts in a very speedy manner. He sets angels to work at moving the heavenly bodies, and these make them go as they do go (however

1 Mario Guiducci to Galileo, April 18, 1625.
2 Monsignor Virginio Cesarini to Galileo, October 28, 1623.
8 Galileo to Prince Cesi, June 8, 1624.

that may be) without the slighest difficulty or entanglement.   And certainly this ought to be enough for us."

Of the greater part of the year 1625 we have but scanty details.   Galileo's time was divided between attendance on the young Grand Duke, whose *Galileo instructs the* aptitude for mathematics seems to have been *Grand Duke* remarkable, and the composition of the " Dia- *in mathematics.* logue," which, he complains in a letter to Prince Cesi, got on but slowly, owing to his constantly recurring indispositions.   It is probable, from the paucity of his daughter's letters at this time that he had frequent interviews with her.   Her note of the 19th December is worth recording, not for its cleverness, but because it seems to give us an insight into her simple nature. A winter rose, found in the convent garden, is made the pretext for sending the note, and seems to be a good occasion for a little of what she herself would call sermonizing.   But so artlessly is the sermon introduced, that we feel sure that her "dearest lord and father" could not have been offended with it.   The greatest fear that Sister Maria Celeste seems *Sister Maria* to know is that her father's thoughts and *Celeste's letter.* desires should be too much bound down to earth.   Yet hers was no contemplative life.   The care of the sick, the preparation of rosemary water and preserved citron, and the baking of cakes and biscuits, occupied a large portion of her time and thoughts ; but heaven had its place in her heart too.   " Of the preserved citron you ordered," she writes, " I have only been able to do a small quantity.   I feared the citrons were too shriveled for preserving, and so it has proved. I send two baked pears for these days of vigil. But as the greatest treat of all I send you a rose, which ought to please you extremely, seeing what a rarity it is at this season. And with the rose you must accept its thorns, which represent the bitter Passion of our Lord, while the green leaves represent the hope we may entertain that through the same Sacred Passion we, having passed through the darkness of this short winter of our mortal life, may attain to the brightness and felicity of an eternal spring in heaven, which may our gracious God grant us through his mercy.

" Here I must stop. Sister Arcangela joins me in affectionate salutations ; we should both be glad to know how you are at present.

" I return the table-cloth in which the lamb was wrapped : you have a pillow-case of ours in which we sent your shirts, also a basket and a coverlet."

Of Vincenzio we only know that he was still study-
Vincenzio's extravagance. ing at Pisa, and spending more money than his father could afford to allow him. " For the future," Galileo wrote to Castelli, "he is to be content with three crowns a month for pocket-money. With this he can buy plaster figures, pens, paper, or anything else he likes ; and he may consider himself lucky to have as many crowns as I at his age had groats." [1]

[1] Galileo to Castelli, December 27, 1625. There is a sentence in this letter from which we may infer that Vincenzio was quarrelsome, and wanting in self-control.

CHAPTER VII.

DURING the Carnival of 1626, Galileo, relieved for the time from attendance on the Grand Duke, remained at Bellosguardo, absorbed in the preparation of the "Dialogue." At St. Matthew Sister Maria Celeste, though immersed in the business of still-room and pharmacy, yet found time to long for a sight of her father, and to grieve when day after day passed and her beloved visitor appeared not in the convent parlor. The Carnival passed, and Lent came, but no Galileo. Then the bitterness of her disappointment found vent in words, and she wrote, telling him that, in spite of all his past kindness, she could not help fearing that his love for his daughters must be on the wane, or else that for some reason he was dissatisfied with them, and therefore had left off coming. She entreats him to come, if not to please himself, to please them. Yet, if he will not or cannot come, she says, not the less will they pray for his happiness in this world and the next.

Galileo probably did go, or, if not, wrote to his daughters. We know that he sent them a present of eatables, besides rosemary and citrons, of which Sister Maria Celeste required a large supply. It was and is the custom in Italian convents to make conserves and fine pastry for sale, and St. Matthew enjoyed a high reputation for its preserved citron. We learn from Sister Maria Celeste's letter, written on Ash Wednesday, that Vincenzio had been grumbling about his collars, and had sent to ask her for some new ones. But his sister, having no money, is obliged to ask Galileo for the necessary materials. At the same time she begs to know how Vincenzio is, and what he is doing.

In the spring of 1627, Sister Maria Celeste fell ill with what would appear to have been low fever. Self-denying and uncomplaining though she was, yet the *Bad food at the convent.* convent fare was so unsuitable to her invalid state, that at length she wrote to ask her father for a little money to enable her to procure such comforts as were necessary to her recovery. The convent bread was very bad (though there was no reason for its being so, seeing that there was ground enough belonging to the convent to supply wheat for the use of the community), the wine was sour, and the beef coarse and uneatable. Invalid though she was, it was Sister Maria Celeste's rule (unlike her sister) only to wish for what other people would reject as not good enough. Thus we find her writing to beg that if there happens to be a tough old hen in the poultry yard at Bellosguardo, she may have it to make some weak broth.

Since the death of Madonna Giulia, in 1620, the brothers Galilei had communicated but little, if at all, with each other. Galileo's position at the Court of Tuscany was certain, in Michelangelo's esti- *Michelan-* mation, to secure him riches as' well as *gelo Galilei.* honor. The honor he might keep: the riches, his brother considered, ought to be divided freely with those of the family who had been less fortunate. If Galileo chose to cripple himself at the very *His mean-* outset of his appointment by paying his *ness.* brother's share of the dowries still owing to their brothers-in-law, Michelangelo considered that that was Galileo's own affair, but that it did not by any means absolve him from aiding in the maintenance of a numerous and beautiful family of nephews and nieces. Indeed, from the tone of Michelangelo's letters, he would appear to have thought it a privilege for Galileo to be joined to him in the task of filling all these young and lovely mouths. He had written a book — some say it was a dissertation on the flight of swallows — hoping to gain something by it ; but seeing that the title of his work is not known with certainty, even his secondary wish of showing the world that he too knew something would seem not to have been gratified. Finding that the disturbed state of Germany rendered it unlikely that he would ever make a fortune at Munich, where men's thoughts were turned to more serious matters than lute - playing, Michelangelo sounded his brother on the feasibility of returning to

Florence. There had been at one time a thought of Galileo's taking his sister-in-law Clara Galilei's sister, Maximiliana, as housekeeper. But Maximiliana lived in Michelangelo's house, and was useful in attending to the children and to the cooking, so that Michelangelo felt he could not spare her without inconvenience to himself and his wife. Shortly after, finding that his income was getting no larger, while his family was increasing, and the daily necessaries of life were rising almost to . famine prices, Michelangelo offered to send his wife, Clara, to act as his brother's housekeeper. "This arrangement," he wrote, *Michelan-* / *gelo's letter.* " would be good for both of us. Your house would be well and faithfully governed, and I should be partly lightened of an expense which I do not know how to meet ; for Clara would take some of the children with her, who would be an amusement to you and a comfort to her. I do not suppose that you would feel the expense of one or two mouths more. At any rate, they will not cost you more than those you have about you now, who are not so near akin, and probably not so much in need of help as I am."[1]

Galileo, desirous to help his brother to the utmost of his power, offered to take him and his whole family in, and maintain them, in part at least, till Michelangelo should succeed in procuring work of some sort. *Michel-* / *angelo* / *brings his* / *family to* / *Florence.* In September accordingly they came to Belosguardo, accompanied by a German nurse — a party of nine. The sister-in-law, Maximiliana, had not been able to make up her mind to quit Germany, and Michelangelo had left his eldest girl behind to console her. We are assured that Clara

[1] Michelangelo Galilei to Galileo, May 5, 1627.

was quite as good a cook as Maximiliana, and that she would cook Galileo's dinner for him with her own hands, so that he should have no doubt of its being cleanly prepared. Shortly after the installa- *Galileo maintains them.* tion of his brother's family at the villa, Galileo sent his eldest nephew, Vincenzio, to Rome to study music. Michelangelo had sent him to Paris in 1627, and from Paris he now wished him to go to Rome, Galileo defraying the expense. The instability of Michelangelo's character is evident in every step of his own career, and not less evident in his direction of his family. Every transaction in which he had a part serves to illustrate Galileo's long-suffering, and his own egotism, and arrogance, and vacillation.

For Galileo's sake, Castelli took charge of this boy Vincenzio as if he had been his old friend's son. He introduced him to the ambassador of Venice and to other public characters who might prove useful at a later period, as well as to his own private friends. He saw to the replenishing of his wardrobe, even to the requisite number of pairs of shoes and slippers, "so that he might have wherewith to change and keep dry-footed." "I took him," he wrote, "to Monsignor Ciampoli, who will keep him until he can be received into the house of a friend of his, where he will be comfortably lodged for six crowns a month, which will include board, lodging, washing, and getting up of his collars ; everything, in short, that he can want. I assure you I should have paid more than eight crowns for this accommodation anywhere else."[1]

Monsignor Ciampoli was pleased with the youth's appearance and manner, and augured that he might do

---

[1] Castelli to Galileo, January 8, 1628.

great things in the musical profession.   But Vincen-

Ill-conduct of his nephew Vincenzio. zio's true character soon became apparent. In less than six months Galileo's friends were writing to complain of his ill-behavior ; idleness and impertinence were the least of his failings. The gentleman who had taken him as a boarder at Ciampoli's request declared that he could keep him in his house no longer.   Castelli's affectionate exhortations were thrown away upon him.   Not long before, Castelli had been grieved by the refusal of Galileo's son Vincenzio to take orders.   It augured ill for his friend's orthodoxy that his friend's son should refuse to take a step which was necessary to the enjoyment of the long-promised pension of sixty crowns. "I shall have no longer any pleasure in serving him," he wrote, "for it does not appear to me right that those who will not serve the Church should receive benefits from the Church."   The pension had been by Galileo's desire transferred to his nephew. "But," wrote Castelli of the latter, "he has little devotion.   I found

Castelli's complaints.   it very hard to persuade him to take orders, and with great difficulty have I induced him to recite the Office of the Blessed Virgin, which he must do under pain of incurring the loss of the pension and committing. mortal sin besides.   My words enter in at one ear and go out at the other.   He wants to buy a diamond ring, and declares that he is neither friar nor nun, and will hear none of my sermons.   He is obstinate, impudent, and dissolute.   The insolence of his replies is such that I believe he must be mad as well as vicious."[1]

The pension was not forthcoming, owing to the

---

[1] Castelli to Galileo, May 27, 1628.

death of the Vicar of Brescia, whose place it was to pay it, and there was some delay in procuring an order for payment from the Bishop of Brescia. Michelangelo, who had returned to Munich, wrote, *Michelangelo's son Vincenzio's debts.* desiring Galileo to pay his son's debts, lest he should be taken to task by the Elector of Bavaria for not paying them himself. While Castelli was writing to Galileo full of anger and grief and anxiety, declaring that he had done more for Vincenzio than if he had been his own brother's son, Michelangelo's greatest complaint was that there was no one at Rome capable of instructing Vincenzio in the lute. He had expected that Galileo would provide for the instruction of all his nephews and nieces at Bellosguardo ; and complained bitterly that Albertino and the rest would forget all the music they had learnt at Munich. " If you really mean,"[1] he wrote arrogantly, " that there is (as you seem to say) no remedy to this disorder except by my taking them back again, I must do it, even if I come to Florence on foot. What my troubles are, nobody knows better than myself. You may say that you too have your own anxieties, and I believe you. I should think that among them that of seeing the ruin of these unhappy children would not be the least." He complains loudly of his poverty and of the expense of the journey to Florence, 800 florins. But, notwithstanding his want of *Michelangelo's selfishness.* funds to keep up a house, he did not choose to economize as he might have done by giving it up, because " the discomfort of lodgings would have been unbearable." And although provisions were at famine prices, he felt it necessary to drink good wine for

---

[1] Michelangelo Galilei to Galileo, June 8, 1628.

his health's sake. Wine in a beer-drinking country was of course a luxury in the best of times, but it was sufficient to Michelangelo to desire a thing, and a luxury became a necessity.

Sister Maria Celeste took every opportunity of showing by trifling presents and kind messages to her aunt and cousins how deeply she felt obliged to all who were in any way capable of supplying her place in the household. On Christmas Eve she writes a few lines *Sister Maria Celeste's letter.* to her father, wishing that "in these holy days" the peace of God may rest on him and all the house. She had sent a basketful of presents. "The largest collar and sleeves," she writes, "I mean for Albertino; the other two for the two younger boys; the little dog for baby (*la bambina*), and the cakes for everybody, except the spice-cakes, which are for you. Accept the good-will which would readily do much more."

Galileo's Christmas gift to her consisted of wine, *Christmas gifts.* and rhubarb for the convent pharmacy, of which his eldest daughter had constant charge, though as a rule the offices in the convent were held by rotation.

Worn with mental labor, sleepless nights, and the anxiety of providing for his brother's family, Galileo fell seriously ill. Michelangelo wrote in April to express his joy at hearing that he was out of danger. *Michelangelo's letter.* "From what I know of our brother-in-law," he continues, "I tremble to think what would have become of poor Clara, if you had died! I think now, that, with your good leave, I shall have all my family back, for I do not wish them to be in danger of suffering unkind treatment one of these days. I beg that you will see that the maid-servants pay Clara proper respect and obedience, as I could on no account suffer her to be maltreated in any way whatever." [1]

Michelangelo's letters must have been anything but a comfort to Galileo. When at last Vincenzio had been dismissed from Rome, his father wrote, desiring Galileo to keep him till he came, as he intended to relieve him of the burden of maintaining his family. Galileo had endeavored to procure a place for Albertino in the grand-ducal household, but Michelangelo objected that Albertino's tender age made it *His arro-* more proper that he should be served than *gance.* that he should serve others. It would please him better if his Highness would make some provision for the boy, so that he might remain at home and learn to play the lute. Consequently, he desires Galileo to settle nothing with the Grand Duke till he could see him. As for Vincenzio, he was past praying for. *Michel-* "But," Michelangelo consoles himself by *angelo's ex-* *cuse for his* saying, "I know he did not learn his wicked *son.* ways from me or any one else belonging to him. It must have been the fault of his wet nurse!"

Galileo, notwithstanding his brother's arrogance, desired to help him as far as lay in his power. He advised him to leave his wife and children at Bellosguardo, where at least there was comfortable board and lodging for them. But Michelangelo, though confessing that he had not wherewith to maintain them, had become as anxious to have them back as he had been to get rid of them.

He went to Florence in the August of 1628, and

<hr>

[1] Michelangelo Galilei to Galileo, April 5, 1628.

took Clara and all the children back to Munich.

Michel-angelo dies at Munich, and leaves his family to be main-tained by Galileo. That his step was a cause of displeasure to Galileo, who had finally lost patience with a man who would only allow himself to be helped in his own way, seems probable from the cessation of their correspondence and from a letter of Petrangeli in the latter part of December, 1630, telling Galileo that his brother had begged his pardon on his death-bed for his ill-behavvior in 1628, and for all the trouble he had caused him during his life.

From a letter of Galileo's daughter while these unpleasant matters were still disturbing her father, we learn that she too was sick and miserable,—jealous, perhaps, for a moment, of the aunt and cousins : —

" I believe that it is possible for paternal love to diminish in consequence of children's ill-behavior. *Sister Maria Celeste's letter.* And this belief is confirmed by some signs which seem to tell me that your affection for us is not so cordial as it was in times past. For now you do not pay us a visit once in three months, which to us seem three years and more. Besides which, though you are well now, you never, never write me a line.

" I have closely examined myself to see what fault of mine has merited this chastisement, and I can accuse myself of one, which however is involuntary. It is that for some time I have treated you with neglect in not sending oftener to inquire after your health by message or letter. This having been wanting on my side, joined to the many demerits which I possess, is enough to make me fear that your affection is diminished through displeasure. But indeed you must not account my silence as a sign of my want of respect, but rather as a sign of want of strength, which prevents my making the least exertion. For more than a month I have suffered day and night from headache, and can get no relief. Just now, the Lord having mercifully mitigated the pain, I seize my pen to write you this long lamentation, which you may take as a burlesque if you like. At all events you will not forget that we want to see you as soon as ever the weather permits. Meanwhile I send a few preserved fruits which were given me. They have hardened in keeping, for I have had them by me many days in hopes of being able to give them to you myself. The sweetmeats are for Anna Maria and her little brothers. I send a letter for Vincenzio just to remind him of our existence, which I think he must have entirely forgotten, seeing that he never writes us a single line." [1]

Vincenzio, still a student at Pisa, was at home for the Carnival vacation. We may suppose that, seeing he had forgotten his sisters' existence, he was well supplied with collars !

When scarcely convalescent, Galileo had a relapse which caused his daughter the greatest anxiety. Unable to see for herself whether he were better or worse, she sent the steward on one pretext or another, charging him to bring her word, and if possible see her father himself. The steward must have been devoted to this sweet, gentle nun, else we think he would have remonstrated at being made to take the long walk to Bellosguardo so frequently, bearer of such trifles as a baked quince, a couple of pears, preserved citron, and phials of cinnamon-water.

[1] Sister Maria Celeste to Galileo, March 4, 1628.

The nun herself had the greatest confidence in him, and would rather take his word than any one's, aunt or cousins, on the important subject of her father's health. In one of the affectionate little notes written at this period, she says: "Only in one respect does cloister life weigh heavily on me; that is, that it prevents my attending on you personally, which would be my desire were it permitted. My thoughts are always with you, and I long to have news of you daily. As you were not able to see the steward the day before yesterday, I send him again to-day with these two pieces of preserved citron as an excuse. You will be able to tell him if there is anything we can do for you, and if the quince was to your liking, because, if so, I might prepare another for you. I, Sister Arcangela, and our friends here, pray the Lord without ceasing for your restoration to health."

As soon as Galileo was convalescent, Sister Maria *Sister Maria Celeste's illness.* Celeste fell ill again; so much so that by the physician's orders she was forbidden to keep Lent, and, the convent fare being exceedingly meagre, she wrote to ask for wine and meat, and "some little dainty that would do for Sister Arcangela's supper." All this was sent without fail, together with a present of citrons for Sister Luisa, Sister Maria Celeste's friend and helper in the still-room. In return Galileo received a present of preserved fruit, of which it would appear he was extremely fond.

Besides her occupations in the still-room and pharmacy, Sister Maria Celeste was Infirmarian. We *The sick mistress.* learn from a letter written in April that her mistress[1] was ill, and she was much taken up

---

[1] To each younger nun was given a mistress, or "mother," chosen among the senior sisters.

with attending on her and on three other sick nuns. As Sister Infirmarian it was her duty to be present during the physician's visits; a duty which could be delegated to no other sister. In this letter she begs for a flask of her father's good wine for the sick mistress. She also requests that he will get her some cloth at the fair at Pisa, for two "poor little nuns" who had begged her to do them this kindness. The kind of stuff they wanted was to be bought cheaper at Pisa than elsewhere. So she sends the pattern of the stuff and the eight crowns which her father is to spend in the purchase.

We have advanced considerably since 1628. What would an Astronomer Royal say nowadays to such a request? It speaks equally well for the simplicity of Galileo's character and for the simplicity of the times, that, though he was in constant attendance at Court, and was the intimate friend, during his whole life, of secretaries of state, noblemen, and prelates of distinction, such requests as the above were frequently made and granted.

According to the convent regulation, the whole sisterhood were obliged to change from their winter to their summer habits in April, with-*Convent rules.* out regard to the temperature or the feelings of individuals. To Sister Maria Celeste, born in the soft, enervating climate of the lagunes, the keen air at Arcetri was a constant source of suffering. Many are the complaints in her letters, of toothache, rheumatism, cold, and fever. But the rule being in existence, she had to observe it, and take the bodily suffering as a matter of course. Not even her value as adviser and secretary to the Mother Abbess, nor her attendance in the infirmary, nor the fact of her father being the personal friend of the Pope, could absolve her from obedience to the rule. The utmost she was allowed was to put on some wrap under the summer habit.

One of the rules of the Franciscan Order required a second Lent to be observed in preparation for Advent. Sister Arcangela (who seems to have been somewhat dainty) makes frequent acknowledgment, through her *Sister Arcangela's daintiness.* sister, of her father's presents of caviare and other provisions for fast-days. At the same time we gather that when the basket happened to contain other than the food she had a fancy for at the moment, Sister Arcangela was not best pleased; for the elder sister, in one of her letters, begs her father to send Sister Arcangela some Dutch cheese, because she had been expecting some, and had been extremely disappointed on finding that the basket only contained caviare.

We gather also from a sentence in one of his sister's *Vincenzio a sloven.* letters, that Vincenzio had been a slovenly youth. She says: "Vincenzio is in great want of collars, and never thinks about it till he requires a clean one to put on. All he has are very old, and we have great trouble to get them up. I should like to make him four new ones trimmed with lace, and cuffs to match. Having neither time nor money at my disposal, I should feel glad if you would kindly send me a braccio of fine cambric, and nineteen or twenty lire to buy the lace. I could get it from Sister Hortensia, who makes it beautifully. The collars are worn so large now that it takes a great deal of lace for the edging; and since Vincenzio is now so obedient to your wishes as always to wear cuffs, he deserves to have handsome ones, therefore you must not be surprised at my asking for so much money."

In July, 1628, after having remained six years at Pisa, studying law and mathematics, Galileo's son, *Vincenzio quits Pisa.* then twenty-two years of age, took his doctor's degree, which Galileo himself, more than thirty years before, had abstained from taking on account of the unavoidable expenses which attended it. Among his papers there is a letter from the Rector of the University containing a list of the different fees which he would have to pay for Vincenzio.

It was Galileo's wish to see his son employed in some branch of the civil service, for which he might be supposed, from his legal studies, to be peculiarly fitted. But Vincenzio, as it soon appeared, preferred living an idle life at home under pretense of *Vincenzio's idleness.* aiding his father in his experiments, to gaining his bread by his own exertions.

It will be remembered that, on his return to Tuscany, Galileo had been appointed professor extraordinary at Pisa. About this time (1629), the question *Attempt to deprive Galileo of his stipend.* was mooted by his opposers, whether it had been in the power of Grand Duke Cosmo I. to assign a pension from the University funds without attaching corresponding duties to the enjoyment of it. For nineteen years Galileo had held this sinecure, created expressly for him by the above-mentioned sovereign, in order that, being freed from the necessity of teaching, he might be better able to pursue those studies which had already led to such marvelous discoveries. It was thought by the orthodox or anti-Copernican party that the reigning Grand Duke, brought up *Ferdinand II.* under the influence of his grandmother and

Austrian mother, in their turn influenced by the Jesuits, would be found more scrupulous and less attached to his teacher than his predecessors had been. To aid Cosmo I. in the endowment of the Pisan University, the reigning Pope had given up a certain portion of the tithe. This formed (in the main, if not wholly) the yearly revenue of the University, from which fitting provision was made for the various professors. Not only was the office of professor extraordinary a sinecure, but Galileo, the man who held it, was a layman. This being the case, it was hoped that an appeal might be successfully made to the conscience of the young Grand Duke, and that he might be brought to see the impropriety of allowing any portion of a revenue derived from ecclesiastical sources to be enjoyed except by an ecclesiastic. But a portion (2,000 crowns) of this same revenue had been employed in the equipment of the grand-ducal fleet; and this was felt by Galileo's friends to be a strong argument in his favor. The opinion of the most eminent jurists in Tuscany being taken, and being universally in favor of Galileo's retaining his stipend, the question was entirely set at rest, and the anti-Copernicans once more defeated. In addition, Galileo was shortly after elected one of the magistrates of the University.

Guido de' Ricci and Giulio Arrighetti, advocates, and Niccolò Cini, theologian, Canon of Santa Maria del Fiore.

In the beginning of November, 1628, Sister Maria Celeste writes again in great distress. Her sister's health had been worse than usual, but she had thought little of it, ill-health being the normal condition of most of the nuns at St. Matthew's. But certain symptoms had appeared which were both unusual and alarming. She knows her sister ought to be

Sister Arcangela's illness.

bled, and had therefore sent for the surgeon ; but she has neither money to pay him, nor to procure the necessary comforts for the poor invalid, "who had fallen into her usual melancholy mood." In this extremity she entreats her father "for the love of God" to send Vincenzio, if the weather will allow, that she may tell him her troubles, "which yet cannot be sent for nothing, since God sends them." She remembers, even in the midst of her anxiety for her sister, to send her father a pear, cooked after a new receipt, which she thinks he will approve of, and begs that the dish in which it is sent may be returned, as it does not belong to her.

During all this time Galileo's own health was so indifferent as to put a stop to his visits at the convent. Such strength as he had was devoted to his scientific labors.   On the 10th of December his daughter writes again : —

"You may think from my long silence that I had forgotten you, just as I might suspect that you had forgotten the road to our abode, from the length of time which has elapsed since you came that way. However, as I know that the reason of my silence is that I have not a single hour at present which I can call my own, so I think of you, that not forgetfulness, but press of business, keeps you from coming to see us. It is some comfort to have Vincenzio's visits, as by this means we get news of you which we can rely on. The only thing which I am sorry to hear of is that you are in the habit of going into the garden of a morning. I cannot tell you how grieved I am to hear this, for I feel sure that you are rendering yourself liable to just such another lingering illness as you had last winter. Do pray leave off this habit of going out, which does you much harm ; and if you will not give it up for your own sake, give it up for your daughters', who desire to see you arrive at extreme old age ; which will not be the case unless you take more care of yourself than you do at present.   As far as my experience goes, if ever I stand still in the open air without some covering on my head, I am sure to suffer for it.   And how much more hurtful must it be for you !

Sister Maria Celeste's advice to her father.

" When last Vincenzio was here, Sister Clara asked him for eight or ten oranges.   She wants to know if they are pretty well ripened by this time, as she requires them on Monday morning.   I send back the dish, with a baked pear, which I hope you will like, and some pastry.   If you and Vincenzio have collars which require getting up, you might send them when you return the other basket and the cloth you have of ours."

A daughter of Signor Geri Bocchineri of Prato, major-domo of the palace, has already been mentioned as Sister Maria Celeste's best friend in the convent. Shortly after Vincenzio's return from Pisa, he paid his addresses to a sister of this lady, and was accepted. From some reason, which we are unable to fathom, Vincenzio had kept his intentions a secret from his sister, neither was Sister Luisa Bocchineri, the bride's sister, acquainted with them. From Sister Maria Celeste's little note to her father on this occasion, we learn that she was most agreeably surprised : —

Vincenzio Galilei marries Sestilia Bocchineri.

" This unexpected news our Vincenzio has just given me about his marriage, has given me so much joy that I do not know how to express

Letter of congratulation.

what I feel except by saying that my pleasure at your contentment just equals the love I bear you ; and I should suppose that you are extremely pleased at his making such a good connection. I write now to congratulate you, praying the Lord to preserve you, and give you length of days, in such comfort as Vincenzio promises to give you. He has many good qualities, and my affection for him increases every day. Indeed, he appears to me a very quiet, prudent young man.

"I should much prefer being able to talk to you about this ; but since I cannot do so, will you please write and let me know what I ought to do about sending some one to pay my compliments to the bride ; whether I ought to send to Prato when Vincenzio goes, or wait till she comes to Florence? She has been in a convent, so she will know what the usage is among us nuns on such occasions. I wait to know your wish on the subject, and meanwhile I salute you heartily."

On the 4th of January, 1629, she writes about the wedding present : —

"I suppose that your being so very busy is the reason of our not seeing you. Wishing to *Letter about the wedding present.* know about one or two things, I have resolved to write again. About sending to congratulate the bride, I will wait till you think fit, only please let me know a few days beforehand. As I have not the means to do as my mind prompts me, I must take advantage of your kind offer of help towards the wedding present.

" I send a list of the principal ingredients for making a batch of cakes ; the smaller things, which will cost but little, I can get myself. Besides these I will, if you like, make some chocolate biscuits, or something of that sort. I really think it would come cheaper for you than if you were to buy them, and we would take every care in the baking.

"I also wish that you would tell me what sort of present would be most fitting for the bride. I only care to give what meets with your approval. I was thinking of making her a handsome apron, which, besides being useful, would be less expensive to us, as we could work at it ourselves ; and the collars that are in fashion now we do not know how to make. I should be afraid of acting foolishly in asking questions about such trifles, if I did not know that in small things as well as in great your judgment is so much better than ours."

Sister Maria Celeste's satisfaction at the match con-
Sister Maria Celeste's satisfaction. cluded between her brother and Sestilia Bocchineri was increased by her first interview with the bride. She thought she perceived in her such signs of dawning affection toward her father as augured well for the comfort of his declining years. Writing on the 22d of March, she says : —

"Both my sister and I were much pleased with the
Sister Maria Celeste's letter. bride's affable manner, and with her good looks. But what gave me the greatest joy was to see that she was fond of you, since from that we may judge that she will not be wanting in such loving attention and duty as it would be our delight to render you were it permitted. But we will never give up our own peculiar part, that is, to recommend you to our Lord God continually ; which indeed is our duty, not only as daughters, but as desolate orphans, which we should be if you were taken from us.

"O, if it were but given me to explain what I feel !

Then indeed I should be certain that you would not doubt my loving you with a tenderness beyond what any daughter ever had for a father. But I do not know how to express myself, except by saying that I love you better than myself. For, after God, I belong to you; and your kindnesses are so numberless that I feel I could put my life in peril were it to save you from any trouble, excepting only that I would not offend His Divine Majesty.

" Pray your lordship pardon me if I am tedious; my love for you carries me sometimes beyond bounds. I did not sit down to write about my own feelings, but to tell you that if you could manage to send back the clock on Saturday evening, the sacristaness, whose duty it is to call us to matins, would feel much obliged. But if you have not been able to set it to rights yet, never mind; for it will be better for us to wait a little longer than to have it back before it has been properly put in order.

" I want to know whether you would mind making an exchange with us, namely, to take back a lute which you gave us many years ago, and give us instead thereof a breviary apiece; for those we had when we became nuns are quite torn to pieces. They are the instruments we use every day, while the lute remains hung up and covered with dust; and I fear that it may come to harm, as I am forced sometimes to lend it out of the house, in order not to be thought discourteous.

" If you like to do this for us, will you send me a message to send the lute back? As for the breviaries, we do not care for their being gilt; it will be quite enough if they contain all the saints lately added to the calendar, and if the print be good, as they will then be useful to us if we live to be old.

" I want to make you some rosemary conserve, but I must wait till you send back some of my glass jars, because I have nothing to put it in. At the same time, if you have any empty jars or phials which are in the way, I should be glad to have them for the pharmacy."

From another letter we learn that the clock, " which had been sent first to one and then to the other," with no improvement, was going well now that Galileo had set it to rights. We learn, too, that this spring was a season of sickness at the convent. Sister Maria Celeste remarks that it would appear as if she were destined always to be the messenger of bad news ; nevertheless she will not complain, but thanks God for everything, as she knows not a leaf turns but by his will.

CHAPTER VIII.

IT has been already said that the vow of poverty,
heavy enough at all times under the Franciscan rule,
yet weighed disproportionately on some members of
the community. At St. Matthew it was the custom, as
in some convents in the present day, for the *Inequalities*
nuns to have such comfort and accommoda- *among the*
sisterhood.
tion as they chose to pay for. There appears to have
been no fixed sum for the dowry of women taking the
veil, nor did those who possessed the larger income
give up the surplus to enrich the common stock.
They were allowed to pay rent for, or to purchase for
their life-time, private rooms, which they fitted up
according to their means. The common dormitory
and common living room were therefore only occupied

by such of the sisters as were too poor to pay for privacy. Of course the rent from these private rooms helped the scanty revenues of the convent, and thus indirectly the poorer nuns benefited.

From Sister Maria Celeste's letter of the 8th of July, 1629, we gain an insight into the innermost workings of the convent life in one of the best-ordered establishments of the time : —

"Your lordship partly knows to what inconvenience I have been put ever since I first came here, because of the scarcity of cells. Now, I must explain that the small cell for which (according to the custom among the nuns) we paid the mistress thirty-six crowns, two or three years ago, I have been obliged to give up entirely to Sister Arcangela, in order that she may be, *The mis-* as much as possible, separated from the *tress.* said mistress; for I feared that, owing to the extraordinary eccentricities of the latter, her constant society would prove most detrimental to Sister Arcangela. Besides, as Sister Arcangela's disposition is very different to mine, being rather odd and whimsical, it is better for me to give up to her in many things, in order to preserve that peace and unity which accords with the exceeding love we bear each other. Wherefore I find myself by night in the tiresome company of the mistress. Nevertheless, by the Lord's help, by whom doubtless these trials are permitted for my good, I get through it most joyfully : and by day I am quite a pilgrim, having no corner of my own wherein to pass a quiet hour.

"I do not wish for a large or handsome room, but *Sister Maria* merely for a little cabinet just the size of *Celeste's letter.* the small cell in question. There is one now which the nun to whom it belongs wishes to sell, being in need of money. Thanks to Sister Luisa, who kindly spoke of me, she will give me the refusal of it in preference to many others who wish to become purchasers. But as the value of the cell is thirty-five crowns (7*l.* 15*s.* 5½*d.*), and I have but ten, which Sister Luisa has lent me, and five which I expect from my own income, I cannot take possession of it, and fear it may be lost to me altogether, unless your lordship is able to supply the sum wanting, namely, twenty crowns.

"I explain my wants to your lordship with filial security and without ceremony, that I may not offend that kindness which I have so often experienced.

"I will only say further, that in the monastic condition I could have no greater necessity for anything than what I have already explained (that is, *Her wish to* to possess some place where I could be quite *be alone.* private and retired). Loving me as I know you do, and wishing above all things my happiness and comfort, you will feel that to have a cell of my own would be greatly conducive thereto ; and also to desire only a little peace and solitude is a proper and honest desire.

"You might say that the sum I ask is large, and that I might content myself with the thirty crowns (6*l.* 13*s.* 3*d.*) which the convent still has of yours. To this I answer that, besides its being impossible for me to get that money paid back at this moment, and the nun who wants to sell being in great want, you promised the Mother Abbess that you would not ask for the money unless the convent happened to receive relief from some quarter, and that only if such an occasion arose was it to be paid down at once. But I do not think that for the sake of these thirty crowns you will hesitate to do me this great kindness, which I ask for the love of God. For indeed I belong to the number of those poor wretches laid in prison. And I may call myself not only poor, but also ashamed ; for, indeed, I should not dare express my wants so openly in your presence, or Vincenzio's either. I only venture on writing this letter, having full assurance that you can and will help me. In fine, I recommend myself affectionately to you, as well as to Vincenzio and his bride. May the Lord give you length of days and happiness."

Galileo gave the thirty crowns, but Sister Maria Celeste was no better off. The community *Galileo's liberality.* was large, and the Abbess at her wits' ends to make both ends meet. From the nun's letter of the 22d of November, 1629, we gain an impression that Galileo was a very easy man to deal with in regard to money matters. Such at least seems to have been the impression of the Lady Abbess of St. Matthew. Sister Maria Celeste tries to keep the matter to herself, and for some weeks only discourses of such trifles as a pattern of a new collar, of which she is making a set for her father, or of cinnamon-water, or of the Brescian thread which she wanted for embroidering her sister-in-law's handkerchief, or of the phial containing scorpions preserved in oil, which Galileo had sent as a present to her and Sister Luisa, probably to adorn a shelf in the pharmacy. But the concealment weighs on her, and at length she resolves to make a clean breast of it.[1]

---

[1] Sister Maria Celeste to Galileo, November 22, 1629.

"Now that the tempest of our many troubles is somewhat abated, I will no longer delay telling you all about them ; hoping thereby to lighten the burden on my own mind, and desiring also to excuse myself for writing twice in such a hurry, and not with the respect I owe you. The fact was, that I was half out of my senses with fear (and so were the other nuns) at the furious behavior of our mistress, *Madness of Sister Arcangela's mistress.* who during these last few days has twice endeavored to kill herself. The first time she knocked her head against the floor with such violence that her features became quite monstrous and deformed. The second time she gave herself thirteen wounds, of which two were in the throat. You may imagine our consternation on finding her all over blood and wounded in this manner. But the strangest thing of all was, that at the time that she inflicted these injuries upon herself, she made a noise to attract somebody to her cell, and then she asked for the confessor. In confession she gave up to him the instrument with which she had cut herself, in order that nobody might see it (though, as far as we can guess, it was a penknife). It seems that, though mad, she is cunning. And we must conclude that this is some dark judgment upon her from God, who lets her live when according to human judgment she ought to die, her wounds being all dangerous in the surgeon's opinion. In consequence, she has been watched day and night. At present we are all well, thank God, and she is tied down in her bed, but has just the same frenzy as ever, so that we are in constant terror of something dangerous happening.

"Now I have told you of our trouble, I want to tell you another which weighs me down. Some time ago you were so kind as to give me the thirty crowns I asked for (I did not venture to tell you my mind freely when you asked me the other day whether I had got the cell). I went with the money in my hand to find the nun to whom the cell belonged. She, being in great distress, would willingly have taken the money, but she loved her cell so dearly that she could not bear to give it up. This being the case, we could not agree ; so the matter fell to the ground, as I for my part only wished for the cell in order to have a little place to myself. Now, as I had assured you I was going to have it, I was greatly grieved ; not so much at having to go without my little room, as for thinking that you would think I had been deceiving you, though indeed such was not my intention. And I do wish I had never had this money, for it has been a great anxiety to me. It so happened that just then the Mother Abbess was in need of money, and I lent her these twenty crowns ; and now she, out of grati-tude and kindness, has promised me the cell of the nun who is ill, as I told you. This room is a fine large room, and the price of it is one hundred and twenty crowns, but as a particular favor she would let me have it for eighty. In this, as on many other occa-sions, she has always favored me. But as she well knows I cannot pay eighty crowns at once, she offers to take in account those thirty crowns of yours that the convent has had so long ; this, of course, will only be done with your consent. I can scarcely doubt of your giving it, knowing as I do that you like me to be comfortable, and this opportunity being one that will not occur again.

"Please let me have an answer to give the Mother

Abbess ; she quits office in a few days, and is engaged in making up her accounts.

" I should like to know how you feel now the weather is milder. Having nothing better, I send you a little quince marmalade, made poor man's fashion ; that is, mixed with apples. If you do not care for it, perhaps others will. If you have a fancy for any dish made by us nuns, please let us know, for we shall be glad to do something to your liking. I have not forgotten my obligation to Porzia (Galileo's housekeeper), but for the present I can do nothing for her. If you have any more scraps (of cloth), I should be glad of them, as I have been waiting for them to begin working with what I have already.

" While writing the above, I hear that the sick nun has had such a fit that it is thought she cannot live long. If this be the case, I shall have to give the rest or the money for the burial expenses.

" I have a chaplet of agate which you gave me long ago, which is quite useless to me ; but I think it would do nicely for our sister-in-law. I send it for you to look at, and if you like it, would you take it back, and send me a little money for my present wants ? I hope, please God, this will be the last time I shall trouble you for such a large sum ; but in truth I have none to turn to for assistance, except your lordship and my most faithful Sister Luisa, who does all she can to assist me ; but we are shut up here, and, in short, have not that power to act which ofttimes we want. Blessed be the Lord, who never forgets us ! For his sake I pray your lordship to pardon me if I weary you. I trust that He will not leave unrepaid the many benefits which you have conferred and still confer upon us. I pray for this with all my heart, and I beg you to excuse all mistakes ; for I have no time to read over this long effusion."

In the beginning of January the sisters were again *Illness at* in trouble.   One of the mistresses, an aged *the convent.* nun in her eightieth year, Sister Giulia by name, whom Galileo had noticed during his Christmas visit to the convent on account of her liveliness and activity, was suddenly taken dangerously ill of fever, as also another of the nuns, Sister Violante.   Sister Luisa, Sister Maria Celeste's faithful friend, was overcome with grief at the prospect of losing her beloved mistress.   Sister Giulia was kind and motherly, and did not keep her " child " awake all night, like Sister Arcangela's poor mad mistress.   Though ill herself, Sister Maria Celeste equaled her friend in affectionate assiduity at the aged nun's bedside.   Galileo's cellar, as it had often done before, supplied the good old wine for the invalid's support.

In the midst of her duties as sick-nurse, Sister Maria Celeste found time to think of every one.   She sent fresh eggs for her father's supper, and worked kerchiefs for Porzia.   Sister Maria Grazia, a nun now mentioned for the first time, wanted to write a letter of ceremony, a begging letter it might be, to some high personage.   Being no scribe herself, she applied to Sister Maria Celeste, who did her best, and submitted it to her father for approval.   If he did not think it properly written, another should be indited according to his directions, though indeed, as Sister Maria Celeste complains, the day is not half long enough for what she has to do.   Another nun, Sister Brigida by name, had been asking her father a service, nothing less than a contribution to the dowry of some poor girl in whom she was interested. If Galileo's pocket was thus made to suffer every time he visited St. Matthew's, can we wonder if sometimes those visits were suspended? In one of her letters, his daughter expresses her fear lest his displeasure at something said or done by some one not named should be the reason of his keeping away.

There was need of great tact in Sister Maria Celeste's dealings with the different members of the community. Sister Clara, her cousin, was given to take offense and to be suspicious on slight grounds. *Tact necessary to enjoy peace in the convent.* On one occasion we find Sister Maria Celeste begging her father to let Sister Clara have the loan of his little mule, because else she would think that she had asked him not to let her have it, and then there would be discord and heartburning. As the mule could not have been required for the use of a cloistered nun, it is probable that Sister Clara wanted it for some member of her own family.

At all events, Sister Maria Celeste is careful to keep the peace with everybody, as far as may be. She begs for some Dutch cheese for Sister Arcangela, who will not be happy till she gets it. The clock has been in Vincenzio's hands, and goes *The clock wrong again.* worse than ever. She sends it to her father in despair; if any one can make that clock go, he will be the one to do it. Yet perhaps its not going is more her fault than Vincenzio's; or else it is because the cord is bad. At all events, mended the clock must be, and Galileo must mend it, and quickly too, "for those nuns will let her have no peace else." For herself, she only begs for more scraps for her patchwork.

Galileo's great work, the " Dialogue on the Ptole-
Galileo con- maic and Copernican Systems," was finally
cludes the
" Dia- concluded in the beginning of March, 1630.
logue,"
March, 1630. As a mark of the affection he felt for his
pupil and patron, and also that the work might appear
under the most favorable auspices, it was dedicated to
the Grand Duke Ferdinand.

But neither the astronomer's fame nor the Grand
Duke's protection was sufficient to insure the appearance of the book.   The sanction of the authorities
was necessary ere it could be printed, and, in order to
obtain this with as little delay as possible, Galileo was
advised by Ciampoli and Castelli to go himself to
Rome.   Riccardi, Master of the Sacred Palace, had
given his word that, as far as he was concerned, Galileo
Cardinal should meet with no difficulty in obtaining
Antonio, the
Pope's the desired license.[1]   The Barberini were all
brother;
Cardinals well disposed.   The Pope had expressed his
Francesco
and An- regret to Campanella[2] at the prohibition
tonio, his
nephews. (by the Decree of 1616) of the Copernican
theory, and had said distinctly, that, had it depended
on him, that decree would not have been published.[3]
Ciampoli, though he could not venture to speak with
absolute certainty, yet was of opinion that the surest
way to success lay in Galileo's own personal influence
and in his rare powers of persuasion.[4]   While his

---

[1] Castelli to Galileo, February 6, 1630.

[2] Fra Tommaso Campanella, a Calabrian by birth, had been
confined in the dungeons of Naples for twenty-five years, under
suspicion of designs against the Spanish Government.   He was
liberated by Urban VIII., and lived for some time at Rome, but
afterwards went to Paris, where he died.

[3] Castelli to Galileo, March 16, 1630.

[4] *Ibid.,* February 6, 1630.

friends were thus urging him to come, his daughter, knowing how frail he was, contemplated the journey with anxiety. In her letter of the 14th March she hopes he will come and see her and her sister before he goes. Then, after telling him how busy she is, and reminding him that he had promised her a "Polite Letter Writer," comes the practical housewifely postscript, "If you want any collars washed, please send them, and eat these fresh eggs for love of me."

For many days Sister Maria Celeste went on hoping to see her father; but Galileo, absorbed in the revision of his work, found no time to go to St. Matthew's, even to wish his daughters the customary "happy Easter." Sister Maria Celeste, hearing how deeply her father was immersed in study, could not refrain from an affectionate remonstrance. She does not wish him to shorten his precious life, she says, for the sake of immortal fame. He must take care of himself for his children's sake. She reminds him tenderly that though they all love him, yet she loves him with a love far surpassing theirs, and suffering to him is affliction and torment to her.

On the 12th of April, Galileo found time to pay the long-wished-for visit. He was made to promise another, which was to be a kind of family gathering, before his departure for Rome. There was to be a repast in the parlor. The two sisters would be there expecting their father, sister-in-law, and brother at the convent dinner hour; but the dinner to which he was invited was to be of Galileo's own providing. Sister Maria Celeste, finding that between Ptolemy and Copernicus her father was becoming strangely forgetful of such trivialities as *entrées* and removes, sends a little note to remind him that she does not want either lemons or rosemary, but that she does want something substantial ; in particular a flask of wine, two cream-cheeses, and some other dish that will do to come after the roast.

The Mother Abbess could not let pass such an opportunity of detailing the needs of the convent, and entreating Galileo's good offices towards procuring relief from Rome. She neither felt ashamed of making such a request, nor doubted its being granted. Gallileo, the Pope's friend, could surely ask alms for her, as well as mend the convent clock, and lend money, and give the sick nuns wine from his well-stocked cellar. Sister Maria Celeste had her own private opinion on the matter.

Galileo set out for Rome in the beginning of May. *Galileo sets out for Rome, May 1.* Personally, he had no reason to be dissatisfied with his reception at the Papal Court. Cardinal Barberini had declared that he had no better friend than the Pope ; and a person who had ventured to bring to his Eminence a vile and mendacious report concerning Galileo's private life, was met with a stern *Disappointment.* and well merited rebuff. But in the object of his journey he was doomed to disappointment. The result of his audiences with the Pope showed him that the recognition of the Copernican system, so ardently looked for by him under this pontificate, was as far off as ever. The Pope, however, did not object to the publication of the " Dialogue," if certain conditions were complied with. These were, first, that the title was to show forth plainly that the Copernican system was treated as a mere hypothesis. Secondly, that the book itself was to conclude with an argument of his own, which his Holiness considered unanswerable. Rather than forego the publication of a work which had been the daily and nightly labor of so many years, Galileo consented. He doubtless felt that such minds as were capable of following his train of reasoning in favor of the truth of the Copernican system, would be no more convinced of the falsity of it by the Pope's argument than he himself was. The manuscript was returned to him with the necessary license, after a careful examination by Riccardi and his colleague Visconti, and he returned to Florence about the end of June. During his stay at Rome, *Galileo's return home.* his daughter had been desired by the Mother Abbess to remind him of her request that he would seize any available opportunity of asking alms for the convent. She obeyed this order, but, at the same time, added her opinion as to the request. "It appears to me," she says, "a most ridiculous thing for people to ask favors of strangers, who probably have their own friends and country people to relieve. It is nevertheless true," she adds, "that we are in penury, and if it were not for the alms we get sometimes, we should be in danger of dying of hunger."

Galileo had returned to Florence intending to complete the index and the dedication, and then send the manuscript to his friend Prince Federigo Cesi, who had offered to superintend the printing of it. Riccardi was to revise the proof-sheets after Cesi. But in the month of August the Prince died. In him Galileo lost the best and most influential, as well as the most enlightened friend he possessed out of Tuscany.

The plague had broken out with such virulence that communication between Rome and Florence *The plague.* was suspended. Galileo, anxious for the ap-

pearance of his book, endeavored to obtain permission
Difficulty of obtaining a license to print at Florence. from the papal authorities to have it printed in Florence. Fresh difficulties arose in consequence of this request ; but at last permission was given him to print the " Dialogue," provided he obtained the license of the Inquisitor-General and the Vicar-General of Florence.[1] To this end he was obliged to go almost daily into the city. No slight undertaking this from Bellosguardo on a summer's day, even when there was no fear of plague infection. Sis-
His daughter's anxiety. ter Maria Celeste, anxious at his silence, miserable because of the length of time he allowed to elapse between his visits, thought, as usual, that his love for her must be waning ; that the sister-in-law, always present, was making him forget the absent
Her jealousy. daughter. Her evident jealousy would be ridiculous were it not so clear that it only arose from her humble opinion of herself. She does not for a moment think that she possesses any right to her father's love, much less to help from his purse and larder. At length Galileo, having obtained the desired license from the inquisitorial and clerical authorities, was able to take rest and write to his daughter.

Her answer is dated the 21st of July, 1630 : —

" Just as I was thinking of sending you a long lamentation because of your never coming to see me, I receive your most loving letter, which shuts my mouth entirely. I must accuse myself of being fearful and suspicious, for I did doubt whether the love you have for those nearest you might not be the cause of some coolness and diminution in your love for us who are

[1] Pietro Niccolini and Clemente Egidi, Inquisitor and Vicar-General.

absent. I know truly that this fear of mine shows that I possess a mean, cowardly soul, for I ought generously to feel persuaded that as I allow myself to be equaled by nobody in my love for you, so in like manner your love for me surpasses that you bear your other daughters. I believe my fear arises from my knowledge of the small merit I possess. But enough of this. We were grieved to hear of your being ill, but really, after taking a journey at this time of the year, I do not see how it could be otherwise. I was astonished to hear of your going into Florence every day. Pray take a few days' rest; do not even come to see us. We would rather you kept well, than have the pleasure of your company.

" Will you see whether by chance you have a chaplet left? If so, would you bring it when you do come next? I should like to send it to Signora Ortensia, to whom I have not written for a length of time. It is a long time, too, since I wrote to your lordship. I could not write before, for I was quite overpowered with weakness and lassitude, and had not energy enough to move my pen. Thank God, since the abatement of the heat I have been better. I pray continually that we may both be preserved in health. I had been keeping these twelve sweet biscuits for you, but send them now, lest they should spoil. We thank you for the wine and the fruit, both extremely acceptable. The little biscuits are for Virginia."

It is not clear who this Virginia is. All we can tell with certainty is that she was a young relative of Galileo's, and that about this time she came to live in his house. Probably she was one of the Landucci family.

The Mother Abbess for the time being was a woman
Energy of the Abbess. of greater energy than her predecessors.
She at least was determined to lose nothing
for want of asking. Accordingly she sends petitions
to various great personages, not forgetting the Grand
Duke and Grand Duchess. When relief of any sort
arrives in answer, she sends to ask Galileo's advice as
to the most proper way of making her acknowledg-
ments. Galileo gives advice, and sends dainties for
the poor, sick nun, Sister Violante, such as a dish of
frogs or a melon.

In a letter written on the 10th of September, 1630,
Galileo's versatility. we get another glimpse of Galileo's delight-
ful faculty for turning his hand to everything
and anything. He has already appeared as artist,
musician, mathematician, physician, glass-blower, astronomer, and poet. Now we hear of him as a gla-
zier ![1]

" Yesterday evening," his daughter writes, " the
Serenissima (Grand Duke Ferdinand's consort) sent
us a present of a fine stag, which was most joyfully
received. I do not think the hunters who killed it
could have made so much noise over it as the nuns
made when it was brought in.

" Now that the weather is getting cooler, Sister Arcangela and I, together with those of the nuns whom
we love best, have planned to sit at work together in
my cell, which is very roomy. But the window being
very high, it wants glazing, in order that we may see a
little better.[2] I should like to send you the panels for

---

[1] On one occasion he was asked to furnish a design for a new
coach which Cardinal Barberino wished to have built.

[2] The common window of this period was no more than an

you to glaze them with waxed linen, which, even if old, will answer the purpose quite as well as if it were new. But I should like to know first whether you have any objection to do this for me. Not that I doubt of your kindness, but because it is a piece of work rather fitter for a carpenter than for a philosopher. So please to say exactly what you think about it."

The plague, already rife within the city gates, now began to spread to the suburbs. Even Bellosguardo, the fashionable suburb, whose reputation for salubrity equaled the beauty of its view over the Val d'Arno, was not spared; one of Galileo's own household, a glass-blower, was taken. Vincenzio, seized *Vincenzio's* by a panic unworthy of the son of Galileo, *flight.* fled with his wife to Prato, leaving his father alone, and his child out at nurse in the neighborhood of the villa.

On the 18th of October, 1630, Sister Maria Celeste writes : —

" I am troubled beyond measure at the thought of your distress and consternation at the sudden death of your poor glass-worker. I entreat you to omit no possible precaution against the present danger. I believe that you have by you all the remedies and preventives which are required, so I will not repeat. Yet I would entreat you, with all due reverence and filial confidence, to procure one more remedy, the best of all, to wit, the grace of God, by means of true

opening in the wall, fitted with a shutter, in which was a hole, letting in a ray of light when the shutter was shut to keep out the extremes of heat and cold. Such unglazed windows still exist in out-of-the-way, poverty-stricken localities in Italy and France.

contrition and penitence. This is without doubt the
Consoling letter of sister Maria Celeste. most efficacious medicine both for soul and body. For if, in order to avoid this sickness, it is necessary to be always of good
cheer what greater joy can we have in this world than
the possession of a good and serene conscience ?

" It is certain that once having this treasure we shall
fear neither danger nor death. And since the Lord
sees fit to chastise us with these plagues, let us by his
help stand prepared to receive the stroke from his
Almighty hand, who, having given us life, may take it
from us when and how it pleases Him.

"I pray your lordship to accept these few words,
Her frame of mind. prompted by the deepest affection. I wish also to acquaint you of the frame of mind in
which I find myself at present. I am desirous of passing away to the next life, for every day I see more
clearly the vanity and misery of this present one. And
besides that I should then no longer offend our blessed
Lord, I would hope that my prayers for your lordship
would have greater efficacy. I do not know whether
my desire be a selfish one ; may the Lord, who sees
all, in his mercy supply me where I am wanting
through ignorance, and may He give you true consolation.

" Here we are all in health except Sister Violante,
who lingers on from day to day. Poverty weighs
heavily on us, but, by God's help, not to our bodily
detriment.

" I am writing at seven o'clock (1 A. M.), therefore
Her daily occupations. I hope you will excuse mistakes. By day I have not a single hour that I can call my
own, for now, in addition to my other occupations, by

Madonna's order I have to instruct four of the younger sisters in choir-singing, besides which I have to arrange the choral service every day. From my having no knowledge of Latin, I find this no small labor. It is true that all these occupations would be to my taste were I not obliged to work in order to earn money. But in one way I am a gainer, for I never have a quarter of an hour's idleness, except when I am asleep. If your lordship could tell me the secret which enables you to do with so little sleep, I should be much obliged, for seven hours seem a great deal too much, and yet I cannot tell how to manage with less on account of my head."

About this time a new Archbishop[1] was appointed to the see of Florence. The Abbess of St. Matthew, not feeling herself capable of inditing a proper letter, delegated the duty to Sister Maria Celeste, who, not being accustomed to write to Archbishops, and not finding a model of a letter in her "Polite Letter Writer," applied to her father. Galileo sent back a copy of such a letter as the Abbess wished — we may suppose that the strain of it was a fine mixture of congratulations and begging — saying at the same time he feared it was not well done. His daughter replies : "Though you say you have not done it nicely, still it will be a great deal better than anything I could have done alone, and I am infinitely obliged to you for writing it."

Galileo writes a letter for the Abbess.

After discoursing on the merits of some quinces which she hoped to get for her father, she says : —

" I should be glad to know whether or not Vincenzio was really gone to Prato. I was thinking I would

[1] Pietro Niccolini.

write and give him a piece of my mind on this subject, and advise him not to go, or at any rate not to leave the household so inconveniently situated. His going away in this manner really seems exceedingly strange at this present juncture, as there is no saying what may happen. But fearing to make the embroilment worse, I did not put my intention into effect. I have the assurance that Almighty God will supply you by His providence where men fail you. I would not say that the failing in this case was for want of affection, but rather for want of understanding and consideration.

" Our friends here join me in hearty greetings, and my poor prayers accompany you unceasingly."

From the next three letters we learn that Vincenzio was still away, leaving his aged father with a scanty *Vincenzio's* household. His idleness had already been *idleness.* a great source of pain to Galileo. Finding that he could not obtain such a post in Florence as was commensurate with his ideas of his own importance, he preferred to live at his father's expense rather than seek employment in some humbler neighborhood. We also learn that the petitions and begging letters of the Mother Abbess were successful, though it would appear that Galileo's request at Rome had failed to procure alms for the convent.

His daughter's exhortations during this time are most touching. She entreats him sweetly not to brood over his enforced loneliness, not to chafe inordinately at Vincenzio's ill-behavior, but to fix his thoughts steadfastly on heaven. Remembering the daily danger hanging over their heads, this pious nun seeks earnestly to speak of spiritual things so as to attract and not offend or disgust her dear and learned father, the greatest man in all Italy. Her exhortations, *Sister Maria Celeste's pious exhortations.* though vastly similar to other sermons, lay and clerical, on the same subject down to our own day, still become strangely touching when we reflect that these commonplaces were not commonplace to her ; that they were no empty echoes of sermons she had heard or good books she had read. Except her breviary, the only book we know of her reading was her father's "Saggiatore" for which she was probably very little the wiser. We know that the nuns would have two courses of sermons in the year, one for Advent and the other for Lent. But Sister Maria Celeste's pious teachings are no fag-ends of last Sunday's discourse. They come straight from the depths of her tender heart, and are delivered with a diffidence and humility most unconventual. Spiritual arrogance, we must remember, was not the least of the abuses of the monastic system in the seventeenth century.

"I know," she says,[1] "that your lordship knows better than I do that tribulation is the touchstone whereon is proved the genuineness of our love to God."

Then again : "I pray you not to take the knife of these crosses and disturbances by the wrong end, so that you may not offend because of them. But rather take it by the haft, and use it to cut through all the imperfections which you may discover in yourself, that being thus freed from all impediments, you may in like manner, as with a lynx-like eye you have penetrated the heavens, so, penetrating the things of this lower world you may come to know the vanity and fallacy of all earthly things. . . . . For neither the love of children,

---

[1] Sister Maria Celeste to Galileo, November 2, 1630.

nor pleasures, nor honor, nor riches, can give us true happiness, seeing that all these things are by nature too unstable. Only in our gracious God can we find true rest. O, what rejoicing will be ours, when the thin veil that enfolds us is rent, and we are able to see the Most High face to face !"

Then after reminding her father of the short span of life that yet remained to enable them to make their peace with God, she continues, as if she feared that her foregoing words might in some way offend his *amour propre :* —

" Now it seems to me, dearest lord and father, that your lordship is walking in the right path, since you take hold of every occasion that presents itself to shower continual benefits on those who only repay you with ingratitude. This is an action which is all the more virtuous and perfect as it is the more difficult. This virtue seems to me, more than any other, to render you like to the same God who (as we have often experienced), though we daily offend His Divine Majesty, still continues to grant us infinite benefits. If He sometimes chastises us, it is for our good, even as a wise father takes the rod to correct his son. Thus it seems to be the case with our poor city at present, in order that, through fear of the impending danger, we may amend our lives."

After mentioning that an acquaintance, Messer Matteo Ninci, had died of the plague, leaving his family in deep grief, Sister Maria Celeste adds : —

" But I will not be the bearer of bad news alone, but tell you that the letter I wrote for Madonna to my lord Archbishop [1] was extremely agreeable to him.

____

[1] Pietro Niccolini, Archbishop of Florence.

He has sent us a courteous reply, offering to help us in any way he can, and promising his protection.

"Also, there has been a good result to the two petitions I sent last week to the Serenissima[1] and to Madama.[2]

"On All Saints' day we had three hundred loaves from Madama, and an order to send for a bushel of wheat. So Madonna's grief at not having wherewith to sow is lightened now. *Alms to the convent.*

"Pray your lordship pardon me if my chattering becomes wearisome. You incite me to it by telling me you are pleased to have my letters. I look upon you as my patron saint (to speak according to our custom here), to whom I tell all my joys and griefs. And finding you always ready to listen, I ask (not indeed for everything I want, for that would be too much), but just for what I find most needful at the time. Now the cold weather is coming, and I shall be quite benumbed if you do not send me a counterpane, for the one I am using at present is not mine, and the person to whom it belongs wants it returned. The one you gave me, as well as the woolen one, I have let Sister Arcangela have. She prefers sleeping alone, and I am quite willing she should do so. But in consequence I have only a serge coverlet remaining ; and if I wait till I have earned money enough to buy myself a counterpane, I shall not have put by enough even by next winter. So I entreat my most beloved *Devoto*, who I know well enough cannot bear that I should want for anything. May it be the Lord's pleasure (if so it be for the best) to preserve *Winter privations.*

---

[1] The Grand Duke's consort.
[2] The Grand Duke's mother.

him to me for many a year, for he is my only earthly treasure.

"But it is grief to me to be able to give him nothing in exchange! At least, I will endeavor so to importunate our gracious God and the most Holy Madonna, that he may be received into Paradise. This will be the best recompense I can give for all the kindnesses so constantly received by me."

"I send you two pots of electuary as a preservative against the plague. The one without the label consists of dried figs, walnuts, rue, and salt, mixed together with honey. A piece of the size of a walnut is to be taken in the morning, fasting, with a little Greek wine (or any other good wine). They say its efficacy is wonderful. It is true that what is in the pot is baked rather too much; we did not take into account the tendency the figs have to get into lumps. The other pot is to be taken in the same way; the taste of it is rather more tart. If you like to continue taking either of them, we will try to make it better next time.

"You said in your letter that you had sent the telescope, but I think you must have forgotten to put it in, and therefore remind you of it, also of the basket in which I sent the quinces, because I want to send you some more if I can meet with any."

All through the month of November the plague *Increase of* gradually increased. Sister Maria Celeste, *the plague in and around* like every one else in the panic-stricken *Florence.* neighborhood, sought anxiously for such panaceas as were most in vogue, with this difference, that while others thought only of their own preservation, she thought only of her father's. Among these panaceas, one more highly vaunted than the rest, per-haps from the difficulty with which it was procured, was a strong water or liqueur made by Abbess Ursula, a Pistoian nun who enjoyed a great reputation for sanctity. From the rank of lay sister, this nun, though unable to read, had risen to the highest grade a nun could enjoy, and had brought the community over which she ruled into a state of excellent discipline. So great a demand was there for her manufactures, that Sister Maria Celeste found it most difficult to ob-tain a phial of this strong water ; such of the nuns as possessed any looked upon it as a relic, and were for-bidden to part with it. Sister Maria Celeste, how-ever, obtained a small quantity of this liqueur, as a favor, and hastened to send it to her father, begging him to take it. By the same messenger she sent a little note, in which, as a further inducement to faith in the contents of the phial, she assured him that she had by her four or five letters of this blessed Mother, and other writings, which she had read with much profit, and that she had heard from persons worthy of credit many accounts of her singular perfection. "Therefore," she continues, "I pray your lordship to have faith in this remedy. For if you have so much faith in my poor miserable prayers, much more may you have in those of such a holy person ; indeed, through her merits you may feel sure of escaping all danger from the plague."

We are not able to say from his daughter's succeed-ing letters whether Galileo took Abbess Ursula's liqueur, or whether he preferred the electuary made of nuts, dried figs, rue, salt, and honey. The next letter, dated 26th November, gives an account of the death of poor Sister Violante.

"On Sunday morning, at the fourteenth hour, our Sister Violante passed away to a better life. We may hope that she is now in a state of blessedness, having borne a painful and lingering illness with much patience and submission to the Lord's will. Truly for the last month she was reduced to such a distressing state of weakness, being unable even to turn in her bed, and taking nourishment with extreme difficulty, that death appeared to her almost desirable, as a termination to her many sufferings. I wished to tell you of this before, but had no time to write; I have only time now to add that by God's grace we are all well, and that I want to know whether it is the same with you and your scanty household, particularly our little Galileino.[1] The counterpane you sent is really too good for me. I thank you for it, and pray the Lord to repay you your constant kindness by giving you an increase of his grace now, and the glory of Paradise hereafter."

Sister Violante's death.

We now first hear of Dame Piera, a discreet and prudent woman, who had succeeded Porzia as housekeeper, and whose presence in Galileo's house lightened in some degree the burden of anxiety always on Sister Maria Celeste's mind. It may be fairly concluded that Madonna Piera was an old acquaintance, or even a humble friend, of the family; and it may be said with an approach to certainty, that Galileo and his house were better looked after under her government than when superintended by Porzia or Vincenzio's wife. After her coming there are no longer such constant complaints in Sister Maria Celeste's letters of baskets and dishes which ought to be returned,

Galileo's housekeeper.

---

[1] Galileo's infant grandchild.

and which must be lying about somewhere in the house. "Knowing her great judgment and discretion," she writes, "I shall regain that peace of mind which else were wanting, whenever I thought of you, deprived in in this most perilous time of all other and dearer company and assistance. Nevertheless, I think of you day and night, and many a time do I mourn over the distance which prevents my having daily news of you.

"Nevertheless, I trust by God's mercy that you may be kept free from harm. For this I pray with my whole heart. And who knows? perhaps you might be more exposed to danger if there were more people in the house. I know that whatever happens is by God's providence, and is permitted for our good ; and with this reflection I quiet myself.

The new Archbishop had ordered the Abbess of St. Matthew's to send him a list of the names of the nearest relations belonging to each nun in the convent, in order that they might be requested to contribute to the relief of the sisterhood during the winter. As Sister Maria Celeste had obtained the Abbess's permission to warn her father beforehand, "in order that the thing might not come upon him unawares," it would appear that it was expected the Archbishop's request to the nuns' relatives would savor somewhat of command.

"I should be much pained," she continues, "at your being put to inconvenience ; yet, on the other hand, I cannot with a good conscience prevent any help and relief which is in contemplation for this poor and truly desolate house. I would, however, suggest to you a reply to my lord Archbishop, which contains in it a

well-known fact. This is, that it were a very good and
Money owing to the nuns. proper thing if the relations of many of the
nuns here were forced to disburse the sum
of two hundred crowns which they have kept back
from their dowry, and not the two hundred crowns only,
but the interest of the same, which has been owing for
many years. Amongst the number of these is Messer
Benedetto Landucci, who is a debtor to his daughter,
Sister Clara. If something is not done, I fear that you,
being Messer Benedetto's surety, will have to pay that
sum, or else it will fall upon our Vincenzio's shoulders.

"If those who owe money could be made to pay,
the convent would be relieved in a much better way
than by the donations of relatives, few of whom are
rich enough to subscribe. The intention of the superiors is good ; they help us as best they can, but the
wants of the convent are too great. I, for my part, envy
none in this world but the Capuchin fathers, who are
placed beyond all the cares and anxieties which come
upon us nuns. For we have not only to supply the convent charges, and give grain and money every year,
but also to supply our own private necessities by the
work of our hands ; and our gains are so small, that
the relief they afford is but scanty. And if I were to
tell the truth, I should say that these gains were rather
loss than profit in the end, for we hurt our health by
sitting up working till seven o'clock (1 A. M.), and con-
sume oil, which is so dear. Hearing from Madonna
Piera to-day that you said we were to ask for anything
we wanted, I will make so bold as to ask for a little
money to pay a few small debts which make me uneasy.
As for the rest, we have enough to eat and to spare,
for which God be praised.

" I hear that you have no present intention of coming to see us, and I do not press it, for a visit now would give but little satisfaction to either of us, as just at present we could not have an hour together in private."

Then follows a discourse on preserved citron, and a reminder that Dame Piera has the list of all the boxes and phials she wants her father to get for the pharmacy. Then she winds up her long letter : " I say good night, it being nine o'clock of the fourth night of December (3 A. M.). When you have seen my lord Archbishop, I shall be glad to know the result."

Galileo had promised his daughters a visit in the beginning of December, but the *tramontana* (the cold wind from the Apennines) was blowing hard, and the old man dared not brave it. In consequence his eldest daughter sends one of her little notes and some of the never-failing preserved citron. She also asks for the wherewith to make a Christmas pres- *Christmas presents.* ent to Virginia and Dame Piera, and to her beloved friend, Sister Luisa. The presents are extremely modest. For Sister Luisa she desired stuff sufficient to make a door-curtain for her cell. Either leather or colored cloth would do, so as it answered the purpose of keeping out the cold wind. To this she would fain add a few trifles, such as bobbins, a bundle of sulphur matches, some wicks and tags, and laces. But on no account was Galileo to send out to purchase these things. If he had them not in the house, she would be content to go without rather than run the risk of the plague being brought back from Florence by the person sent to buy them.

CHAPTER IX.

In spite of *tramontana* and wintry weather, the plague continued in Florence, steadily, though slowly, increasing. At their wits' ends, the board of health *Quarantine.* at length ordered a quarantine of such strictness as to put a stop even to neighborly communication. The general panic became greater in consequence of this, as none knew who of their acquaintance might be dead or dying, and, as might be supposed, reports were rife and full of falsities.

Galileo, mewed up between the four walls of his villa, scarcely felt the restriction. He had his beloved tower, his telescope, and his own thoughts. Often did his daughter remonstrate affectionately with him for his merciless usage of that poor servant, his body, which she tells him will most surely take its revenge on his mind, sooner or later, if he does not allow it needful rest. Vincenzio and his wife were still at Prato, on *Vincenzio's ingratitude.* such ill terms with Galileo that, during this period of sickness, his only knowledge of

their being in health arose from the fact of his hearing
nothing whatever of them. The solitary old man's
only pleasure consisted in the prattle of his infant
grandchild and the perusal of his daughter's almost
daily letters. Once, long before, she had told him
that she had kept all his, and read them during such
moments as she could snatch from her many duties.
Now, in his turn, he looks out for her letters, and
keeps them, discourses on preserved citron and all;
and, amid many labors and anxieties, he finds time to
write to her and keep her assured of his own well-
being and the child's, and to send money and give
medical advice, besides presents of such Lenten food
as his daughters liked best. In one letter she says,
after speaking of Vincenzio's behavior as being " the
fruit of this ungrateful world," " I am quite confused
at hearing that you keep my letters ; I fear that your
great love for me makes you think them more perfect
than they are. But let it be as you will ; if you are
satisfied, that is enough for me."

At last, Sister Maria Celeste appears convinced of
the reality and depth of her father's affection. Her
letters no longer read like a piteous wail of entreaty.
She says no more of her own many demerits as an
excuse for his waning love. It is not too much to
suppose that in truth Galileo's affection for his daughter did increase towards the last years of her life.
When stung by Vincenzio's ingratitude, it must have
been a singular relief to him to turn to one whose
whole life seems to have been a mingled hymn of gratitude and blessing. It must have soothed his *Galileo finds*
aching heart to know that there was one be- *comfort in*
his daugh-
ing in the world who would never misunder- *ter.*

stand his motives and actions, and whose sympathies were his, whether in joy or sadness.

Chilled and repulsed by Vincenzio's ungeniality and sullen reserve, may it not have occurred to Galileo, as it does to the readers of his daughter's loving letters, that he had been a happier man, and that she had been a happier woman, if, instead of consigning her from her childhood to the cloister, he had kept her with him to be the angel of his house?

The panic which, with the increase of the plague, spread from the lower to the higher classes in Florence, explains the fact that during the winter of 1630–1 *Donations to St. Matthew.* donations of all kinds poured in upon the needy inmates of St. Matthew. On the 24th of January, 1631, Sister Maria Celeste writes that the convent has had an alms from the officers of the board of health to the amount of two hundred and four crowns. "God never fails those who trust in Him," she observes. "I think this was given by command of their Serene Highnesses, who show the greatest kindness to the convent. Now, for some months at least, our poor Mother Abbess will be free from anxiety. I think she has obtained this result through her constant prayers, and by the supplications and petitions she has made to divers persons."

Galileo, with that excessive wariness and prudence which he knew by experience to be necessary in dealing with the authorities, ecclesiastical or secular, had been careful to keep his patron the Grand Duke fully informed of the slow progress made in obtaining the license for the printing of the "Dialogue" in Florence. It would seem either that Riccardi had in the first instance signed the permission without due consideration, or that he had changed his mind after signing it. For, not satisfied with the decision of the Inquisitor at Florence, he sent to tell Galileo that he wished to look at the book a third time. This caused *Further* still further negotiation and delay. With *delay.* rare patience the author waited, comforted by the opinion of a friendly Inquisitor on the intrinsic merit of the work. But weeks and months passed, and still the preface and index were not returned, and the printing was at a stand-still. Galileo, anxious and uneasy at the delay, at last wrote to Cioli, the Grand Duke's secretary, as follows : —

" As your illustrious lordship knows, I went to Rome for the purpose of getting permission to pub- *Galileo's let-* lish my ' Dialogues,' and to this end I put *ter to Cioli.* them in the hands of the most Reverend Father the Master of the Sacred Palace, who committed them to the care of his colleague, Father Raffaello Visconti, that he might look at them with the most particular attention, and note if there were any doubtful matter, or any conceit of imagination which required correction : which, at my own request also, he did most thoroughly. And as I entreated the Reverend Master to give the required license, and affix his name thereto, his Reverence signified his wish to read the whole book through once more. This was done, after which he returned me the book, with the permission signed with his own hand. Whereupon I, having been at Rome for two months, returned to Florence, intending to send back the book (as soon as I had written the index, the dedication, and a few other necessary things) to the most illustrious and eminent Prince Cesi, head of the Lyncean Academy, who had always superintended the printing of my other works. But, owing to the death of this Prince and the interruption of communication, I was hindered from printing my work at Rome, and decided on having it done here. I had found and arranged matters with an able printer and publisher, and procured the permission of the Reverend Vicar and of the Inquisitor,[1] and also of the Illustrious Signore Niccolò Antella. I informed the Reverend Master of the Palace of all that had taken place, and of the impediments in my way touching the printing of my book at Rome. Whereupon he sent to tell me through my lord Ambassador (Niccolini), that he wished to have another look at the book, and that I was to send him a copy. On this, I came to you, as you know, to ask whether it were possible to send such a large volume to Rome with security. And you answered, Certainly not ; and that letters were hardly safe. On this I wrote again, declaring the impediment, and offering to send the preface and the end of the book, to which the Superiors might add if they saw fit, or take away, or, if it so pleased them, add notes of explanation. For I myself do not refuse to call these thoughts of mine chimeras, dreams, paralogisms, and vain imaginations : submitting the whole to the absolute wisdom of my Superiors. As to the revision of the book, I suggested it might be done here by some person named by the Reverend Father. He was content that it should be so, therefore I sent the preface and the end, which the Master gave on this occasion to a fresh person to revise, namely, Father Jacinto Stefani, Counselor of the Inquisition, who (also by me requested) revised the whole work

---

[1] Pietro Niccolini and Clemente Egidi.

with the greatest care, observing even the minutest
points, which neither to him nor to my most malignant
adversary could give the slightest umbrage. Indeed,
this Reverend Father declared that the reading of my
work had drawn tears from him more than once, when
he considered with what humility and reverent submission I submitted myself to the authority of the
Superiors ; and he declares, as do all those who have
read the book, that I ought to be entreated to publish
it, instead of being hindered in so many ways ; of
which I need not here adduce examples. Weeks and
months ago I heard from Father Benedetto Castelli,
that he had often met the Reverend Master, who had
given him to understand that he was going to send
back the preface and the end, arranged to his entire
satisfaction. But this has not been the case, and I
hear no word of its being sent back : the book has
been thrown aside into some corner, and my life is
wasting away, and I am in continual trouble. I went
to Florence yesterday at my Serene Master's command, to see the designs for the façade of the cathedral, and also wishing to have recourse to his kindness,
so that, taking counsel with your Excellency, *Letter to*
some means might be found for making the *Cioli.*
Reverend Master explain himself ; and that, if it were
his pleasure, the Ambassador be desired to speak
to the Master, and signify to him his Highness's
desire for a termination of this business, and to let
him know what sort of man his Highness had for his
servant. But so exceedingly troubled was I, that I
could neither speak to his Highness about this business nor look at the designs. Just now a messenger
from Court came to know how I was ; and truly I am

in such a state, that I should not have risen from my bed had I not wished so particularly to tell your lordship of this business, and to beg you to do for me that which I was unable to do yesterday ; and also to take the matter into your own hands, and act as you shall think best : in order that I may, while life yet remains, see what result I may expect from all my lengthy and heavy labors. I send this by the hand of the Court messenger, and shall await your decision through Signor Geri Bocchineri (the Grand Duke's private secretary). And since his Highness is kindly anxious to know the state of my health, I beg you to tell him that I should be pretty well in body, if I were not so afflicted in mind."[1]

At the commencement of the year (1631) Galileo's anxieties had been augmented by the death of his brother Michelangelo, leaving his family totally dependent on him for support. With the view of lightening his burden in some slight degree, he sounded his daughter on the feasibility of placing Virginia, the young niece who was then living in his house, in the convent under her rule and protection. *Galileo's desire to place his niece Virginia under the care of Sister Maria Celeste.* Thus Sister Maria Celeste would in her turn have become a mistress, and would have had a "child" to take care of her in her old age. It may at first sight appear strange that Galileo should have desired to place his niece in a convent where the scarcity of means was such that the inmates were often only kept from starvation by a timely alms. But it must be remembered that poverty was the normal condition of all convents belonging to the Order of St. Francis ; and that the poor convents were free from

[1] Galileo to Cioli, March 7, 1631.

the reproach of sloth, and misrule worse than sloth, which, with scarcely an exception, was justly applicable to the wealthier Orders.

Doubtless Galileo felt that at St. Matthew's his niece would find an honorable asylum. He knew that at his own death his stipend would cease, and Government was scarcely to be expected to pension his relations. Vincenzio had not yet begun to help himself; it was not to be supposed that he would bear the burden of maintaining a number of younger cousins.

But, eager as she always was to satisfy her father's wishes, Sister Maria Celeste was unable to comply in this particular instance. Such was the poverty at St. Matthew, that the Superiors had forbidden the reception of any new members into the community, whether as novices or as serving sisters. So strict was the commandment, that Sister Maria Celeste declared she would not venture to ask for an exception to be made in her favor, though the reigning Abbess was her very good friend. Had it been possible, she would have liked to have Virginia, whom she loved because she had helped to amuse and console her father, so cruelly forsaken by Vincenzio and his wife. She suggests timidly, that perhaps if Vincenzio had some- *Employ-ment for Vincenzio.* thing to do, he and Sestilia would cease to annoy her father so constantly. Upon Galileo seems naturally to fall the task of finding this something; Sister Maria Celeste does not appear for a moment to imagine that Vincenzio is bound to search for employment himself as well. She says, " I do not doubt but that peace and quietness will follow, if you would but find him some employment. He always talks as if he were very anxious to maintain himself." In the same letter she says, " I am much grieved to hear of your being so out of health. I would that I were able to take all your pain upon myself; but since that cannot be, I do my best by praying for you continually. May the Lord hear and answer me ! "

Writing on the 12th of March, in answer to a letter of Galileo's which had accompanied a basket of provisions, she again laments her inability to take Virginia, though she would do anything to give her father satisfaction. Galileo had probably been making fresh complaints of Vincenzio, for she reminds him that it will be good for him in one respect that Vincenzio should consider the neighborhood to be infected, for that now people will not even take money from persons suspected of plague taint; and since Vincenzio is so timorous, he will probably leave off asking for money.

The new Archbishop being well-disposed towards Galileo, he, with that readiness to help which was such a distinguishing feature in his character, asked the Abbess, through his daughter, whether there were any favor which his interest at the archiepiscopal palace could procure them. Accompanying this letter was a Lenten dish, — of what nature is not specified, — which he had prepared for Sister Maria Celeste with his own hands.

It is not clear what the favor was which the Mother Abbess, taking counsel with Sister Maria Celeste, thought fit to ask. But from the context of one of her letters it would appear that it had to do with the visits of the fathers and brothers of the nuns. Her words are : " Mother Abbess says that doubtless it would give great pleasure to all the nuns, if my Lord Archbishop would grant this favor to the brothers as well as to the fathers, but she thinks it would be best not to ask it till after Easter. Meanwhile your lordship can talk to her about it when you come to see us. You will find her a very discreet and prudent person, but extremely timid."

In the same letter she says: "I send back the collars ; they are so worn out that it was impossible to get them up as exquisitely as I wished. If you want anything else, please remember that I have no other pleasure in this world than to be employed in your service ; I think that you too have none greater than to please me and give me everything I ask for." Shortly after this, Virginia, for whom she says there is a little present in the bottom of the basket, ceased to be a member of her father's household.[1]

In a letter dated the 11th of April, she says, "I think the few cakes I send will be enough, as *Galileo left* you have no one with whom to share them, *alone.* except perhaps little Galileo."

This is the last time the grandchild is mentioned. It is probable that his parents took him back to Prato at Easter. We learn from a note containing a few lines only, written on the 22d of April, that Vincenzio had sent his sisters an Easter present of two doz- *Easter gifts.* en eggs and half a lamb ; and that Galileo, not being well enough to go himself as far as the convent, had sent his Easter present, consisting of four piastres, by the hand of Piera.

Galileo getting no better, but rather worse, his daugh-

---

[1] From a letter of Galileo to Benedetto Guerrini, we learn that the Grand Duke was paying for the education of a niece — perhaps Virginia — at the Convent of S. Giorgio, in 1639.

ter looks through all her recipes, and at last finds one which has been much vaunted for its strengthening powers by the physicians.   She makes him a small

The elixir. quantity of the elixir, feeling sure that even if it does no good, it can do no harm.   She tells him that the ingredients are sugar, pomegranate wine, and vinegar ; and he is to take two or three spoonfuls every morning in a small quantity of cinnamon-water.   This elixir, she thinks, will surely remedy his low spirits and want of appetite.

Feeling age and infirmity creeping surely over him,

Galileo con-templates a change of residence. Galileo about this time began seriously to contemplate a change of residence from Bellosguardo to the neighborhood of the convent, where he would be able to enjoy his daughter's society more frequently.   Sister Maria Celeste's letters show how instantly she was on the alert to hear of a house which should combine vicinity to the convent with good situation and a rent more suitable to her father's much-drained purse than that of the villa at Bellosguardo, for which he paid a hundred crowns yearly.

" As far as I have been able to learn, the priest of Monteripaldi has no jurisdiction over Signora Dianora Landi's villa, except over one field.   But I understand that the endowment of one of the chapels of the Church of Santa Maria del Fiore [1] is secured on the house, and it is on this account that the said Signora Dianora is now having a lawsuit brought against her. From the bearer of my letter, a most sagacious woman, who knows everybody in Florence, you may be able to find out by whom this suit has been instituted, and

[1] The Cathedral Church of Florence.

from him you will get some information respecting the business.[1]

"I have also heard that Mannelli's place is not yet let on lease, but they are willing to let. This place of Mannelli's is very nice and large, and they say the air up there is the best in all the country. I should think you would be allowed to go over it to see whether it would be likely to answer our wishes."

The next letter contains a request for a loan of twenty-four crowns, not for herself, but for her friend Sister Luisa, who is in need of *Galileo lends money.* money, and has none coming in till the end of July. "If I were not certain," Sister Maria Celeste writes, "that she were a person who would rather repay before than after the time she promised, and also that she is certain of getting her own money in July, I would not ask you to become a lender, for fear of such a thing happening again as did happen the last time you lent money; on which occasion you were put to much inconvenience, and I was greatly distressed."

The usual present which accompanied this letter was varied this time ; instead of preserved citron and baked quinces, it consisted of aloes and rhubarb from the convent pharmacy.

The idea of hiring Mannelli's house was not carried out, possibly from the rent not being within Galileo's means. House-hunting in the neighborhood of Florence was not easy work, such villas as then existed being mostly the residences of their well-to-do proprietors. Vincenzio, having got over his sulky fit, was again in communication with his father, and helped in

---

[1] Sister Maria Celeste to Galileo, May 18, 1631.

the search for a house. "Vincenzio will tell you all about this house of Perini's which is for sale. Pray do not let this opportunity escape, for Heaven knows when we shall meet with another, as in this neighborhood no one ever thinks of selling, except under pressure of circumstances. If you could make up your mind to come and look at this house, you might pay us a visit at the same time." In this letter, poor melancholy Sister Arcangela is mentioned as naving been "reduced at last to take to her bed."

Sister Luisa's probity and delicacy in money matters had not been overrated by her friend. Receiving *Sister Luisa's promptness in paying her debts.* her own money earlier than she expected, she hastened to pay Galileo the twenty four crowns he had advanced, with a message transmitted through Sister Maria Celeste, expressive of the deepest gratitude for his kindness in making the loan. And her gratitude was no empty phrase ; for, as Sister Maria Celeste wrote, her friend's kindness, which was great before, was redoubled now : she could not be kinder had she been her mother. The expression, " Con maniera tale che più non potria fare se mi fosse madre," is the only one of the kind throughout Sister Maria Celeste's correspondence. We do not know that Marina Bartoluzzi died before 1623 ; it is probable indeed that she was alive, else there would have been some request, throughout so long a correspondence, for money to pay for masses for her soul. But dead or alive, the sisters were not *Ill-health of the sisters.* the less motherless. Constantly ailing, first one, then the other, often both together, these poor young women stood peculiarly in need of a motherly tenderness beyond that of the *maestra,* the "mother" assigned them by the rule of St. Francis. At the time when Sister Luisa sent back the money lent her by Galileo, Sister Arcangela was so ill that her recovery was despaired of. Various expensive remedies were ordered her, and Sister Maria Celeste's pockets being empty, as usual, she was forced to beg assistance from Galileo. From an allusion to her own health in this letter, we see that summer was no more propitious to her than winter.

In August another opportunity occurred for the hire of a house near St. Matthew's. Sister Maria Celeste writes eagerly to her father on the 12th : —

"I am so anxious to have you in the neighborhood, that I am constantly inquiring whether there is any place near here to be let. I have just heard of a villa belonging to Signor Esau Martellini, which is situated on the Piano de' Giullari, and bounds our place. I write to tell you, that you may find out whether it is to your liking. I should be glad indeed if it were, as then I should not be obliged to remain so long without news of you, as is the case at present. Truly I find it hard to bear ; but counting this, along with a few other grievances, as taking the place of the mortifications I neglect through carelessness, I go on bearing it as well as I can, as it pleases God to give it me. But you, doubtless, find no lack of worries and perplexities of quite another kind, so I will keep silence as regards my own.

"Sister Arcangela, about whom I was so anxious, is somewhat better, though extremely weak. She has a fancy for salt fish, so pray send some for the next fast-days. Take care of yourself during these great heats, and do pray write me just one line. Our friends greet you affectionately, and I pray the Lord to give you his heavenly grace."

Shortly after this, Dame Piera, going to the convent with a basketful of provisions besides the salt fish, rejoiced Sister Maria Celeste's heart by telling her that there was every prospect of her father having Villa Martellini.

We cannot help reflecting, as we peruse these letters, how much better it would have been for Galileo's oft-drained purse had he kept his two daughters at home. This good provision, of which Sister Maria Celeste makes grateful acknowledgment, was to be divided among her friends that same evening. For the rule, though it allowed a nun to receive, forbade the keeping of any gift to herself. " Only of the curds," says she, in her little note, " I do not promise to give to very many." We are not told whether the relatives of other nuns were as liberal as Galileo. It is certain that there is no mention of presents received by Sister Maria Celeste from her companions, though she distinctly states the obligation she is under of dividing gifts fairly among the different members of the community. It is equally certain that she shrank from asking a favor from any of the sisterhood, with the exception of her " most faithful Sister Luisa."

The letter dated August the 30th is one of the *Sister Maria Celeste's begging letters.* frequent begging letters, most touching of all perhaps when we notice the difference of tone, no longer abject and timorous, but secure and serene in the full consciousness of possessing the largest share of her father's love.

" If the sign and measure of the love one bears a person," she writes, " is the confidence one feels in him, your lordship should be in no doubt as to my loving you with all my heart, as in truth I do. For indeed such confidence and security have I in you that sometimes I fear that I overstep the bounds of filial modesty and reverence, especially as I know you to be burdened with many expenses and anxieties at present. Nevertheless, being certain that you remember my necessities quite as much as those of any other person whatever, and indeed before your own, I am emboldened to pray you to be so kind as to lighten my mind of its present disquietude, because of a debt of five crowns which I have been forced to incur in consequence of Sister Arcangela's illness. On her account I have been obliged, during the last four months, to incur expenses little in accordance with the poverty of our condition. And now, finding myself in extreme necessity of satisfying my creditor, I recommend myself to him who both can and will help me.

"I want one flask of your white wine to make steel wine for Sister Arcangela ; I believe, however, that the faith she has in the medicine will do more good than the medicine itself. I have so little time that I can add no more than that I hope these six large cakes may please you."

Here the correspondence breaks off. In the autumn of the same year (1631) Galileo took up his abode at Villa Martellini, on the slope of the Piano de' Giullari, over against the convent. There he was able to have almost daily intercourse with his daughters, and Sister Maria Celeste no longer found difficulty in procuring a messenger to send, if necessary, with affectionate inquiries after her father's health, and humble presents from still-room and pharmacy.

CHAPTER X.

GALILEO'S great work, the " Dialogue," appeared in
Appearance of the "Dia-logue." January, 1632. In the various hindrances
which had met its author at every step ere the
final authorization of the book was granted, there had
been a slight foretaste of the persecution which was
to be his lot for the remainder of his days.

The first edition contained two frontispieces engraved
on copper. In that on the left hand, the words " Dia-
logo di Galileo Galilei al Serenissimo Ferdinando II.
Gran Duca di Toscana" are placed on the field of a
pavilion surmounted by a ducal crown and surrounded
by the *Palle*, the armorial bearings of the house of
Medici. Below, on the shore of a sea dotted with
ships, stand three personages disputing, — Ptolemy,
Copernicus, and Ser Simplicio, each with his name
written on a fold of his mantle. On the right-hand

page the title of the book is printed in full, as follows : [1] —

"Dialogue by Galileo Galilei, Mathematician Extraordinary of the University of Pisa, and *Title of the* Principal Mathematician and Philosopher of *"Dialogue," as ordered* the Most Serene Grand Duke of Tuscany, in *by the Pope.* which, in a conference lasting four days, are discussed the two principal systems of the world, proposing indeterminately the philosophical arguments on each side." [2]

According to custom, the first page was devoted to the Imprimatur, as follows : —

"Imprimatur si vidibitur Rev. P. Magistro Sacri Palatii Apostolici : A. Episcopus Bellicas- *Imprimatur.* tensis Vices gerens."

"Imprimatur : Fr. Nicolaus Ricardus Sacri Apostolici Palatii Magister."

"Imprimatur Florentiæ, ordinibus consuetis servatis : Petrus Nicolinus Vic. Gen. Florentiæ."

"Imprimatur : Die 11 Septembris, 1630.   Fr. Clemens Egidius, Inquisitor generalis Florentiæ."

"Stampisi, a di 12 Settembre, 1630.   Nicolò dell' Altella."

---

[1] "*Il Padre Maestro* (Riccardi) salutes you, and says that he is pleased with the work (the *Dialogue*), and he will speak to the Pope to-morrow about the title." — *Letter of Father Raffaelo Visconti (Riccardi's colleague) to Galileo*, June 16, 1630.

[2] The copy of this work preserved in the library of the Seminary at Padua, contains marginal notes in Galileo's handwriting concerning the earth's motion, which is treated as an absolute truth, in spite of the decrees of 1616 and 1633. When the third or Paduan edition was printed, about a century after the first appearance of the work, the editors, from prudential motives, either omitted or altered the sense of these notes, so as to reduce Galileo's certainty to hypothesis.

The preface was in substance[1] the work of Riccardi and the Pope, by whom it was imposed on Galileo. Had he not accepted it, he would never have obtained the Imprimatur.

Of all Galileo's friends and followers, only one was *Foresight of Paolo Aproino.* far-sighted enough to see how fraught with evil was this great work to their master. Blinded by admiration, they had, with one solitary exception, urged him on, forgetful of possible consequences.[2] This exception was Paolo Aproino.

Having read a copy of the "Dialogue," which Galileo had sent in manuscript to his friend Micanzio, at Venice, he imparted his opinion to the latter, begging him to write and advise Galileo to pause ere he printed a book which contained such startling doctrine. Micanzio did not refuse, but nevertheless desired Aproino to write himself, and explain his objections to Galileo. The letter came too late, as the " Dialogue " was actually printed before it reached Galileo.[3]

We may, however, assert with safety that, even had the work not been so far advanced, Aproino's letter

[1] "Conformably to the order of our Lord (Pope) respecting Signor Galileo's book, besides what I remarked to your Reverence concerning the body of the work (May 24), I send you the preface, with liberty to the author to alter or embellish it as to the words, so as the substance is preserved." — *Riccardi to the Inquisitor of Florence*, July 19, 1631.

[2] Niccolò Aggiunti, writing in April, 1628, in reference to an illness which had caused Galileo to neglect the *Dialogue*, then about half finished, declares that the completion of the work was a duty Galileo owed to the great God who had given him a genius hitherto unknown in the history of mankind. He entreats him also to think of posterity, affirming that all he had done yet was but a slight sample of what he could do.

[3] Paolo Aproino to Galileo, March 13, 1632.

would not have made Galileo alter his purpose, while at the same time the probability is that by following his disciple's advice he would have escaped the censure of the Holy Office. Aproino's plan *Aproino's* was, for Galileo to send copies of his work *plan.* in manuscript to the public libraries in the capitals of Europe ; with permission for copies to be taken at the demand of any person who might wish to possess the work. This plan, Aproino thought, would prevent the dissemination of the doctrine among the ignorant and ill-disposed, who, instead of taking advantage of Galileo's labors, would make them serve to ruin him. As for his followers, none of them would grudge the expense of a manuscript copy of such a precious work. Half hoping that his old master would fall in with this plan, Aproino began himself to make a copy, but desisted, on being reminded by Micanzio that he ought to obtain the author's permission. This letter is another instance of the undying attachment which Galileo's pupils felt for their great teacher. Aproino refers to the time he spent at Padua when studying mathematics under Galileo in terms of enthusiasm,[1] and thanks God daily " that he had for his master the greatest man the earth had ever seen."

Copies of the " Dialogue " were sent by Galileo to his friends and disciples throughout Italy. There was some delay in the presentation of the book to the various dignitaries in Rome, in consequence, as he says in a letter to Castelli, of the difficulty of transmission, owing to the fresh sanitary restrictions in force at the Roman frontier. Castelli and the Jesuit fathers had already received their copies. The great personages must

---

[1] " . . . . Quel beato tempo di Padova ! "

wait till the plague should be abated; "for," says Galileo, "having gone to the expense of having the books bound and gilt, I shall wait till I can send them bound."[1] Probably there was greater fear of infection from leather binding than from the common paper wrapper. Thus the "Dialogue" entered the precints of the Papal Court amid the applause of all Italy.[2]

Favorable reception of the "Dialogue."

Suddenly, in the beginning of August, in consequence of a report sent in to the Inquisition by the Jesuit Inchofer, one of the Consultori, came a stringent order from the Master of the Sacred Palace to sequestrate every copy in the bookseller's shops, not only in the States of the Church, but throughout Italy. Landino, Galileo's publisher, received an injunction to suspend the publication of the book, and to forward to Rome all copies he might have in his possession. To this Landino answered that he had not a single copy left; a proof, if any were needed, of the popularity of the "Dialogue," for it would have been useless and unwise to prevaricate when the Inquisitor of Florence could at any hour of the day or night make a descent on the premises, and satisfy himself of the real state of things.

Order for its sequestration.

Surprised and displeased, the Grand Duke ordered Francesco Niccolini, his ambassador at Rome, to demand an explanation of the

Displeasure of the Grand Duke.

[1] Galileo to Benedetto Castelli, May 17, 1632.

[2] The following may serve as a sample of the reception the *Dialogue* met with : "I had scarcely had time to devour your book before it was taken from me and lent from one to the other. And to-day no sooner do I get it back by main force than I am obliged to send it to the Commissary Antonini, at Verona, one of our cleverest men, and one who admires you above all the literati of the age." — *Micanzio to Galileo*, July 3, 1632.

Pope's sudden caprice. This demand was embodied in the dispatch written by Andrea Cioli, the Grand Duke's Secretary of State, to the Tuscan Ambassador, on the 24th of August, 1632. It is as follows : —

" I have orders to signify to your Excellency his Highness's exceeding astonishment that a *Cioli's* book, placed by the author himself in the *dispatch.* hands of the supreme authority in Rome, read and read again there most attentively, and in which everything, not only with the consent but at the request of the author, was amended, altered, added, or removed at the will of his Superiors, which was here again sub-jected to examination, agreeably to orders ·from Rome, and which finally was licensed both here and there, and here printed and published, should now become an object of suspicion at the end of two years, and the author and printer be prohibited from publishing any more."

Cioli went on to say, that, considering the manner in which Galileo had handled his subject, the Grand Duke strongly suspected that this suspension of the book was not so much caused by zeal for purity of doctrine, as by dislike to the person of the author. He therefore desired that the reasons of the suspen-sion be set forth clearly in writing, and forwarded to Galileo, who felt strong in the consciousness of his own innocence, and had declared this to be only a fresh instance of his enemies' malignity. He had, moreover, offered to leave Tuscany and forfeit the Grand Duke's favor, if the charge of holding heretical doctrine could be fairly proved against him.

Niccolini's astonishment at the Pope's sudden change of sentiments was such that " he thought the world must be going to fall to pieces." At the mention of Galileo's name, the Pope interrupted him an-*The Pope's anger.* grily, saying that Galileo had dared discuss matters on which it was his duty to have kept silence. Niccolini reminded his Holiness that the book had only been published after obtaining the consent of the necessary authorities in Rome and Florence. The Pope answered hotly, that Galileo and Ciampoli had both deceived him ; that Ciampoli had had the audacity to assure him that Galileo was inclined to do everything as he had commanded ;[1] which he had believed, not having himself seen the manuscript. Then he complained of Ciampoli again, and of the Master (Riccardi), though, as for the latter, he believed that he, too, had been deceived ; for that Galileo, with his art of persuasion, had got him to write the permission, and that the license to print at Florence had been obtained in the same artful manner, for that the Master had nothing to do with licensing what was printed beyond Rome ; and moreover, the form given to the Inquisitor had not been observed, but had been altered in the printing. Niccolini begged that Galileo might at least know clearly of what he was accused. The Pope answered that it was not the custom of the Holy Office to give its reasons to those who fell under its censure ; that Galileo knew well enough in what way he had transgressed, for that they had spoken on the subject (the Copernican theory), and he had himself pointed out to Galileo

[1] Concerning the argument which Urban himself believed to be unanswerable, and which he desired should conclude the fourth (and last) Dialogue, which it did, Galileo having placed it in the mouth of Simplicio the Peripatetic. At this period Urban certainly had not read the book.

the difficulties he would have to avoid.   His Holiness
further desired Niccolini to tell the Grand *The Pope's arrogant message to the Grand Duke.*
Duke that in a matter such as this, he ought,
as a Christian prince, to aid, instead of hin-
dering him, to bring the offender to pnnishment ; and
that he had best not meddle in this business as he
had in Alidosi's,[1] because he would not come out of it
with honor.   He had formed a Congregation of theologians and other learned persons, all grave and saintly
men, who would weigh every word in the book ; for
it contained the most perverse matter that could come
into a reader's hands.   The Pope also gave it to be
understood that he had acted with extraordinary kindness to Galileo in not sending his book at once to the
Inquisition, and that Galileo ill-deserved this leniency,
for that he had dared to deceive him.   " I found the
Pope greatly incensed, and indeed full of ill-will to
our poor Signor Galilei," says Niccolini ; " so your
lordship may think in what a state of mind I returned
home yesterday morning " (September 5, 1632).

Meanwhile, Galileo's followers, Micanzio among the
number, scrupled not to stigmatize these "learned,
grave, and saintly men," in whose judgment Pope
Urban placed such confidence, as a set of " unnatural,
godless hypocrites."   They bade him be of *Opinion of Galileo's followers.*
good cheer, reminding him that the world
was not restricted to a single corner, and that this
persecution was one of the surest means of handing
the " Dialogue " down to posterity.   " But what a
wretched set this must be," Micanzio exclaims, " to
whom every good thing, and all that is founded in
nature, necessarily appears hostile and odious ! "

[1] A Florentine nobleman, whose estate Urban had wished to
confiscate for heresy.

As soon as the matter was put into the hands of a
Warning from friends at Rome. Congregation, great secrecy was affected ;
but Galileo was not without friends at Rome,
who kept him informed of all the *on dit.* Among
these was Magalotti, whose letter to Mario Guiducci is
worth reading, if only to show what miserable trifles
had their share in causing the condemnation of Galileo's work.

" On Monday morning," he writes,[1] " I was in the
Church of S. Giovanni, when the most reverend
Father (Riccardi), having heard that I was there, came
to seek me. He signified to me that it would be
agreeable to him were I to give up the whole of the
copies of Signor Galileo's book of ' Dialogues ' which
I had brought from Florence, promising to return them
in ten days at the farthest. I answered that I regretted infinitely not being able to comply with his wish,
for of the six copies which I had brought, five were for
presentation, and his Reverence knew that they had
already been presented ; that is to say, one to his
Eminence Cardinal Barberino, one to himself, one to
the Ambassador of Tuscany : and the other three, one
to Monsignor Serristori, a member of the Congregation of the Holy Office ; one to Father Leon Santi, a
Jesuit ; and lastly, one for myself. I told him that it
was impossible to ask to have back again those copies
from the persons to whom they had been presented ;
and as for my copy, it was in the hands of Signor
Girolamo Reti, the Prefect's Chamberlain, and I was
not sure but what his Excellency himself was reading
it. He must know that in this particular it was impossible for me to satisfy him. At the very utmost I

[1] Magalotti to Mario Guiducci, August 7, 1632.

could only have given him my own and Monsignor
Serristori's copy. He appeared sensible of the difficulty, but assured me that it was only for the sake of
the book and its author that he had wished to have
the said copies. Then I took occasion to ask why
such diligent perquisition should be made to have
the books, since I was sure that if the author were
written to, and given to understand the feeling of
the Superiors, he would have divined that it was a
case for obedience ; and that having re- *"La Santità
ceived the permission of our Lord's Holi-* *di Nostro
ness and of the Sacred Congregation to publish the* *Signore."*
work, as any one might see by the Imprimatur in
the beginning of it, it was not to be believed that he
would fail to give every possible satisfaction. I also
hinted that he had already been written to on the subject. To this he answered in the affirmative, but
without any specification. This, as you know well,
was because the dealing of the Holy Office cannot be
revealed, even the very smallest particle, under pain
of the severest censures. He just added that what
had been written and ordered was in a spirit of kindness and leniency, and with no object but the glory of
God and the tranquillity of Holy Church ; and that
no damage should accrue to the reputation of the author, whom he looked upon as one of his best friends.

" Then he proceeded to disclose another reason for
wishing to have these copies of the 'Dialogue.' I
should be ashamed to repeat it to you, for the sake of
his reputation and for the inventor's, only that I know I
can speak to you in confidence. It is this. *Trivial ob-
Under the seal of secrecy he told me that* *jections.*
great offense had been taken at the emblem which was .

on the frontispiece, if I recollect aright (I say this because I paid no great attention to the frontispiece, and
have not the book by me just now). This emblem,
unless I am mistaken, consists of three dolphins holding each other's tails in their mouths, with I know not
what motto. On hearing this I burst out laughing,
and showed him plainly how astonished I was; and
said I thought I could assure him that Signor Galileo
was not the man to hide great mysteries under such
puerilities, and that he had said what he meant clearly
enough. I declared that I believed I could affirm
that the emblem was the printer's own. On hearing
this he appeared greatly relieved, and told me that if
I indeed could assure him that such was the case (now
see what trifles rule our actions in this world) the result
would be most happy for the author. I thought I had
by me a small book written by the Portuguese doctor,
about a preventive for the plague, which would convince him of the truth of what I was saying. He said
my word as a gentleman was quite enough. But I
answered that in case this book had not the emblem
on its title-page (which indeed it has not, though it is
printed by Landino), I would send to Florence for
what would convince him clearly enough, and he was
extremely glad to accept my offer.

" So the matter stands. Other motive for censure
I do not think there is, except that already mentioned
by the Master of the Sacred Palace ; namely, that the
book has not been printed precisely according to the
original manuscript, and that, among other things, two
or three arguments have been omitted at the end,
which were invented by our Lord Pope himself, and
with which he says he convinced Signor Galileo of the

falsity of the Copernican theory. The book having fallen into his Holiness's hands, and these arguments having been found wanting, it was necessary to remedy the oversight. This is the pretext; but the real fact is that the Jesuit fathers are working most valiantly in an underhand way to get the work prohibited. The reverend Father's own words to me were: *Riccardi's* 'The Jesuits will persecute him most bitterly.' *opinion.* This good Father, being mixed up in the matter himself, fears every stumbling-block, and wishes naturally to avoid bringing trouble on himself for having given the license. Besides which, we cannot deny that our Lord's Holiness holds an opinion directly contrary to this (of Galileo's).

" Now, if it is true that the original manuscript was altered, I know not what to say; but if not, it will be easy to convince the authorities, and once convinced, they can go no further, I should think. . . .

" But if some omission has been made through inadvertence, particularly the omissions I have mentioned, I would advise that the utmost readiness be shown to add, take away, or change, so as to save appearances. Meanwhile do not fail to send me as soon as possible some publication of Landino's, were it but an almanac, that I may be able to show it to the reverend Father, and if possible get me one which was published before the publication of the " Dialogue." If you cannot do this, let me have an affidavit signed by some gentlemen of note ; perhaps it would be well to apply for this to the President of the Academy, Signor Tommaso Rinuccini."

Magalotti did not finish his letter without impressing upon Guiducci the necessity of keeping his name a profound secret. He wished to serve Galileo, but he did not wish to incur the displeasure of the Barberini, with whom he was closely connected. Castelli, too, though anxious and eager to serve his old friend, felt strongly the necessity of walking circumspectly in the midst of so many Jesuitical nets and pitfalls. When at length the Jesuits had succeeded in instilling into the Pope's mind that Galileo had meant to hold him up to ridicule in the character of Simplicio, it was *The Pope's mind poisoned by the Jesuits.* felt by every one of Galileo's followers that no circumspection, no dexterity, could save their master from the Pope's wrath. To their honor be it said, that when that time came, not one denied his master.

Fra Tommaso Campanella, who for years had been an ardent admirer of Galileo, wrote to him in September, 1632, as follows : —

"I learn with the greatest annoyance that a Congregation of angry theologians is being *Letter of Fra Tommaso Campanella.* formed for the purpose of condemning your "Dialogue," no single member of which has any knowledge of mathematics or familiarity with abstruse speculations. I would advise you to procure a request from the Grand Duke, that, among the Dominicans, and Jesuits, and Theatines, and secular priests who are in this Congregation, they should admit also Castelli and myself."

The required letter was procured, and forwarded to Niccolini for presentation. Niccolini's opinion, however, was that the request would be worse than useless, Campanella having already written a work of similar tendency to Galileo's,[1] which had been prohibited, and

---

[1] The work in question was an *Apology for Galileo.* It was

Castelli being absent at Castel Gandolfo.[1] Both Galileo and the Grand Duke had the greatest confidence in the Ambassador's judgment, and followed his advice in this instance, as in many others.

Riccardi confided to Niccolini, that he had got himself into serious trouble in consequence of his having given Galileo the permission to print; that there were a few phrases in the book which certainly wanted alteration, and that the end was not at all in accordance with the beginning; besides which, the pages containing the license to publish were printed in a totally different type to the rest of the book. It is not easy to conceive what difference this could make, though the fact of its being so seemed to be as important a charge as any brought against Galileo.

Niccolini advised great caution on the Grand Duke's side; menace and remonstrance he *The Pope's* declared to be equally unavailing, for his *irascibility.* Holiness was not the man to brook contradiction; and if he imagined that his Highness intended to brave his authority, it would be the worse for Galileo. They must gain over his ministers to Galileo's side, and temporize as much as possible. Thus, Niccolini ventured to keep back an official note of Cioli's in

addressed to Cardinal Gaetano, an Inquisitor, and published in Germany; as, though Campanella wrote it in 1616, it was not ready for publication till after the promulgation of the edict prohibiting the discussion of the Copernican theory, that is, after the month of March.

1 " And for other reasons," Niccolini says, without further explanation (dispatch of 11 September, 1632). The fact was, that it was feared Castelli's logic and eloquence would prove too powerful in Galileo's behalf. He had already won over the Commissary Fiorenzuola to his side.

which his Holiness was to be informed of the Grand Duke's displeasure, because "by making a great ado, they should only exasperate him and spoil everything."

Though he professed complete ignorance of all scientific matters, Niccolini nevertheless thought it a great honor for Florence that the "Dialogue" had been published there. He and Riccardi both hoped that after Riccardi had altered such phrases as were contrary to Scripture, the suspension might be withdrawn. For the present, Riccardi declared that the less said in defense of Galileo the better; and told Niccolini moreover, under the seal of secrecy, that he had found *Riccardi's discovery of the prohibition of 1616.* a minute in the books of the Holy Office, which alone was sufficient to ruin Galileo, — namely, that sixteen years before he had been absolutely forbidden to hold or discuss the opinions which he had discussed in the "Dialogue."

On the 1st of October, the Inquisitor of Florence, *Galileo's citation to appear and answer to the charge of heresy, Oct. 1, 1632.* in the presence of the Protonotary apostolic and two monks as witnesses, transmitted to Galileo the order from the Inquisition at Rome. Galileo promised obedience, and signed the order, which then received the signatures of the Protonotary and witnesses.

Galileo wrote to Cardinal Barberino,[1] to beg for a delay, and sent the letter open to Niccolini, in order that the latter might have cognizance of its contents before presenting it to his Eminence. Niccolini's opinion of its tenor was such that he refused to present it, alleging that the Cardinal was so situated as to have no alternative but to lay it before the Congregation; that there it would be scrutinized and pondered over,

---

[1] This Barberino was Francesco, the Pope's nephew.

and that Galileo would infallibly have to explain the meaning of a certain dark passage in it, whether he would or not.

But though Niccolini would not undertake to present Galileo's letter to Cardinal Barberino, he solicited, unasked, the protection of two other cardinals, Ginetti, the Pope's intimate friend, and Boccabella, Assessor of the Congregation. "To these," he writes, "I represented his advanced age (seventy-five[1]), his weak health, and the danger of travelling at this time, besides the discomfort attendant on performing quarantine. But as these are men who hear and answer not, this morning I spoke to his Holiness on the subject, placing strongly before him Signor Galileo's prompt submission, and begging him to take compassion on the poor man, so very aged, and whom I so love and revere." His Holiness answered that it was absolutely necessary for Galileo to *The Pope's harshness.* appear in person before the Inquisition. Niccolini suggested that so extreme was the old man's weakness that if his Holiness insisted on his coming, he would, in all probability, fall ill and die by the way. The Pope answered that he might perform the journey as slowly as he pleased, but that come he must. He had brought all this trouble on himself; for he (Urban) had warned him when Cardinal. Niccolini declared that the approbation the book had received from Riccardi and others had caused all the trouble. Here he was interrupted by the Pope, who *Complaints of the Pope.* recommenced his former complaints of the

---

[1] This was, perhaps, an intentional mistake of Niccolini's. Galileo was born in February, 1564, and was, consequently, in his sixty-ninth year.

heresy of Galileo's doctrine, and the deceit of Ciampoli and Riccardi.

Finding from Monsignor Boccabella that the order *Galileo cited again to appear before the Inquisition.* for Galileo's appearance was actually being drawn up,[1] Niccolini hastened to advise both Galileo and Cioli of it, adding that since matters had gone so far, it would be Galileo's best policy to comply with the order as speedily as possible.   He had endeavored to discover whether Galileo would be placed in confinement on his arrival at Rome, but in vain ; from the friendly cardinals he could learn absolutely nothing.   Every one was afraid of incurring censure if he so much as opened his mouth.

On the 19th of November, Galileo was again called before the Inquisition of Florence.   He declared himself ready and willing to obey ; and said that his only reason for delaying his journey to Rome had been his age and infirmities, which were at that moment of a serious nature, requiring medical treatment.   The Pope accorded a delay of one month.   On the 18th of December the Inquisitor of Florence wrote that his vicar had seen Galileo, who was confined to his bed, and declared himself utterly incapable of undertaking a journey until his condition should be somewhat ameliorated.   The Pope and the Congregation chose to treat this statement as a mere subterfuge.[2]

[1] Niccolini to Cioli, November 13, 1632.

[2] " Sanctissimus mandavit Inquisitori rescribi quod Sanctitas Sua et Sacra Congregatio nullatenus potest et debet tolerare hujus modi subterfugia et ad effectum verificandi an revera in statu tali reperiatur quod non possit ad urbem absque vitæ periculo accedere. Sanctissimus et Sacra Congregatio transmittet illuc commissarium una cum medicum qui illum visitent ut certam

Fearing from the silence observed on the subject by the Cardinals that there was an intention of placing Galileo in prison, Niccolini, in concert with Monsignor Boccabella, advised Galileo to procure *Galileo's medical certificate.* and forward a medical certificate of his state of health. This was accordingly done, and Niccolini waited on Boccabella to know the result. It would seem that the more strenuous the representations of Galileo's friends as to the impossibility of his performing the journey, the stronger the determination of the Pope and Congregation to have him at Rome. Boccabella said that the certificate had been received with shakes of the head ; that the members of the Congregation had declared it to have been drawn up to please Galileo ; that, in short, like his statement to the Inquisitor at Florence, it was a subterfuge.[1] If

et sinceram relationem facient de statu in quo reperitur, et si erit in statu tali ut venire possit illum carceratum et ligatum cum ferris transmittat. Si vero causa sanitatis et ob periculum vitæ transmissio erit differenda, statim post quam convaluerit et cessante periculo carceratus et ligatus ac cum ferris transmittat. Commissarius autem et medici transmittantur ejus sumptibus et expensis quia se in tali statu et temporibus conticuit et tempore opportuno ut ei fuerat preceptum venire et facere contempsit." — *MS. of the Trial,* fol. 409.

[1] Galileo's Medical Certificate, dated December 17, 1632. The original is among the other papers relating to the trial, which, after being carried to Paris in the time of the First Empire (1809), were lost, or supposed to be lost, and only restored to the Vatican in or about 1846. — " Noi infranscritti medici facciamo fede d'haver' visitato il Sig. Galileo Galilei e trovatolo con il polso intermittente a tre e quattro battute, dal che si conjettura la facultà vitale essere impedita e debilitata assai in questa età declinante. Riferisce il detto patire di vertigini frequenti, di melancolia hipocondriaca, debolezza di stomaco, vigilie, dolori vaganti per il corpo, si come da altri può essere attestato. *Co se*

Galileo would take his advice, Boccabella concluded, he would set out at once ; and if he fell ill on the way, it would be all the better for him. "In spite of the threatened censure," Niccolini wrote, "I do not conceive that I should be acting rightly were I not to acquaint you of this. Beside, I do not wish this poor old man to be worse used than he is already." (15th January, 1633.)

Even the Grand Duke was at length convinced that Galileo would only damage his own cause by further delay. The greatest kindness he could confer on him was to show as publicly as possible that he had no intention of withdrawing his friendship from his venerable teacher, notwithstanding his being in disgrace with the Pope. Galileo set out on his weary journey in one of the grand-ducal litters on the 20th of January, 1633.

Widely different were the circumstances attending *Journey to Rome.* this journey to those which had attended that of eight years before ! Federigo Cesi, his princely entertainer and counselor at Acquasparta, was dead. His health, never good, was now a constant source of annoyance to him ; already his eyesight had begun to fail. Not only was the time of year most unpropitious (from January to February being the season when the *tramontana* is most biting and most persistent), but the region through which he was

anco haviamo riconosciuto un hernia carnosa grave con attentatum del peritoneo. Affetti tutti di considerazione, che per ogni piccola causa esterna potrebbe apportarli pericolo evidente della vita.

(Signed) Vittorio de' Rossi, *Medico fisico, mano propria.*
Giovanni Ronconi, *Medico fisico, mano propria.*
Pietro Cervieri, *Medico fisico, mano propria.*"

compelled to pass was singularly bleak and inhospitable, and its inhabitants as wild as the winds that howl across its wastes.

The country round Ponte Centino, where he was forced to perform a quarantine of eighteen days, was infested with brigands and malefactors. From this place, as well as from each halting-place before reaching Ponto Centino, he had written to his daughter, notwithstanding his dim eyesight. In her answer, Sister Maria Celeste, after expressing her grief at her father's having been forced to remain so long in such a wretched habitation, deprived of every comfort, entreats him " to keep up his spirits, and put his whole trust in God, who never forsakes those who trust in Him."

Galileo had lent his house to a friend, Signor Rondinelli; but as this gentleman was detained in Florence by a lawsuit, the confessor of the convent failed not to give a look at house and garden from time to time, to see that all went on well.

On the evening of the 13th of February, Galileo[1] arrived at Rome, and was received as the honored guest of the Tuscan Ambassador. On the following

---

[1] Niccolini sent a litter to meet Galileo at Ponte Centino, and wrote as follows to Cioli, to know whether the Grand Duke chose to pay for it or not : —

" I sent a litter to Ponte Centino, as Signor Galilei asked me. It was hired by the day, and my major-domo paid thirty-six Tuscan crowns, as it had had to wait some days at that place. I do not know whether this expense is to fall on him (Galileo), or whether my Serene Master chooses to take it on himself; therefore I pray your lordship to let me know what I am to do. The litter which brought him to Ponte Centino was not allowed to pass the frontier, so he was obliged to send it back."

day he paid a visit to the Ex-Assessor of the Holy
*Galileo ar-
rives in
Rome, Feb. 13.* Office, Monsignor Boccabella, who received
him with great kindness, and gave him some
advice as to the behavior which would be most pru-
*Visits the
members of
the Congre-
gation.* dent under the circumstances. Cheered by
Boccabella's expressions of sympathy, the
old man went on to pay the new Assessor of
the Inquisition, and the Commissary, the necessary
official visit. The Commissary was not at home ; but
as a certain Girolamo Matti, a great friend of the Commissary, was in the way, Niccolini judged that a visit
to him might be useful, particularly as Signor Girolamo had expressed his admiration for Galileo, and had
offered his services.

"For this day," Niccolini writes, "it was impossible to do more. To-morrow I shall endeavor to see
Cardinal Barberino, in order to recommend Galileo to
his protection. I shall also ask his Eminence to intercede with the Pope for him to be allowed to stay in
this house, instead of sending him to the Holy Office,
in respect to his age, his reputation, and his readiness
in obeying the mandate."

Two days after Niccolini wrote again, saying that,
as far as could be gathered from men whose very essence was secrecy, the tribunal did not seem inclined
to act with severity. The Commissary of the Holy
Office had promised to represent to his Holiness Gal-
*Cardinal
Barberino's
message.* ileo's extreme readiness to obey. Cardinal
Barberino had sent a message that he was
not to pay visits, nor to admit everybody who would
wish to see him ; for that such a course could only be
to his great prejudice and harm : therefore, until he
had further notice, he was to remain within doors, and

keep himself quite retired. The Cardinal had been seen going to the Congregation of the Holy Office that morning, and as it was contrary to his custom to attend to it on a Wednesday, it was just possible that Galileo's affair was being discussed; but this was only Niccolini's private conjecture. Galileo ventured to go out for the purpose of asking the protection of the Cardinals Scaglia and Bentivogli; but the Commissary of the Holy Office insisted on his keeping within doors, and seeing literally no one. His message, similar to Cardinal Barberino's, yet had greater weight, as, from its wording, he might be supposed to speak out of friendship to Galileo, when strictly his duty as Inquisitor would have been to remain silent.

Monsignor Serristori, one of the counselors of the Inquisition, and an old friend of Galileo, came twice under pretense of paying him a visit, but as he talked all the time of nothing but the trial, it was thought with some reason that he had been sent by the Holy Office to discover Galileo's private opinions. "I think," Niccolini continues, "that I have succeeded somewhat in cheering up the good old man, by what I have told him of the steps being taken in his favor. Yet he constantly expresses his wonder at this persecution."[1]

We cannot sufficiently admire Niccolini's zeal in Galileo's behalf. He spared neither time nor pains to shield him from the Pope's displeasure; and that the Pope was more to be feared than the Holy Office was but too evident. His Holiness lost his *The Pope's* temper every time the Ambassador spoke of *temper.* Galileo, yet Niccolini persisted in speaking. If his

<hr>

[1] Niccolini to Cioli, February 19, 1633.

Holiness interrupted — Pope Urban would seem to have had this irritating habit — Niccolini waited quietly till he had said his say, and then began again. There must have been a comic side to these interviews, in spite of the terrible fact that a man's liberty and life were hanging on a turn of the Pope's irascible temper. Notwithstanding his frequent protestations of friendship to the Grand Duke, Niccolini felt that, once within the walls of the Holy Office, it might go hard with the Grand Duke's servant. An unsubmissive look or word before his judges might be his ruin. Niccolini seems to have thought that he never could sufficiently impress upon Galileo the necessity of complete submission. Knowing the men, watching them daily, drawing conclusions from their silence more than from their speech, he felt that, to the ears of the Sacred Congregation, even the good old man's querulous wonderment at being brought to Rome instead of being let alone at Arcetri would sound contumacious and heretical. Niccolini had been long enough in Rome to know that Rome was like no other place in the world. From the very beginning, he suspected that, in spite of the alleged leniency to Galileo, the Holy Office might have severity in store. Its present kindness might be but a blind, to make Galileo

The Inquisitors' opinion on the state of the public mind in Florence. incriminate himself. The feeling of the Inquisitors was that the state of the public mind in Florence was already sufficiently unsatisfactory; that there were too many subtle intellects, eager for new doctrine; and that Galileo, whether he had intended it or not, had given greater weight to the arguments for than to those against the earth's motion. It might be, as Niccolini

once ventured to suggest, that the nature of the arguments required it to be so, and perhaps Galileo could
not help himself. To which Cardinal Barberino re-
joined that he knew well enough what a rare writer
Galileo was ; that he knew how to express himself exquisitely, and also had a marvelous power of persuad-
ing people to believe anything he chose. Which being most undeniable, Niccolini held his peace, and
wisely attempted no rejoinder.

In a dispatch dated February the 27th, Niccolini
gives an account of the audience in which *Niccolini's dispatch.*
he had notified to his Holiness the fact of
Galileo's arrival, of which doubtless the Pope was
already aware.

" I added that I hoped his Holiness was inclined
to be persuaded of his most devout and reverent ob-
servance of ecclesiastical things, especially in the
matter now under consideration ; that he was resolved to submit himself wholly and absolutely to the
learned judgment and prudent opinion of the Sacred
Congregation ; and that I myself had been greatly
comforted and edified by his devout submission. His
Holiness answered that, in allowing Galileo to remain
at my house instead of consigning him to the dungeons
of the Holy Office, he had conferred a favor the like of
which had never yet been granted ; and that *Niccolini's interview with the Pope.*
he had proceeded with this leniency because
Signor Galileo was the accepted servant of
our most Serene master, and for no other reason.
For in consequence of the esteem he bore his Highness, he had been willing to consider Signor Galileo
a privileged person. He bade me remember that in
the late case of a gentleman of the house of Gonzaga,

a son of Ferdinand,[1] far different measures had been taken. For that he had been not only taken to Rome in a litter by the officers of the Inquisition, but was kept closely imprisoned for a long time, till judgment was pronounced."

Niccolini, after returning humble thanks for his Holiness's goodness, proceeded to set before him Galileo's great age and many infirmities, as an additional reason for expedition in passing sentence. The Pope answered that the Holy Office was not wont to make haste, and he did not know whether Galileo's affair could be settled within a short space of time; but that the indictment was being drawn up. His Holiness went on to complain of Galileo's book. It was a book which never should have been written; Ciampoli had deceived him. Niccolini replied cautiously, feeling that he was treading on dangerous ground. His Holiness was firmly impressed with the *The Pope suspects Galileo of believing his own doctrine.* opinion, not only that Galileo's doctrine was bad, but that Galileo himself believed his own doctrine; "a nice piece of work, truly." And to sum up all, Niccolini expresses his firm belief that, even if Galileo succeeded in making them believe he was right, they (the Inquisitors) would never let it be known that they felt themselves to have been in the wrong.

Yet so little were the subtle Florentines able to guess the intention of the Sacred Congregation, that during February a report arose in Florence that Galileo had been acquitted of every charge, and was free to go where he would.

---

[1] Cardinal Ferdinand Gonzaga, on whom the Duchy of Mantua devolved on the death of his brother, Francesco IV., without male heirs, in 1628.

CHAPTER XI.

WHILE expecting daily to be brought up for examination before the Inquisition, Galileo's mind was further harassed by his domestic affairs. Vincenzio *Pecuniary* Landucci, his nephew, was pressing for pay- *anxieties.* ment of a sum of money which Galileo owed him, and had served a notice on his uncle. This was felt to be a great insult; but by Signor Rondinelli's advice Sister Maria Celeste paid it, "lest the creditors should offer some worse affront." From the trifling amount of the sum, six crowns, it would appear that this was the interest on a loan which had to be paid monthly, a very common arrangement in Italy.

Signor Rondinelli took the money, intending to deposit it with the clerk of the tribunal till Galileo himself could be communicated with. But the clerk informed him that the money must be paid to Vincenzio Landucci at once: which was therefore done. The costs of the notice of course fell on Galileo.

This little episode is one of the many instances of the small consideration which Galileo experienced at the hands of his relatives. We know that he had crippled himself to pay his brother's share of his two sisters' dowries, that he contributed largely, and at last wholly, to the maintenance of his brother's family. We learn also from his correspondence that he had used his interest to procure Benedetto Landucci a place at Court, and employment at Rome for another of the Landucci family. He was surety for his niece Sister Clara Landucci's dowry, which her father had only paid in part. His son Vincenzio was like a leech, crying, "Give, give;" and it seems that Galileo did give, as long as he had a florin in his purse. Even when Vincenzio had employment, he seems to have been as much in need of help as when he had none. A clerkship had been procured for him at Poppi in the

Vincenzio's inefficiency and carelessness. Casentino, but his inefficiency and careless-ness were so glaring that he ran a risk of being deprived of it, from which he was only saved by the interest of some of his father's friends, who, knowing what was in store for him, managed to stave off the blow; he was, however, forced to send in his resignation. "I wish," wrote Geri Bocchineri to Galileo, "that you would write and tell him to mind his business, and not waste his time over his new invention — a tuning-fork or some such thing, which might serve well enough to employ him after business hours were over, but which ought not to be the principal occupation of the day."

Meantime Sister Maria Celeste was diligently endeavoring to lessen her father's expenses, and to turn the garden to some account during his absence. In

Tuscany it was the custom to clothe servants, as well as feed and lodge them. "The boy tells me," she writes,[1] "he shall want shoes and stock- ings soon. I am going to knit him some stockings of coarse thread. Piera tells me that you had often said you were going to buy a bale of flax. I had intended to let them begin weaving a piece of coarse cloth for the kitchen, but shall await your lordship's orders. *Custom of clothing servants.*

"The garden vines can be pruned now, as the moon is in the right quarter. Giuseppe's father understands all about it, they tell me, but Signor Rondinelli will not fail to look after him. I hear that the lettuce is very fine, so I have ordered Giuseppe to carry it round for sale before it gets spoilt or destroyed. Seventy large oranges [2] have been sold; they got four lire [3] for them, a very fair price, as I under- stand it is a fruit which does not keep well. The oranges [4] were fourteen crazie the hundred, and two hundred were sold. *The garden.*

"I still continue giving Brigida the giulio [5] every Saturday; I consider this to be an alms exceedingly well applied, for she is a very good daughter, and is in great want."

Of Sister Luisa we hear that she had been ill, but was better. Sister Virginia Canigiani was dead. Sister Maria Grazia del Pace, one of the mistresses, a truly kind and peaceful nun, was dying, and the sisters were overcome with grief at the thought of losing her.

[1] Sister Maria Celeste to Galileo, February 26, 1633.

[2] *Melangole*, an enormous fruit, sometimes called "Adam's apple."

[3] A *lire* is equal to 8*d*.

[4] *Arancia*, the common orange.

[5] A coin worth about 4*d*.

Among the names of the women who loved and
Signora Maria Tedaldi. honored Galileo, that of Maria Tedaldi has
come down to us. To judge from her letters
to him during his enforced stay at Rome, she must
have been an old and intimate friend. She was neither
high-born like Caterina Niccolini, nor pious like Sister
Luisa, nor witty like Alessandra Buonamici. Apparently of the same social standing as the Galilei and
Bocchineri, it is evident that she is an exceedingly uneducated, unenlightened person. Vehement to extravagance in her expressions of friendship and sympathy
to Galileo, she interlards her consolatory phrases with
accounts of herself, her own concerns, those of her
family and acquaintance, and those of all Florence generally; all of which she narrates in a hurried trivial
manner, exceedingly characteristic in its way. As we
read these letters, we wonder whether Signora Maria
talked as she wrote ; and if so, how Galileo felt when
he saw her inside the gate of his villa. Yet we do not
wonder at his having preserved these letters. Situated
as he was, advised by his most powerful friends to give
the lie to his whole life for the sake of peace, this silly
woman's friendship for and faith in him must have become invested with a certain value. Signora Maria
Tedaldi says not a word in favor of his submission.
On the contrary, she hopes that God will give him the
victory over all his enemies.

In spite of his own despondency, Galileo was careful
to write in such a strain as to calm his daughter's anxiety throughout this weary time. Thus on the 13th of
Sister Maria Celeste's letter. March she writes back to him : " As matters
are going on so favorably, I will not mind
though your return be delayed, for indeed my being

disappointed for once is a small thing, if staying where you are redounds to your reputation and advantage. And what makes me still more easy is to hear how honorably you are treated by these excellent gentlemen, and in particular by her Excellency the Ambassadress, my lady and mistress. I am well now, because my mind is at rest. Nevertheless I do not cease praying for you." Then, after giving an account of the invalids at the convent, and naming the persons who desired to be affectionately remembered to her father, she says : " I pray your patience if I have been tedious ; but you must remember that I have to put into this paper everything that I should chatter to you in a week."

Sister Maria Celeste's mind would not have been at ease had she known of the interview which *Niccolini's interview with the Pope.* Niccolini had had with the Pope on the same day she wrote. Niccolini had persisted in asking for a dispensation for Galileo ; he felt that a great point would be gained if he could only be kept outside the walls of that terrible Holy Office. He entreated the Pope to add another favor to that which he had already granted, assuring him that his master would be doubly grateful if this further leniency were extended to Galileo. But in vain did Niccolini dilate upon his age and his many infirmities ; the Pope was not to be moved. " And might God pardon him for discussing such matters, for," said his Holiness, repeating what he had said before, " it was altogether a new doctrine, and contrary to Holy Scripture, and Galileo would have done better had he held the popular opinion. And might God pardon Ciampoli too, for he was a friend of this new philosophy, and had a hankering after new doctrine. As for Signor Galileo, he had been his friend, and he had even admitted him to intimacy, and was sorry to displease him, but he must do what was for the furtherance of the Christian faith." Niccolini ventured to say that he thought Galileo's opinion only went as far as that, God being omnipotent, it was as easy to him to make the world go round as not:[1] whereat the Pope flew into a passion. " See-

[1] The following extract from the *Dialogue* may serve as an illustration of the breadth of Galileo's views, compared with those of his opponents : —

" *Simplicio.* . . . It is not to be denied that 'the heavens may surpass in bigness the capacity of our imaginations, nor that God might have created them a thousand times larger than they really are ; but we ought not to admit anything to be created in vain, or useless, in the universe. Now we see this beautiful arrangement of the planets, disposed round the earth at distances proportioned to the effects they are to produce on us for our benefit. To what purpose, then, should a vast vacancy be afterwards interposed between the orbit of Saturn and the starry spheres, containing not a single star, and altogether useless and unprofitable ? to what end ? for whose use and advantage ?

" *Salviati.* Methinks we arrogate too much to ourselves, Simplicio, when we assume that the care of us alone is the adequate and sufficient work and limit beyond which the Divine wisdom and power does, and disposes of, nothing. I feel confident that nothing is omitted by God's providence which concerns the government of human affairs ; but that there may not be other things in the universe dependent upon his supreme wisdom, I cannot, with what power of reasoning as I have, bring myself to believe. So that when I am told of the uselessness of an immense space interposed between the orbits of the planets and the fixed stars, empty and valueless, I reply that there is temerity in attempting by feeble reason to judge the works of God, and in calling vain and superfluous every part of the universe which is of no use to us.

" *Sagredo.* Say rather that we have no means of knowing what

ing this," Niccolini writes, " I ceased from a disputation on matters which I did not understand ; and, fearing that I too might be accused of heresy by the Holy Office, I turned to other subjects."   But Niccolini did not take leave without again entreating the Pope to

is of use to us. I hold it to be one of the greatest pieces of arrogance and folly that can be in this world, to say, because I know not of what use Jupiter and Saturn are to me, that therefore these planets are superfluous ; nay, more, that there are no such bodies in existence. To understand what effect is worked upon us by this or that heavenly body (since you will have it that all their use must have a reference to us) it would be necessary to remove it for a while, and then the effect which I find no longer produced in me I may say depended upon that star. Besides, who will dare say that the space which they call too vast and useless, between Saturn and the fixed stars, is void of other bodies belonging to the universe? Must it be so because we do not see them? Then in that case the four Medicean planets and the companions of Saturn came into the heavens when we began to see them, and not before ! And, by the same rule, the innumerable host of fixed stars did not exist before men saw them. The nebulæ, which the telescope shows us to be constellations of bright and beautiful stars, were, till the telescope was discovered, only white flakes. O, presumptuous ! nay, rather, O, rash ignorance of man !"—*Dialogue on the Two Great Systems: Conversation the Third.*

As an example of the style of his opponents, an extract may be given from a book written in 1632, by Chiaramonti, then Professor of Philosophy at Pisa, against the Copernican system : "Animals, that are capable of motion, have joints and limbs ; the earth has neither joints nor limbs, therefore it does not move.

" The planets, the sun, and the fixed stars, are all of one substance, that is to say, of the substance of stars ; therefore they either move together or stand still together.

" It is to the last degree unseemly to place among the celestial bodies, which are divine and pure, the earth, which is a sewer full of vile filth," etc., etc.

allow Galileo to remain a prisoner at his residence during the examinations. His persistence so far succeeded, that the Pope deigned to inform him that Galileo should be lodged, not in the dungeons, but in the best and most comfortable rooms of the Holy Office. " I did not tell Galileo that it was probable his case was soon coming on," Niccolini says ; " because I knew it would make him uneasy till the time came, and there is no knowing how long they may keep him waiting. The Commissary of the Holy Office told my secretary some days since that they were talking of having him examined. But the Pope's humor pleases me not ; it is as bad as ever." [1]   Acting on Niccolini's advice, the Grand Duke wrote letters to the Cardinals S. Onofrio, Borgia, S. Sisto, Barberino, Gessi, Ginetti, and Verospi, recommending Galileo to their good offices.

The Grand Duke sends recommendatory letters to the members of the Congregation.

This step, according to Niccolini, was rendered necessary by his Highness having already written to Bentivogli and Scaglia, both cardinals and members of the Congregation, for the express purpose of entreating their favor for Galileo. These letters had had a good effect, but if the other cardinals discovered that the Grand Duke had written to two of their number to the exclusion of the rest, their self-love would be wounded, and Galileo would be the sufferer. [2]

The Ambassador's wife, Caterina Riccardi, was in no degree behind her husband in kindness to Galileo. Fearing that, notwithstanding her anxious endeavors to put him entirely at his ease, he still felt in some measure under constraint, she kindly wrote to Sister

[1] Niccolini to Cioli, Secretary of State, March 13, 1633.
[2] *Ibid.*, March 10, 1633.

Maria Celeste, begging her to persuade her father to behave in all respects precisely as if he were in his own house.   From Niccolini's care in keeping *Niccolini's caution.* back as much as possible from Galileo's knowledge the difficulties which beset him at every turn of the negotiations he had undertaken on his behalf, Galileo's daughter was as far from having any just appreciation of his situation at this time as were his friends at Florence.   Thus, before Galileo had ever been called up for his first examination, she writes : " I want you to bring me a present on your return, which I trust is not far off.   I am sure that at Rome copies of good pictures are easily obtained, and I should like you to bring me a little picture the size of the inclosed piece of paper. I want the kind they make to shut up like a little book,[1] with two portraits, one an *Ecce Homo*, and the other a Madonna, and I wish them to have as tender and heavenly an expression as possible.   I do not care for ornaments.   A plain frame will be quite good enough, for I only want it on purpose to keep it always by me."

The day before Signor Rondinelli had been invited to dine with the Mother Abbess, and had *A visitor at St. Matthew's.* insisted on Sister Maria Celeste and Sister Arcangela joining the dinner party.   It was Mid-Lent, so they feasted on the best the convent could afford ; even the poor melancholy invalid passed a merry day. Sister Maria Celeste thinks it worthy of particular mention, " how exceedingly Sister Arcangela enjoyed herself."   This was but one of good Signor Rondinelli's many kindnesses to the two sisters.

The personal examination of Galileo was fixed for the 12th of April.   As a special mark of the *Galileo's first examination.* pontifical favor, Niccolini had been informed

---

[1] A diptych.

of it beforehand. Taking advantage of a severe attack of gout from which Galileo was then suffering, he again sought to move the Pope to compassion, but without success. It was alleged that his presence was absolutely necessary; that it was totally without precedent for a defendant to be at liberty while in course of examination before the Holy Office. The reason of this, obviously, was to insure complete secrecy, for Niccolini, ever ready at excuse and expedient, suggested that surely the purpose of the Inquisition would be answered sufficiently if Galileo were forbidden to mention the subject of his examinations under pain of censure. But his Holiness was immovable, and Niccolini wisely desisted, covering his defeat by returning *Niccolini's advice.* thanks for favors already obtained. The Pope again alluded to the contents of Galileo's book in terms of severity. "And yet," Niccolini wrote,[1] "he (Galileo) will have it that he can defend his opinions exceedingly well. But I have exhorted him, in order to bring the matter to an end as soon as possible, not to be careful to maintain them, but just to submit to anything they choose to have, even if he really does hold and believe this doctrine of the earth's motion. This advice of mine has afflicted him extremely: so much so, that ever since yesterday he has *Galileo's mental distress.* been in such a state of prostration that I have my fears for his life. I shall beg that a servant may be allowed him, and as much comfort as the place will admit of. Meanwhile we are all doing our best to console him, and to help him through our recommendations to the most friendly disposed members of the Congregation. For truly he deserves

[1] Niccolini to Cioli, April 9, 1633.

every possible kindness that can be shown him, and I cannot describe to you the grief of the whole house, for every one here loves him exceedingly."

The first examination, which took place before Father Vincenzio Maccolani da Fiorenzuola *His first ex-amination, April 12.* (Commissary-General), Carlo Sincero (Pro-curator-Fiscal), and another not named, only lasted a few minutes. Galileo was asked whether he knew the reason of his being cited before the tribunal. Having answered in the affirmative, he was remanded. From Niccolini's account it appears that Galileo was received with great courtesy by the Commissary-General, who had him installed in the apartments of the Fiscal, so that not only was he in the part of the building devoted to the use of the officers, but he had liberty to take the air in the court. His own servant was permitted to be with him, and his meals were taken to him twice a day from Niccolini's *Good offices of Cardinal Barberino.* house. The Commissary declared to Nic-colini that Galileo owed this gentle treatment in great part to the good-will of Cardinal Barberino, who had been untiring in his endeavors to mitigate the Pope's resentment. It was clear that, Cardinal Barberino being friendly to Galileo, the rest of the Inquisitors would take their cue from him. Niccolini mentions that when he presented these Cardinals with the letters which he had advised the Grand Duke to write, some of them declined the responsibility of taking them, until he assured them that Cardinal Barberino had not refused to take his, after which there was no farther objection.

Tormented with the gout, and deprived of the so-ciety of the Ambassador and his gracious and sympa-

thizing wife, Galileo seems to have borne his imprisonment with a degree of impatience at variance with his
natural serenity. We must bear in mind the ever-
present fear that each forthcoming examination might
end in the application of the torture. Apart from this
he had no cause for complaint. Since the establish-
ment of the tribunal in 1215, no prisoner had ever been
Gentle treat- treated with the leniency accorded to Gali-
ment. leo, the Grand Duke's servant. Princes,
prelates, and noblemen, all had been consigned to the
secret dungeons from the very commencement of their
trial. Had Galileo been a scion of a royal house, he
could scarcely have met with more consideration, or
have been treated with more distinction. Yet he
ceased not to complain of, and to entreat greater expedition in the conduct of his case by, a body whose
power of procrastination was scarcely equaled by its
cold ferocity. Daily letters passed between him and
Niccolini, who, while he exhorted him to patience,
ceased not to recommend him to all the cardinals in
turn. Not only was he allowed to write to Niccolini,
but to Signor Geri Bocchineri, his daughter, and others, Signora Maria Tedaldi among the number. In a
letter of hers dated the 16th of April, we see suffi-
Ignorance ciently how complete was the ignorance of
of the Pope's
real feeling those not behind the scenes as to the real
towards
Galileo. attitude of the Pope towards Galileo. She
begs him to procure her a papal absolution, in order
that, in case of her sudden death from plague, she
may escape the pains of purgatory. This papal absolution was never granted but as a particular favor;
Signora Maria insists that Galileo will not have the
least difficulty in obtaining it. "I am positive," she

writes, " that you can get one for me, for his Holiness often gives them ; and a friend of mine, Signora de' Bracci, got one, so why not you ? "

" I suppose you know that this absolution must be *in iscrittis.* Therefore, my dear sir, I do beg you for Heaven's sake to do me this very great favor, which will enable me to live the rest of my days with a good hope of salvation ; and if I die before you, you will be sure of having as intercessor before the face of His Divine Majesty, for your greater happiness, a person who is deeply indebted to you. *The papal absolution.*

" And if it were possible to obtain the same favor for Sister Serafina, my sister, I should be doubly grateful, for she too prays for you without ceasing. Do pray manage to bring me this most rare present on your return. By so doing, you will indeed make me doubly indebted to you in life and death."

The news of Galileo's imprisonment was told Sister Maria Celeste by her father's friend, Geri Bocchineri. Having learnt none of the encouraging particulars, but only the bare fact, she writes thus,[1] in deep distress, yet with a certain caution, mingled with an absolute certainty of her father's innocence : — *Galileo a prisoner of the Inquisition, April 12.*

" I have just been informed by Signor Geri of your being imprisoned in the Holy Office. This, though on the one hand it grieves me much, feeling sure as I do that you are anxious and uneasy, and perhaps without bodily comfort, yet on the other hand, considering that it must have come to this before the business could be terminated, and considering also the benignancy with which you have per- *Consoling letter of Sister Maria Celeste.*

[1] Sister Maria Celeste to Galileo, April 20, 1633.

sonally been treated, and, above all, the righteousness of your cause, and your innocence in this particular matter, I feel comforted, and hope for a prosperous ending with the help of Almighty God, to whom I cry without ceasing, recommending you to his care with the greatest love and confidence."

" Only be of good cheer. Do not let yourself give way to grief, for fear of the effect it would have on your health. Turn your thoughts to God, and put your trust in Him, who, like a loving Father, never forsakes those who trust in Him unceasingly. My dearest lord and father, I have written instantly on learning this news of you, that you might know how I sympathize with you in your distress. Perhaps when you know this, it will not be quite so hard to bear. I have mentioned what I have just heard to no creature in this house, choosing to make my joy and gladness common to all, but to keep my troubles to myself. Consequently, everybody is looking forward joyfully to seeing you back again. And who knows? Perhaps even while I am writing, the crisis may be past, and you may be relieved of all anxiety. May it be the Lord's will in whose keeping I leave you."

Three days later she writes again :—

" Though in your last letter you give no particulars whatever respecting your business,[1] perhaps because you do not wish to make me a partaker of your troubles, yet I found out how matters stood from some one else, as my letter of last Wednesday will

---

[1] It is to be observed that the proceedings against Galileo are always alluded to in mild, vague terms, as the " business," the " matter," the " affair," never as *il processo.* The prisons of the Holy Office are the " rooms," *le stanze.*

have told you. Till your letter came I was in deep distress of mind, but now, being assured of your health, I again breathe freely. Your orders shall be strictly carried out. We thank you for your kindness in allowing Sister Arcangela and myself to have what money we want. Here in the convent we are all well, thank God ; but I hear that there is contagious sickness in Florence, and also in some parts of the suburbs. Therefore, even if your business be soon finished, pray do not set out, and so put your life in danger, especially as the exceeding graciousness of your host and hostess will allow of your remaining as long as is necessary. Sister Luisa and our other friends return your salutations, and I pray our Lord God to give you abundantly of his grace."

While Sister Maria Celeste was writing thus, Signora Maria Tedaldi, full of fear lest the plague should seize her before she got the papal absolution, wrote again at length, repeating and enlarging upon what she had said in her former letter to Galileo. She entreats him to excuse her importunity, seeing how grave and urgent is the necessity. The weather had been *Increase of* changeable, and there had been a vast in- *the plague.* crease in the mortality in consequence. The officers of the Board of Health had ordered a strict quarantine ; friends and neighbors were forbidden to enter each other's houses for fear of spreading the contagion. On the morning of the day on which she wrote, another proclamation had been issued, full of warnings and behests. All women and children were *Quarantine* to keep within doors for the space of ten *regulations.* days, to begin on the Sunday morning (April 24th) at the mid-day Ave Maria bell. This injunction appears to have put Signora Maria into a state of uncontrollable panic. She entreats Galileo with much abject iteration to procure her "that blessed papal absolution."[1] Yet, though evidently shaking in her shoes, she cannot help retailing odds and ends of gossip. Vincenzio Landucci and his father had been to law, and Vincenzio had had the worst of it. Vincenzio Galilei had been offered a petty clerkship, which he had refused, preferring to be maintained by Galileo. No other place had been offered him as yet. She has a widowed daughter at home, for whom she wants to find a second husband, and hopes Galileo will help her in the search as soon as he returns. The new Podestà (mayor) had not gone to Fiesole after all. His Highness had ordered that no changes were to be made in the administration, for fear of the plague being carried about to places which were free from it as yet. The Madonna dell' Impruneta had been carried in procession, with her guard of honor on horseback. She had been met at the Porta Romana by my Lord Archbishop, the clergy of the cathedral, all the magistrates, companies, and brotherhoods, and their Serene Highnesses into the bargain. The cannon had roared, the tapers had blazed, the altars at the street corners had never been more beautifully got up. Galileo's house on the hill-side had been ornamented in the most creditable manner. The

Signora Maria's gossip.

The procession.

---

[1] The phrase sounds pious enough, yet we remain in some doubt whether Signora Maria meant "blessed" as she wrote it. The Tuscans, when they wish to express impatience, invariably make use of the adjective "blessed." Thus *Che benedetto tempo!* must be translated, "What horrid weather!" *Che benedetto uomo!* "What a tiresome man!"

whole city had put its confidence in the Madonna. For the honor of Tuscany the plague must be stayed now. Nevertheless Signora Maria wished to make sure of the papal absolution.

Supposing that during Galileo's detention within the walls of the Holy Office his letters to his daughter might be delayed or detained, Caterina Nic- *The Ambassador's wife, Caterina Riccardi-Niccolini.* colini, with a rare thoughtfulness for one so much her inferior in rank, wrote to Sister Maria Celeste, telling her what she knew of her father, but still keeping in view the brightest side, as Galileo himself did, lest the poor daughter should be too much distressed. It would appear from more than one of Sister Maria Celeste's letters that Galileo had spoken so much to the Ambassadress about his daughter as to make her wish for her personal acquaintance, and she had signified her intention of paying the sisters a visit on her return to her native city. We learn from a letter written some time later that Sister Maria Celeste was expecting the Ambassadress with a mixture of pleasure and trepidation. Her father's advice was necessary before she could decide on what kind of present she might venture to offer without offense to the great lady.

It is gratifying to know what staunch supporters Galileo found in Niccolini and his wife. Acting by the advice of his minister Cioli, the Grand *Stinginess of the Grand Duke.* Duke had signified to the Ambassador that Galileo's expenses were not to be defrayed from the Treasury after the first month of his sojourn at Rome. Niccolini's spirited reply must have been a rebuke to both Cioli and the Grand Duke. He declined altogether to discuss the subject while Galileo was in his

house, and declared that he would take all expense on
Niccolini's reply. himself rather than allow it to be borne by the good old man.

The second examination took place on the 30th of
Galileo's second examination. April. Acting by Niccolini's advice, Galileo, on being invited to speak, took the opportunity to endeavor to remove, if possible, from the minds of his judges the impression that he had written in malice prepense on the subject of the earth's motion. His error, he confessed, had been a vain ambition, and pure ignorance and inadvertence, but of willful disobedience he declared himself innocent. With this the examination concluded ; but immediately after he requested permission to speak. The request being complied with, he offered, as a proof of his not holding the forbidden doctrine, to add to his book one or two more dialogues, if necessary, to confute the arguments in favor of the Copernican theory contained in the body of the book, which in fact terminates with the promise of another meeting for the further elucidation of the questions which had been raised.

After this examination, the Commissary of the In-
Father Vincenzio Maccolani da Fiorenzuola. quisition, taking pity on Galileo's sufferings, interceded with the Pope for his release. Urban was so far touched by the Commissary's representations that he consented to his being
Galileo's release, after the second examination. released conditionally.[1] Galileo was therefore sent back to Niccolini's house on the same evening (April 30th), to the astonishment and delight of the whole household. Not less

[1] " . . . De non tractando cum aliis quam cum familiaribus et domesticis illius palatii."

was the rejoicing at St. Matthew's on hearing the good news. "The joy that your last dear letter brought me," Sister Maria Celeste writes, *Joy of his daughter.* " and the having to read it over and over to the nuns, who made quite a jubilee on hearing its contents, put me into such an excited state that at last I got a severe attack of headache. I do not say this to reproach you, but to show how I take to heart all your concerns. And though I am not more strongly affected by what happens to you than a daughter ought to be, yet I dare to say that the love and reverence I bear my dearest lord and father does surpass by a good deal that of the generality of daughters. And I know that in like manner he excels most parents in his love of me, his daughter. I give hearty thanks to our gracious God for the mercies you have hitherto received. You justly say, all our mercies come from Him. And though you consider these now received as an answer to my prayers, yet truly they count for little or nothing ; but God knows how dearly I love you, and so He hears me. And for this we owe Him the greater thanks."

A few days later, she writes : " You will have heard already what joy and comfort your last letter gave me. As I was obliged to give it to Signor Geri that Vincenzio might see it, I made a copy, which Signor Rondinelli, after reading himself, would carry into Florence to read to some of his friends, who he knew would be extremely glad to hear particulars. He returned the copy, assuring me it had given much satisfaction. Piera tells me she never goes out except to hear mass, or to come here to see us ; and nobody comes to the house except Signor Rondinelli. The boy sometimes goes as far as Signor Bocchineri's to get the letters, and nowhere else ; for besides the necessity of keeping clear of plague infection, he is still weak from his late illness.[1]

" I send this old account-book that you may see what I have spent for the servants, and also what money I had for that purpose. The remainder I made bold to take for my own expenses and Sister Arcangela's ; and now I am going to begin a fresh account-book.

Money mat-ters.
" The other disbursements made since your departure consist of seventeen crowns and a half to Signor Lorenzo Bini for the rent of the villa.

" I paid twenty-four crowns at four different times to Vincenzio Landucci, and six lire, thirteen crazie, four soldi, the costs of that notice which was served on you.   I have all the receipts.

" I took twenty-five crowns for Sister Arcangela, as I told you.   I was obliged to take fifteen more, to enable her to get through her tiresome office (*benedetto uffizio*) of purveyor.   By God's help and your kind assistance, she has managed to get through it, apparently to the entire satisfaction of the nuns.   I shall return these fifteen crowns immediately our allowance is paid us.   We ought to have received it by this time.

" This year it was Sister Arcangela's turn to be cellarer, and I felt very anxious about it.   However, through the kindness of Mother Abbess, I have obtained the office of keeper of the laundry for her

---

[1] " . . . E di più pieno di rogna acquistata nello spedale."
— *Letter* 86.   We may hope that the Hospital of S. Bonifazio is better managed than it was in 1633.

instead; so she will have to look after the washing, and to keep an account of all the convent linen."

The next paragraph, contrasted with the Ambassador's letters to Cioli of the same date, is *Galileo's* another instance of the pious fraud Galileo *pious fraud.* practiced on his daughter in order to avoid awakening her anxiety on account of his health.

"I am particularly glad to hear of your being well, for I feared greatly that all your troubles would have had a bad effect on your health. The Lord has indeed granted you a great mercy, in keeping you thus free from pain, both of mind and body. For this may His Name be ever blessed! They say the plague still continues, but that lately few deaths only have occurred, and they hope it will stop now the Madonna dell' Impruneta has been carried in procession.

"I wonder at Vincenzio never having written to you, and I glory in having been beforehand with him in writing constantly, notwithstanding that I too have sometimes found time wanting: to-day I have written this at four different times, having had constant interruptions from the pharmacy, and also from the tooth-ache, which has been troublesome for many days past."

For once Sister Maria Celeste was unjust to her brother. Vincenzio did not write, it was true; but the reason was, that fear of the plague had interrupted all communication between the healthy and the infected districts. Vincenzio had not long been appointed to a clerkship at Poppi, chief town of the Casentino, a district to which the dreadful scourge had not penetrated.[1]

<hr>

[1] Geri Bocchineri to Galileo, May 12, 1633.

CHAPTER XII.

ON the 10th of May, Galileo was called before the Inquisition for the third time, and informed that a space of eight days was assigned to him for *Galileo's defense.* the preparation of his defense. He presented Cardinal Bellarmine's certificate, dated May 26, 1616. From the context of this certificate, he declared that he had believed himself at liberty to write as he had written. It did not contain the words " vel quovis modo docere," and he had had no idea but that it was one and the same thing with the decree of the Congregation of the Index, which, as he had since learnt, did contain those words. His written defense was a repetition of the answers and explanations which he had given during his examinations, and was terminated by a touching appeal to the mercy of the tribunal.

On the part of the Inquisitors there was a strong

inclination to leniency. More than one actually favored the Copernican theory, and nearly all were personally well disposed to Galileo. He had been given to understand[1] that the trial would terminate favorably, and that he would shortly be at liberty to return to Florence and resume his old pursuits. But, as the result soon showed, it was far otherwise.

The papers containing the minutes of the examinations had been given to three consulting theologians of the Holy Office to report upon. The reports were handed in separately, but all three were unanimous in declaring that Galileo had taught, defended, and adhered to the condemned opinion. The Pope's speech to Niccolini will be remembered. *Augustino Oreggi, Melchior Inchofer, a Jesuit, and Zaccaria Pasqualigo, counselors and theologians to the Holy Office.* He had feared not only that the doctrine was bad, but that Galileo himself believed his own doctrine. The reports of the counselors of the Holy Office did away with any favorable impression which might have been made by the prisoner's defense. Besides this belief in the Pope's mind of Galileo's heterodoxy, there was, as we learn from Niccolini's dispatches, a strong feeling against Galileo, altogether private and personal. [At the least the man must be silenced. That was the capital point. A decree was issued by the Pope on the 16th of June, ordering an examination for the 21st, in which Galileo was to be further pressed as to his intention in writing the "Dialogue."] (He was to be menaced with the torture. If the menace had no effect, he was to be made to pronounce an abjuration for suspicion of heresy ("abjuratio de vehementi suspicione hæresis").] He was to be imprisoned during *Galileo menaced with the torture.*

[1] Niccolini to Cioli, May 1, 1633.

the pleasure of the Congregation, and to be enjoined for the future to abstain from discussing the Copernican theory in any way whatever, either for or against, under pain of being treated as a relapsed heretic.

Whether the Pope's intention was that the menace of torture should remain a mere menace or not, Galileo's answer proves that he expected it to become a *His answer.* reality : "I am in your hands ; do as you please with me." "And," as the minute of the examination runs, "as nothing more could be got from him he was remanded" ("Et cum nihil aliud posset haberi in executionem decreti, habita ejus subscriptione, remissus fuit adlocum suum.")

If we contrast this last decree and the subsequent *Dissimula-tion of the Pope.* sentence and abjuration with the Pope's attitude during his interviews with Niccolini, it will take away all doubt as to whether his Holiness was or was not an adept in the art of dissimulation.

To Niccolini, his anger appeared to have melted away in sorrow. He protested that he would willingly have treated Galileo with greater leniency, merely from his regard for the Grand Duke ; but that Galileo's opinion, being contrary to Holy Scripture, must be prohibited. And it would be further necessary to inflict some salutary chastisement on him for having transgressed the decree of 1616. The Congregation were then deliberating on the sentence ; and as soon as it was published, Niccolini was promised another audience, that the Pope and he might consult together on it. The Pope declared that, though it was impossible to give Galileo a free pardon, yet he wished to afflict him as little as possible. He thought he might be confined in a monastery for a time. "Of the per-

sonal punishment I have as yet said nothing to Galileo," Niccolini wrote,[1] " in order not to distress him
by telling him everything at once; also by his Holiness' orders, who did not wish to add to his troubles;
and also because there may be a change of opinion."

On the 22d of June, Galileo was conducted to the
great hall of the Inquisition at Santa Maria sopra Minerva.   There, before the supreme magistracy of the
Holy See, its head alone being absent, he was made
to kneel and hear the sentence, which declared him
vehemently suspected of heresy, and condemned him
to imprisonment during the pleasure of the _The sen-_
Holy Office.   As a salutary penance, he was _tence._
ordered to say the Penitential Psalms once a week for
three years.[2]   He was then made to recite the abjuration dictated beforehand by the Pope.[3]

Galileo had long before made up his mind that his
book would be prohibited, but had hoped by his complete submission to escape punishment himself.   But
the Pope knew the man sufficiently well to be aware
that under an appearance of leniency he could inflict
the severest torture.   For the abjuration which Galileo
was forced to repeat word for word must have wrung
his soul as severely as the torture of the cord could
have wrung the muscles and tendons of his body.

It is said that Galileo, on rising from his knees after
his abjuration, muttered " Eppure si muove !" " It does
move, though !"   This is one of those fine things which
are put into the mouths of great men, but which in
fact are not said except by their biographers.   It is

---

[1] Niccolini to Cioli, June 18, 1633.
[2] See Appendix I.
[3] See Appendix II.

indeed impossible that Galileo should have uttered such words as would have caused his instant consignment to the deepest dungeons of the Inquisition. Alone and without support in the midst of that stern assembly, distressed in mind and suffering in body, we may fairly suppose that, prudential motives apart, his wit, far from being sharpened, had been numbed by despair and anguish at his humiliation.

Immediately after the ceremony, copies of the sentence and the abjuration were dispatched to all the apostolic nuncios. The Inquisitor-General at Florence was ordered to read both documents publicly in the hall of the Inquisition, and to serve notices to attend on all Galileo's disciples and adherents, and on all public professors. Thus Aggiunti, Guiducci, and all who loved their master best, were made to paricipate in his humiliation.

Publication of the sentence.

Not one of the decrees or orders relating to the trial of Galileo is officially ratified by the Pope. They all begin, it is true, with the words " Sanctissimus mandavit," but, being without the Pope's signature, they are to be considered as merely representing the fallible judgment of an assembly of cardinals. This is equally the case with the decree of 1616 as with the sentence of 1633. Neither Paul V. nor Urban VIII. ratified these documents by their signatures. This fact is too important to be lost sight of.

The sentence not ratified by the official signature of the Pope.

If indeed Galileo was persecuted (as he himself and all his followers believed), he was not persecuted by the Pope as infallible Vicar of Christ, but by Maffeo Barberini in his private capacity of a mean, irascible, vain man ; the instrument in his hands being a subservient Congregation of fallible cardinals. Even if we do not choose to style the proceedings against Galileo a persecution, the fact still remains — that he was sentenced, that the Congregation were mistaken, and that he was punished unjustly. By Tiraboschi the Jesuit, and by many other writers belonging to the Church of Rome, this, so far from being considered as a misfortune, has been made a matter for exultation, as a peculiar manifestation of God's providence. The Vicar of Christ not having spoken *ex cathedra*, his infallibility could neither then nor in future ages be called in question. To Galileo, however, though he was a sincere Catholic, this view does not appear to have afforded any consolation.

The names of ten cardinals appear in the preamble of the sentence. Of this number three abstained from signing the document. These were Gasparo Borgia, Laudivio Zacchia, and Francesco Barberini, the Pope's nephew. *The sentence signed by seven out of the ten presiding cardinals.* The Pope had ordered everything, but had signed nothing. Thus he shifted the responsibility from his own shoulders to those of the Congregation, though he found a minority which refused to accept it.

Besides the prohibition of the " Dialogue " it was decreed that all Galileo's works, published and unpublished, were to be placed on the " Index Expurgatorius." Thus did the Pope take *Galileo's works placed on the Index.* effectual measures for silencing a man whose intellect, compared to his own, was as the sun at noonday to the glimmer of a farthing candle ; thus was his wounded vanity soothed, and the triumph of the Jesuits complete.

Ostensibly, however, his Holiness was still full of desire to mitigate the severity of the sentence of the Inquisition. The sentence of perpetual imprisonment was immediately commuted by him to a relegation to the Villa Medici, in the pleasant gardens of Trinita del Monte, where Galileo, years before, had shown a company of wondering cardinals the satellites of Jupiter, and listened to the language of flattery from all those honeyed Roman tongues. " Thither I conducted him," Niccolini writes,[1] " and there he remains awaiting the clemency of his Holiness. He and Cardinal Barberino do not think it fit to grant a free pardon, but they will at all events allow him to go to the Archbishop's at Siena, or else to some convent in that city. I hear that Galileo has been much cast down at the punishment, of which he has just been informed. As to the book, he did not care for its being prohibited, and indeed had foreseen that it would be so."

On the 3d of July, Niccolini saw the Pope again, and entreated that, as soon as the plague abated, Galileo *Niccolini's* might be allowed to live a prisoner in his *negotiations.* own house at Arcetri. But his Holiness said it was too soon to discuss further commutation as yet: to allow him to be a prisoner in the Archbishop's palace instead of in a convent was a great leniency. Cardinal Barberino added that he might attend Divine service in the cathedral. " God grant that we be in *Galileo's* time," Niccolini continues, " for he appears *prostration.* exceedingly distressed and afflicted, and utterly prostrate. And this tempest has not burst on *Disgrace of* him alone ; Riccardi, the Inquisitor at Flor-*Ciampoli,* *Riccardi,* ence, every one is to be punished who has *and others.* had any hand in licensing the book." Ciampoli had been already disgraced and sent to Montalto, where he remained as long as he lived, Galileo's faithful friend to the last.

<hr>

[1] Dispatch to Cioli, June 26, 1633.

Sister Maria Celeste writes thus on the 2d of July: "The news of your fresh trouble has pierced my soul with grief; all the more that it came upon me quite unexpectedly. From not having had a letter from you this week, I feared something must have happened, and importuned Signor Geri to tell me; but what I hear from him of the resolution they have taken concerning you and your book gives me extremest pain, not having expected such a result. Dearest lord and father, now is the time for the exercise of that wisdom with which God has endowed you. Thus you will bear these blows with that fortitude of soul which religion, your age, and your profession alike demand."

Receiving no news from Galileo for some days after the promulgation of the sentence, Geri Bocchineri and Niccolò Aggiunti, fearing that their friend was incarcerated, and that a domiciliary visit might be expected at the villa from the familiars of the Inquisition at Florence, requested the keys of the house from Sister Maria Celeste, that they might do what Galileo had before told them might be necessary to his safety, should certain contingencies arise. Sister Maria Celeste felt that she could not take upon her to withhold the keys. "They feared you were in trouble," she writes, with her usual caution;[1] "and seeing how exceedingly anxious they were on your account, it seemed to me right and necessary to prevent any accident which might possibly happen: therefore I gave them the keys, and permission to do as they thought fit." "Quest' opera," this piece of work hinted at, can scarcely have been any other than the consigning to

[1] Sister Maria Celeste to Galileo, June 13, 1633.

the flames such writings in Galileo's library as might

Burning of papers. be used further to incriminate him. It is probable that much which was precious was destroyed on this occasion : and this may fully account for the disappearace of those incompleted writings of which mention is made in Galileo's correspondence, but of which no trace remains.[1]

At length Galileo was allowed to leave Rome. He set out for Siena on the 9th of July. We learn from the letters of Ciampoli, of Cini, of Rinuccini, and of Archbishop Piccolomini, how great was the relief experienced by his friends on knowing that he was beyond the treacherous boundary of the Holy City.

Arrival at Siena. At Siena every alleviation to his imprisonment which true friendship could devise was freely placed at Galileo's service. To the Archbishop he was a beloved and venerated guest, not a prisoner whose acts and gestures were to be spied upon and reported to the Holy Office.

"I wish," wrote Sister Maria Celeste on the 13th of

Rejoicing at St. Matthew's. July, "that I could describe the rejoicing of all the mothers and sisters on hearing of your happy. arrival at Siena. It was indeed most extraordinary ! On hearing the news, Mother Abbess

---

[1] It is also possible that Galileo may have destroyed his unfinished writings with his own hands, on his citation to Rome in the October of 1632. He wrote to Cardinal Barberino at that time : "When I think that the end of all my labors, after having gained for myself a name not obscure among the learned, has been finally to bring upon me a citation to appear before the tribunal of the Holy Office, . . . I detest the remembrance of the time I have consumed in study. I regret ever having published what I wrote, and I have a mind to burn every composition that I have yet by me."

and many of the nuns ran to me, embracing me and weeping for joy and tenderness."

The Archbishop's house was an earthly paradise, but the remembrance of the cruel edict condemning him to perpetual silence was a serpent-sting to Galileo. Even the society of his pious and benignant host could not soothe his wounded spirit always, or keep him from falling into fits of despondency, when he accused all his friends of having forgotten him. "My name is erased from the book of the living," he wrote in a moment of bitterness. " Nay," came Sister Maria Celeste's ready reply, " say not that your name is struck out *de libro viventium,* for it is not so ; neither in the greater part of the world nor in your own country. Indeed it seems to me that if for a brief moment your name and fame were clouded, they are now restored to greater brightness ; at which I am much astonished, for I know that generally ' Nemo propheta acceptus est in patriâ suâ.' I am afraid that if I begin quoting Latin I shall fall into some barbarism. But indeed you are loved and esteemed here more than ever."

On the 23d of July we find Galileo entreating Niccolini to use his influence with the Grand Duke to procure him permission to return to Florence. Niccolini advised him to be patient. He was certain his Holiness would not give the permission yet, though he had not been able to get the reason from him.

But it was hard for Galileo to be patient, when his daughter, in spite of her resignation to the Divine will, was consumed with longing to see him once more. Her life was one continual prayer for him. Yet, while ever thinking of his

spiritual welfare not one whit did she abate of her diligence in looking after his worldly affairs. She tells him
of the fruit and the wine which have been sold ; she
keeps a strict account of his money. We learn that the
vines had been injured by hail, that thieves had been in
the garden, that " my lady mule " was behaving arrogantly, and would carry no one now her master was
away ; that a terrible storm had carried off one end of
the roof, and broken in pieces one of the vases which
held the orange-trees. There were but few plums, and
The garden the wind had carried away the pears. With
at Arcetri. the money from the lemons, two lire, she had
had three masses said for her father. " There are two
pigeons in the dovecote waiting for you to come and
eat them," she writes ; " there are beans in the garden
waiting for you to gather them. Your tower is lament-
ing your long absence. When you were in Rome, I
Sister Maria said to myself, If he were but at Siena !
Celeste's
resignation. Now you are at Siena, I say, Would he were
at Arcetri ! But God's will be done ! " Then hearing
from Signor Rondinelli that the Ambassador's opinion
had been against Galileo's supplication for further
leniency, lest his judges should be utterly wearied and
reply once for all in a decided negative, she restrains
herself, and writes in this tone no longer, but tells her
father not to wish to hurry away from Siena, where his
prison is an earthly paradise.

Yet before long she goes back to the old strain : [1]—

" If I do not make great demonstration of my desire
to see you, it is because I do not wish to unsettle you,
and make you more uneasy. I have been going about
Her castles lately making castles in the air, thinking
in the air. to myself whether after these two months'

____
[1] Sister Maria Celeste to Galileo, August 20, 1633.

delay, if the pardon be not obtained, I might have re-course to the Ambassadress, to try whether she might not obtain it through her interest with his Holiness's sister-in-law. I know that this is but a castle in the air, yet still it is not quite impossible that the piteous prayers of a daughter might procure the favor of great personages (the Pope is probably meant). Now, think-ing this over, as I said, when your letter came telling me that one of the reasons why I desired your return was that I wanted a present you had for me, O then I can tell you I did get angry! But such an anger as King David speaks of in the psalm, ' Irascimini et nolite peccare.' For it seemed to me that you thought I wanted to see the present more than to see you ; which is as far from my thoughts as darkness is from light. Perhaps I did not quite understand your letter, and I try to keep quiet with that thought. But if indeed you meant that, I do not know what I should say or do. Do see if you cannot come back to your tower, which cannot bear to remain so desolate any longer ! And now, too, it is time to think about the wine-casks. They have been taken up to the *loggia* and taken to pieces by sentence of the best connois-seurs of the neighborhood, who declare that the reason the wine spoils is that you never have them taken to pieces in order to expose the wood to the heat of the sun. Piera can begin making bread again now that the weather is cooler. Of the eight crowns which I got from the wine, I spent three for six bushels of wheat. Piera begs to be remembered to you, and says that if her wish to see you and your wish to *Piera's* return were put in the scales, her scale would *message.* go down to the ground, and yours up to the ceiling.

"I say no more, except that as soon as I have finished reading your last letter, I long for the next post to bring me another, particularly now that we hope for some news from Rome."

Here is another little episode of the cloister life. Sister Polissena Vinta, an aged nun, sent to ask Galileo *Episode of cloister life.* to find out whether a certain Emilio Piccolomini, a son of her niece who had married a Captain Carlo Piccolomini, was living at Siena. It appeared on inquiry that this was the case. Galileo had reminded this gentleman of the existence of his aged relative, and a message had been sent through him offering help if needful. " You may think for yourself," wrote Sister Maria Celeste, " whether or not she is in want, being as she is nearly always ill in bed. She was extremely angry at the message sent through you, declaring that not only had Signor Emilio forgotten her, but that so had her niece, Signora Elisabetta ; and she believes they all think her dead." Shortly afterwards Galileo received from this nun's rich relatives the magnificent sum of one crown to. transmit to her, for which, notwithstanding her previous anger, the poor woman was thankful.

As soon as the quarantine regulations were removed, Sister Maria Celeste sent the servant Geppo on the mule to Siena to see Galileo, and bring her back word how he was looking. " It seems to me a thousand years till I see you back again safe and well ! " she wrote after Geppo's return.[1] " I would not have you doubt that all this time I have never ceased from commending you to God with my whole heart, for indeed I feel too anxious for your spiritual and bodily health

---

[1] Sister Maria Celeste to Galileo, October 3, 1633.

ever to have neglected praying for you. To give you a proof, I will tell you that as a great favor I managed to get a copy of your sentence shown me, and though on the one hand it grieved me to read it, yet on the other hand I was glad to have done so, because I found out a way of being of some slight use to you; namely, by taking upon myself that part of the sentence which orders you to recite the seven Penitential Psalms once a week. I began to do this a while ago, and it gives me much pleasure; first because I am persuaded that prayer in obedience to Holy Church must be efficacious; secondly, in order to save you the trouble of remembering it. If I had been able to do more, most willingly would I have entered a straiter prison than the one I live in now, if by so doing I could have set you at liberty."

In succeeding letters we hear of more convent trials. Sister Luisa was ill of an incurable complaint, and Sister Maria Celeste was in *Illness at St. Matthew's.* daily and nightly attendance on her. Seven of the nuns were down in fever. Sister Maria Silvia, once the loveliest girl that had been seen in Florence for three hundred years, was dying of consumption at the age of twenty-two. Then we hear of poor neighbors sick and starving; recommended, never in vain, as fit objects for her father's charity. From Siena the same kindness *Galileo's kindness to his poor neighbors and to the nuns.* was shown to the convent as when Galileo was at Florence. He takes charge of divers small commissions, he forwards letters for the nuns who cannot pay the courier, buys cheap thread and saffron and flax for the Mother Abbess, chooses sonatas for the organist, Mother Achilea; he sends presents of gray partridges for the invalids, and cream-cheese, and the famous *panforte* of Siena.

At length the weariness and sickness of heart caused by hope deferred began to tell upon Sister Maria Celeste. Worn by continual ill-health, by nightly watchings in the infirmary and daily occupations which could not be neglected, she would appear to have felt *a* sad presentiment of her approaching dissolution. She strove gently to prepare her father, telling him that it was for him to live long to the service and glory of the God who had endowed him with such a wondrous intellect, and to the comfort of many by whom his loss would be severely felt. But as for her, she could neither do much for the glory of God, nor be of much good to any one, and her living or dying would make but little difference.

Sister Maria Celeste's presentiment of her death.

That Galileo was allowed to leave Siena was owing not so much to the strong representations of Niccolini as to the report given to the Pope by the spies who had dogged Galileo even within the precincts of the archiepiscopal palace. Within the space of four months, they declared, Galileo had sown heretical opinions in Siena, which might bear pernicious fruit. Information had also been given that some of his adherents were writing in his defense. Niccolini assured the Pope that even if such were the case, which he did not believe, he could take upon himself to say that Galileo was entirely ignorant of it, and would be the first to desire that his friends should be silent on the subject. But the Pope probably felt that silence would best be secured by shutting Galileo up in the country rather than in a great city where his age and sufferings,

Anonymous information given to the Inquisition respecting Galileo's conduct at Siena.

even setting aside his fame, would naturally command the love and veneration of all who knew him.

When at length the news reached Sister Maria Celeste that her father's prison had been changed to Arcetri, and that he would shortly set out on his return, she had not life enough left in her to be glad. "I do not think," she wrote on the 3d of December, 1633, "that I shall live to see that hour. Yet may God grant it, if it be for the best."

Her last prayer was granted. Before she lay down in her narrow bed side by side with her sister nuns in the little convent cemetery, she was allowed once more to embrace her *Sister Maria Celeste's last prayer granted.* dearest lord and father. The last we know of her may best be given in Galileo's own words to Elia Diodati.[1] "I stayed five months at Siena in the house of the Archbishop; after which my prison was changed to confinement to my own house, that little villa a mile from Florence, with strict injunctions that I was not to entertain friends, nor to allow the assembling of many at a time. Here I lived on very quietly, frequently paying visits to the neighboring convent, where I had two daughters who were nuns, and whom I loved dearly; but the eldest in particular, who was a woman of exquisite mind, singular goodness, and most tenderly attached to me. She had suffered much from ill-health during my absence, but had not paid much attention to herself. At length dysentery came on, and she died after six days' illness, leaving me in deep affliction."

[Sister Maria Celeste died on the 1st of April, 1634.] *Her death, at the age of thirty-three years.*

____

[1] Galileo to Diodati, July 28, 1634.

CHAPTER XIII.

ON the day when Galileo, heart-broken, was hourly
awaiting the messenger to tell him that his daughter
had breathed her last, a familiar of the Inquisition
appeared with an order from Rome.

The pontifical decree permitting Galileo's return to
The pontif-ical decree. Arcetri had been stringent even to harshness. It was a condemnation to perpetual
solitude, inspired by the Pope's remembrance of Galileo's keen enjoyment of wit that sparkled like Sagredo's, of clear and limpid philosophy such as Salviati's, of comedy such as Buonarroti's, nay, of honeyed
compliment such as Maffeo Barberini, Cardinal, had
delighted to render, in the by-gone days in which he
had written Latin sonnets in Galileo's praise, and
had condescended to . sign himself "his affectionate
brother." No more of this should Galileo enjoy.
"Conceditur habitatio in ejus rure," ran the edict of
the 1st of December, "mode tamen ibi, ut in soli-
tudine, stet, nec vocet eo, nec venientes illuc recipiat
ad collocutiones."

Galileo, supposing that this harshness was merely nominal, and that a proper petition would be followed in due course by a removal of the restriction to Arcetri, had applied through Niccolini for permission to go to his house at Florence. He was now informed that the result of any further application of this sort would be his instant consignment to the dungeons of the Inquisition at Rome. "From this answer," he wrote to Diodati, "I may conclude that my present prison will only be changed for that last narrow dwelling common to us all."[1]

Though there is no doubt that Urban was actuated by personal ill-feeling, we must always remember that, while the Congregation of the Holy Office were but instruments in the hands of the Pontiff, he in his turn was, without being aware of it, merely an instrument in the hands of the Jesuits. Father Griemberger, mathematician of the Roman College, said openly, that, if Galileo had only managed so as to keep in the good graces of the Fathers, he would never have brought such trouble upon himself, but would have kept his name untarnished before the world, and might have continued writing on the Copernican theory had he so pleased. Thus his disgrace was not due to his writings and opinions, but to his having stirred up the enmity of the Company of Jesus; but even in the hour of his deepest despondency Galileo never, so far as we know, regretted having assumed an independent attitude towards that all-powerful Order.

[Galileo's health and spirits declined so rapidly after

----

[1] Galileo to Elia Diodati, July 28, 1634.

the death of his beloved daughter, that it seemed to him at first as if he were destined to follow her.] ["I hear her constantly calling me," he wrote to Geri Bocchineri,[1] less than a month after her death.] In the succeeding portion of this letter we have a sad picture of the old man's desolation. From various alarming bodily symptoms, added to the call resounding in his ears, he believed himself to be dying. Vincenzio was living in Florence, in a house which his father had bought for him during his detention at Siena. "I *Letter to* do not think it at all advisable," he wrote, *Geri Bocchi-* "that Vincenzio should undertake a journey *neri.* just now, when every hour something may occur which would render his presence necessary. I tell you this that you may tell him if you think fit; not because I wish to disturb his plans, but because it seems to me that he ought to know. You, who can speak more firmly to him than I can, will say enough to make him take the course which is most advisable. He has been asking for his allowance, twenty-five crowns. I inclose it to you to forward to him, as I do not wish to say a single word for him to turn and twist at his pleasure."

But Galileo was destined to live yet a few years longer. Full of labor and sorrow had his life been, and full of labor and sorrow was it to the end. Though broken down by grief for his daughter's death, the habits of industry acquired in youth could not be laid aside in old age. Work was more than a consolation ; it was a necessity to him. But he felt the gradual approach of mental decay. "My restless brain goes grinding on," he wrote to Micanzio,[2] "in

---

[1] Galileo to Geri Bocchineri, April 27, 1634.

[2] Galileo to Fra Fulgenzio Micanzio, November 19, 1634.

a way that causes great waste of time; because the thought which comes last into my head in respect of some novelty, drives out all that had been there before." He was then engaged in completing the "Dialogues on Motion," wishing, as he told Diodati, that the world should see the last of his labors before his time of departure came. But as he wrote, thoughts crowded thick and fast upon him, so that his work increased, while each day lessened his span of life.

The "Dialogues on Motion" were completed in the summer of 1636, and consigned to Louis Elzevir at Leyden for publication. Galileo dedicated *The French Ambassador, Comte de Noailles.* this, his last work, to his old pupil Noailles, who, in concert with another distinguished pupil, the Duke of Peiresc, had, while French ambassador at Rome, used all the influence he possessed to procure a mitigation of Galileo's sentence. A Latin translation of the letter to the Grand Duchess Christina had been already printed at Paris. Elzevir contemplated publishing a Latin edition of all Galileo's works, with the exception of the ill-fated "Dialogue;" but this project was subjected to various delays, and at last the author's death prevented its accomplishment. Pierre Carcaville, a counselor of the Parliament of Toulouse, generously offered to undertake the publication of all the "Dialogues" at his own cost; but his offer was not accepted, as Galileo then considered himself engaged to Elzevir. The Dutch edition of the "Dialogues" was surreptitiously introduced into Italy, with great success.

Galileo wrote to Micanzio that, besides the copies usually supplied to the author, he desired to buy a hundred more, as they were not to be got anywhere;

while there was such a demand for them, that he had known six crowns to be given for a copy, more than six times its original price; and he had often been obliged to have manuscript copies made, at great trouble and expense.

The condemned "Dialogue" had already been translated into the English tongue, to the gratification of its author, and the rage and mortification of the Jesuits. Mention is made in Galileo's correspondence of the frequent visits of foreigners (*Oltramontani*); amongst others of an English gentleman who had informed him of the "Dialogue" being read in England.[1] It is a significant fact, and one which was not lost sight of by Galileo and his friends, that a perusal of his sentence was sufficient to establish his guiltlessness in the opinion of foreigners who had first heard the Jesuits' side of the question.

No sooner were the "Dialogues on Motion" revised

---

[1] The following reference to Galileo cannot fail to be read with interest. It is to be found in Milton's *Areopagitica* (which is a discourse addressed to the Lords and Commons against requiring all printed books to be licensed). "I could recount what I have seen and heard in other countries, where this kind of inquisition tyrannizes; where I have sat among their lerned (*sic*) men, for that honour I had, and bin (*sic*) counted happy to be born in such a place of Philosophic Freedom, as they suppos'd England was, while themselves did nothing but bemoan the servil condition into which Lerning amongst them was brought; that this was it which had dampt the glory of Italian wits; that nothing had been there writt'n now these many years but flattery and fustian. There it was that I found and visited the famous Galileo, grown old, a prisner to the Inquisition for thinking in Astronomy otherwise than the Franciscan and Dominican Licencers thought." Milton went to Italy on the death of his mother in 1637, and returned in 1639.

and out of his hands, than Galileo's busy brain began to form new projects. "If I live," he wrote to Bernegger at Strasburg, "I intend to put in order a series of natural and mathematical problems, which I trust will be as curious as they are novel."[1]

But though, as appears from his correspondence, he was fully determined to print his works abroad, he had no longer the option of refuting the falsities promulgated industriously throughout Italy by the Jesuits concerning his life and opinions. As soon as it was prudent to introduce the subject, Noailles and Cardinal Antonio Barberino, the Pope's brother, had spoken to his Holiness in Galileo's favor. "They endeavored," wrote Galileo to Micanzio in July, 1636, "to assure his Holiness that I had never had such an iniquitous thought as to vilipend his person, as my wretched enemies had persuaded him ; which was the *primo motor* of all my troubles. At length he pronounced my exculpation, saying : ' *We believe it, we believe it :* ' adding, nevertheless, that the reading of the ' Dialogue ' was most pernicious to Christianity." Thus the embargo remained in full force. To be acquitted of the charge of intentional disrespect was as much and more than Galileo could expect of the Pope's infallibility; on the other hand, his Holiness could afford to express his belief in Galileo's innocence, since he was determined never to give him any further opportunity of being heard. How great was the power of the Jesuits then and later, is evident from the tone taken by Viviani in 1654, in describing this portion of Galileo's life. It being impossible to

Intercession made for Galileo by Noailles and Cardinal Antonio Barberino.

[1] Galileo to Mathias Bernegger, July 15, 1636.

18

deny the fact of the publication of his master's works

Viviani's insincerity. in Germany and Holland, Viviani thinks it necessary to add what was positively untrue: "that this publication was unauthorized, and that Galileo was extremely displeased and mortified on hearing of it, as his writings contained much that he would willingly have altered or expunged, since he had abandoned the Copernican doctrine as became a good Catholic."

" In order to show his gratitude," Viviani continues, " to that Providence which had mercifully opened his eyes to so great an error, Galileo ceased not to promulgate other discoveries of great importance."

How deep in reality was the undercurrent of bitterness in Galileo's heart when stirred by the remembrance of the Jesuits' machinations, his correspondence at this period, of which we give two examples, sufficiently shows. The first is a letter to Peiresc.[1]

" I have said, my lord, that I hope for no alleviation ; and this is because I have committed no crime. If I had erred, I might hope to obtain grace and pardon ; for the transgressions of the subject are the means by which the prince finds occasion for the exercise of mercy and indulgence. Wherefore, when a man is wrongly condemned to punishment, it becomes necessary for his judges to use the greater severity, in order to cover their own misapplication of the law. This afflicts me less than people may think possible ; for I possess two sources of perpetual comfort : first, that in my writings cannot be found the faintest shadow of irreverence toward Holy Church ; secondly, the testimony of my own conscience, which I myself alone

---

[1] Galileo to the Duke of Peiresc, February 21, 1636.

know thoroughly, besides God in heaven. And He knoweth that in this cause for which I suffer, though many men might have spoken more learnedly, none, not even the ancient fathers, have spoken with more piety, nor with greater zeal for Holy Church, than I. Could all the frauds, the calumnies, the stratagems, the deceits, which were made use of at Rome eighteen years ago for the purpose of imposing upon the supreme authority, — could all these, I say, be brought to light, their only effect would be to enhance the purity and uprightness of my intentions. But you, having read my works, will have seen how they justify my assertions of sincerity, and you will have understood the true cause for which, under the mask of religion, I have been persecuted, and which now continually assails me and crosses my path ; so that no help can come to me from without, nor can I myself undertake my own defense. For all the inquisitors have received express orders to allow neither the reprinting of such works of mine as were · published many years ago, nor to grant a license to any fresh work which I may desire to publish. Thus I am not only forced to keep silence towards those who strive to distort my doctrine and make my ignorance manifest, but I must also bear the insults and the contempt and the bitter taunts of men more ignorant than myself, without proffering a word in my own defense. . . . My heart thanks you better than my words can express, for the most pious and humane office which you have undertaken on my behalf. May the Lord reward you for your kindness."

This was in allusion to Peiresc's endeavor to obtain a removal of his restriction to Arcetri. In the same strain of bitterness he wrote to Ladislaus, King of Poland, in 1637.

"I send your Majesty three lenses, according to *Letter to* the command which I received in your most *Ladislaus,* *King of* gracious letter. I have endeavored to the *Poland.* utmost of my ability to serve your Majesty well in this matter; but I am in prison here, and have been for the last three years, by order of the Holy Office, for having printed the 'Dialogue' on the Ptolemaic and Copernican systems; though I had the license of the Holy Office, that is, of the Master of the Sacred Palace of Rome. I know that some copies of the said books have penetrated your Majesty's dominions; and your Majesty and such of your subjects as call themselves scientific men may have judged whether or not it be true that my book contains doctrine more scandalous, more detestable, and more pernicious than is to be found in the writings of Luther, Calvin, and all other heresiarchs put together! Nevertheless, the Pope's mind has been so strongly imbued with this idea, that the book has been prohibited, and I put to utter shame, and condemned to imprisonment during his Holiness's pleasure, which will be perpetual. But where doth passion transport me? Let me go back to the lenses."

Such bursts of anger as the above alternated with fits of deep melancholy. "Alas!" he exclaims to Micanzio, "tristis senectus!" In 1634 his sister-in-law, Clara Galilei, with her three daughters and one son, came to live with him; but they all perished in the plague shortly after their arrival. Some time after their deaths, finding the solitude of his house at Arcetri insupportable, Galileo desired his nephew

Alberto to come and live with him. This boy had lost the little his mother had had to leave him, in the sack of Munich, and was maintaining himself and his young brother Cosmo on the scanty stipend he gained as violinist and lute-player to the Elector. He appears to have been of a far different disposition to his worthless brother Vincenzio. Galileo kept him for some time, but he finally returned to Munich, married, and reëntered the service of the Elector ; so that the old man was again alone.

In 1637, just before his sight failed him, Galileo made his last celestial discovery, known as *Discovery of* *the moon's* the moon's libration. His observations *libration.* were embodied in a treatise, in the form of a letter to Antonini. The only other notice of this discovery is in a letter to Micanzio. Sadly different is its tone to that of his letter to Vinta in 1610, in which he speaks with mingled awe and exultation of his discovery of Jupiter's satellites. " I see," he wrote,[1] "that you suppose I have not given up speculating. It is true. I do go on speculating; but to the great prejudice of my health ; for thinking, joined to various other molestations, destroys my sleep, and increases the melancholy of my nights ; while the pleasure which I have taken hitherto in making observations on new phenomena is almost entirely gone. I have observed a most marvelous appearance on the surface of the moon. Though she has been looked at such millions of times by such millions of men, I do not find that any have observed the slightest alteration in her sur- face, but that exactly the same side has always been supposed to be represented to our eyes. Now I find

[1] Galileo to Fra Fulgenzio Micanzio, November 7, 1637.

that such is not the case, but on the contrary that she changes her aspect, as one who, having his full face turned towards us, should move it sideways, first to the right and then to the left, or should raise and then lower it, and lastly incline it first to the right, then to the left shoulder. All these changes I see in the moon; and the large, anciently known spots which are seen in her face, may help to make evident the truth of what I say. Add to this a second marvel, which is that these three mutations have their three several periods; the first daily, the second monthly, the third yearly. Now what connection does your Reverence think these three lunar periods may have with the daily, monthly, and annual movement of the sea? which is ruled over by the moon, by the consent of all."

This was the last of the long list of discoveries Galileo was permitted to make. His sight rapidly decayed, and blindness was soon added to his other miseries. "I have been in my bed for five weeks," he wrote to Diodati,[1] while there still remained a vestige of hope that the blindness might not prove incurable, "oppressed with weakness and other infirmities from which my age, seventy-four years, permits me not to hope release. Added to this (*proh dolor !*) the sight of my right eye — that eye whose labors (I dare say it) have had such glorious results — is forever lost. That of the left, which was and is imperfect, is rendered null by a continual weeping."

"Alas !" he wrote again to the same friend a few *Galileo's* months later,[2] "your dear friend and ser-*blindness.* vant Galileo has been for the last month

---

[1] Galileo to Diodati, July 4, 1637.   [2] January 2, 1638.

hopelessly blind ; so that this heaven, this earth, this universe, which I by my marvelous discoveries and clear demonstrations had enlarged a hundred thousand times beyond the belief of the wise men of bygone ages, henceforward for me is shrunk into such a small space as is filled by my own bodily sensations."

But when his blindness was known to be without earthly remedy, then complaint ceased, and, instead of enlarging on his misery of mind and body, he only desired his friends to remember him in their prayers. On two occasions only was Galileo permitted to quit Arcetri: once in the spring of 1638,[1] when he was per-

[1] "In order to fulfill more entirely the command of his Holiness," wrote the Inquisitor Fanano to Cardinal Francesco Barberini, on the 13th of February, 1638, "I went myself when I was not expected, accompanied by a foreign physician who was in my confidence, in order to observe Galileo's way of living at Arcetri, feeling persuaded that I should thus be able to judge, not so much of the kind of complaint or complaints he may have, as of his present studies, and of those who frequent his house, with whose aid he might hold gatherings in Florence, and discourses wherein to disseminate his condemned opinion respecting the earth. I found him totally blind, and, though he himself hopes for a recovery, his physician considers that his age renders the disease incurable. Besides the blindness, he suffers terribly from hernia, has continual pains all over his body, and suffers, as he himself declares (and those of his household confirm him), to such a degree from sleeplessness, that he never sleeps a whole hour together in the twenty-four. Moreover, he is so prostrate, that he looks more like a corpse than a living person. The villa is distant from the city, and so inconveniently situated that the attendance of a physician is a difficulty and an expense to him. Blindness has put an end to his studies, though he has himself read to now and then. People do not visit him as much as formerly, for since his health has been so broken, he does nothing as a rule but complain, and relate his symptoms to those around him. I think, therefore, that if his Holiness were

mitted to be in Florence for a very short time for the purpose of consulting the best physicians, but on condition only of not attempting to visit, or receive his friends freely; in spite of which, one at least — Michelangelo Buonarroti — ventured to visit him. The only other occasion was when he went to pay his

to show his infinite pity by giving him permission to go to Florence, there would be no reason to fear the assembling of a great concourse of people at his house. And if there were any such fear, he is so prostrate that a good admonition would be quite sufficient to keep him within bounds."

Galileo had been ordered to present himself at the Holy Office to receive oral directions concerning his conduct. "I signified to him," wrote the Inquisitor to Cardinal Barberini, on the 10th of March, 1638, "the favor accorded him by our Lord (Pope) and the Sacred Congregation, to have himself carried from his villa at Arcetri to his house in Florence, for the purpose of medical treatment. I have ordered him not to go out into the city under pain of imprisonment and excommunication; and have forbidden him to discourse with any one on his condemned opinion of the earth's motion. He is now seventy-four years of age, and brought so low by his blindness and other complaints, that we may easily believe his promise not to transgress this command. Moreover, his house is in a most out-of-the-way place, far away from any habitation; it can scarcely be said to be in the city. Besides this, he has a son, a civil, honest man, who is constantly with him, and whom I have admonished not to admit any suspected person to speak to his father, and to see that those who do visit him do not stop too long. I feel certain that he (the son) will take heed that nothing happen to induce a revocation of his Holiness's permission, for it is to his interest that his father should take care of himself and live as long as possible, since the Grand Duke's pension of one thousand crowns ceases on his death. Notwithstanding, I shall watch narrowly to see that his Holiness's commands are carried out. Galileo has entreated me to forward his request for permission to be carried to hear mass at a little church distant twenty paces from his house; this I do accordingly."

respects to the Comte de Noailles at Poggibonsi. Once or twice he visited the Grand Duke at Petraia with great secrecy, going from Arcetri in a close carriage in the early morning, and returning late at night. But after 1638 it does not appear that he attempted to quit the precincts of his villa ; and indeed, increased feebleness, if nothing else, would have kept him a prisoner.

In 1636 Galileo had addressed himself to the States-General of Holland, offering them freely, and without hope of reward, his method of determining the longitude by means of Jupiter's satellites, the tables of whose motions had been accurately ascertained through his unceasing observations from the moment of their discovery to 1632. Elia Diodati took charge of the negotiation, which was also furthered by the patronage and recommendations of Hugo Grotius, then ambassabor for Sweden at the French Court. The States-General were more favorably inclined to the method than the Spanish Government had been. They named four commissioners to examine its merits, and voted the sum of a thousand francs for the purchase of the instruments necessary to verify its accuracy and utility. But delay followed delay, and it was not till the August of 1638 that a deputation was sent to Arcetri to confer with Galileo in person, on behalf of the States. Hortensius, one of the commissioners, had wished to form one of the deputation, but was dissuaded from his plan by Galileo's desire, news having reached him from Rome of the displeasure which the knowledge of his negotiation with the States had given to the Holy Office. The deputation, consisting of two merchants, the

The States-General send a deputation to Arcetri.

brothers Ebors, went to Arcetri bearing a letter from the States, and a gold chain, sent as a mark of respect. They found the old man in bed, blind and grievously afflicted. He requested them to read the letter aloud, and to give him the box containing the chain. Taking it in his hands, he desired them to thank the States for their courtesy. The box and the letter he kept. The chain he returned to the deputation, saying he did not think proper to keep it, seeing that in consequence of his blindness and increasing infirmities, the negotiation which had so long languished must be for a time, and perhaps forever, at a standstill. Seeing, however, in the fact of the States having sent this deputation, a proof of their desire to adopt his method, Galileo on his recovery put all his writings on the satellites into the hands of Renieri, in order that the revision of the tables and ephemeris might be performed with that nicety of which his blindness rendered him no longer capable.

But before this could be done, three of the commissioners, Real, Blauw, and Goll, died; and *Death of four Dutch commissioners.* their deaths were followed by that of Hortensius in April, 1639; so that this plan was abandoned. In the beginning of the succeeding year, Constantine Huyghens, Secretary of the Prince of Orange, undertook to renew the correspondence with the States-General, who seemed, after the death of the four commissioners, to have forgotten Galileo's existence, and Borel, Counselor of the Provinces and Pensioner of Amsterdam, was requested to remind them of the long-pending negotiation; but though the tables of the periods of the satellites had been examined and approved of by many astronomers, yet their approbation was insufficient to dispel the coldness of the Dutch Government; and Galileo was at length forced, though unwillingly, to abandon all hope of his discovery of the satellites being put to that use of which he for such a number of years had fondly imagined it to be capable.

The last work of Galileo's old age was a short treatise on the secondary light of the moon, in which he combated the opinion of Liceti, a professor *Liceti's* of Padua, who held that the moon was phos- *opinion of the moon's* phorescent, like the Bologna stone. This *phosphores-cence.* treatise was written by Prince Leopold's desire, he having observed that Liceti had, in his work " De Lapide Bononiensi," impugned many of Galileo's opinions. This proceeding, though cowardly enough, considering that Liceti knew that Galileo was prevented from answering him publicly, was aggravated by his impudent misquotation of various passages in Galileo's prohibited works. In some of his private letters on this subject, Galileo makes touching allusions to the inconvenience he suffered from his blindness.

" I am obliged to have recourse to other hands and other pens than mine since my sad loss of sight," he wrote to Prince Leopold.[1] " This, of course, occasions great loss of time, particularly now that my memory is impaired by advanced age; so that in placing my thoughts on paper, many and many a time I am forced to have the foregoing sentences read to me before I can tell what ought to follow; else I should repeat the same thing over and over. Your Highness may take my word for it, that between using one's own eyes and hands and those of others there

----

[1] Galileo to Prince Leopold de' Medici, March 13, 1640.

is as great a difference as in playing chess with one's eyes open or blindfold."

Without entering into the merits of the controversy (about which, indeed, there is no doubt), it is worth while to notice the contrast presented by the tone taken throughout by Galileo to that held by Liceti. In Galileo's correspondence the stately courtesy becoming a philosopher and a gentleman is never once abandoned. In writing, even to his most intimate friends, he mentions Liceti in becoming terms, and alludes to his violent opposition only with the kind of amused contempt which could be expressed without derogating from his own dignity. On the other hand, not only did Liceti contradict and misquote his writings and opinions, but he even ventured to address the aged astronomer in a manner which is unequaled for its arrogance by any other of Galileo's bitterest opponents. Even the commonest phrases of courtesy *Liceti's* are wanting: the "Vossignoria," used to ex- *want of* *courtesy.* press the curt "you," is nearly always pretermitted ; the usual phrase, "le bacio le mani," left out at the end, which, though not rigorously necessary, might well have proceeded from the pen of a man comparatively young, like Liceti, in writing to one so venerable as Galileo. Liceti's correspondence, so far from showing common respect, often takes a tone as from a superior to an inferior. He even ventures to allude in terms of contempt to Galileo's blindness. Displeased at the old man's judgment on some passages in his book, " De Lapide," he says : " I appeal to those who have their own hands to write with, and their own eyes to see with. Learned men are in the habit of not easily believing those whose opinions are in opposition to their own, therefore I am not in the least surprised that you should consider my arguments easily disposed of.   As to our differences of opinion, had I considered your dicta frivolous, I should never have deigned to give them a moment's consideration." "If you order diligent search to be made for the book I sent you, 'De Luminis,' etc., doubtless it will be found either at the Custom-house or at the courier's."[1]

"The book which your lordship's most illustrious excellency has done me the honor to send," *Galileo's answer to Liceti.* Galileo wrote in reply,[2] "has at length been found.   I have sent it to be bound, and as soon as I get it back I will have it read to me.   I hope that with its help I shall shortly be able to understand what many and many hundred hours of thinking have yet not made me capable of understanding: to wit, the essence of light, as to which I have always been in darkness. . . . . . Though it has pleased you to quote and amend various opinions of mine, which I still hold to be most true, nevertheless I trust that I shall never be induced to mention your writings except with proper praise; though, indeed, from my advanced age and unhappy state, it is probable that I may be able to speak but little, and write less, if indeed I am able to write anything."

With this exception Galileo's last years were soothed by the affection and devotion of his friends, and the homage of all to whom his name was known.   The Grand Duke frequently visited him, and replenished his cellar with the best of wines.   Besides the creature comforts which were thus supplied to him — and

[1] Liceti to Galileo, June 8, 1640.
[2] Galileo to Liceti, August 25, 1640.

Archbishop Piccolomini must not be forgotten as a contributor to these — Galileo had the better comfort of once more meeting with his old friend Castelli, and discoursing with that learned and truly pious man on the things of that world to which they both were tending.

Viviani lived in his house, and was to him as a son. Towards the last Torricelli was joined to him as amanuensis and companion. Galileo had formed the plan of adding two chapters, or conversations, to the *Galileo's last work.* " Dialogues on Motion," with various additions and illustrations to those already published. He intended the last of these new chapters to be devoted to the consideration of the nature of the force of percussion, in which he believed he had discovered facts at least as marvelous as any published in his former works. But these labors were interrupted by an attack of low fever, accompanied by palpitation of the heart. After two months' suffering, *His death.* borne with most philosophic and Christian fortitude, he gave back his soul into the Creator's hands on the evening of the 8th of January, 1642.

In addition to such details of Galileo's life as have already been given, the following may not be without interest.

In his will, made in 1638, he had ordered that his *His will.* body was to be buried in the family vault at Santa Croce. His son Vincenzio was left sole heir : to his daughter, Sister Arcangela, he gave an annuity of twenty-five crowns : to his nephews Alberto and Cosmo, then living at Munich, he bequeathed a thousand crowns ; which bequest, however, was revoked in a codicil added the same year. He willed that any of his descendants who might enter into a religious Order were to be by such act deprived of the enjoyment of such property as he otherwise bequeathed to them. In the event of his son's death during the minority of his grandchildren, their mother, Sestilia Bocchineri, was to be guardian conjointly with Mario Guiducci.

Not only was Galileo's power of making a will disputed, but the propriety of laying his body in consecrated ground was loudly questioned by some fanatics, who could only see in the career of this great man the one fact that he had died vehemently suspected of heresy. A legal consultation as to his power of making a will was, fortunately for his family, decided in his favor. It was also ruled by the legal authorities consulted on the occasion, that the survivors had a full right to place his body in consecrated ground.

The corpse was therefore brought from Arcetri to Santa Croce, and preparations were made *Preparations for the funeral.* for such a funeral as might best show the sense of the Court and the whole city of the greatness of their loss. The sum of three thousand crowns was quickly voted to cover the expense of a marble mausoleum. This and other particulars were instantly reported to the Holy Office at Rome. The *Interference of the Holy Office.* Ambassador of Tuscany received orders to communicate to the Grand Duke the Pope's opinion that his intention concerning Galileo's remains would, if carried out, prove most pernicious, and that he must remember that the said Galileo during his life had caused scandal to all Christendom by his false and damnable doctrine. Niccolini advised that the project both of a public funeral oration and a mausoleum be laid aside, at least for a time ; since, as the Pope claimed to be absolute master of all consecrated ground, it was likely that, by persevering to honor Galileo's remains so signally, the Grand Duke might draw down upon himself some such affront as had happened to the Duke of Mantua, on the occasion of the removal of the body of Countess Matilda, which it had been the Pope's pleasure to place in St. Peter's.

The Inquisition was all eyes and ears, fearing that the city would at least insist on the public funeral. The Inquisitor of Florence, Fanano, wrote to assure Cardinal Barberino, that, should it be absolutely impossible to prevent this, he would at least take care to follow out any orders which he might receive from Rome concerning the funeral oration and the epitaph.

So powerful was the opposition, that the Grand Duke felt himself forced to bend to it. The idea of both public funeral and monument was entirely laid aside, and the friends of the great philosopher were *Galileo's resting-place.* constrained to lay his beloved remains apart, in the chapel Del Noviziato, at the end of the corridor leading from the south transept to the great sacristy of Santa Croce. There, in an obscure corner on the Gospel side of the altar, the body rested for nearly a century, only rescued from oblivion by the epitaph placed by Pierozzi in 1656 ; to which was added what, indeed, for the honor of Florence might have well been wished away namely, the bust of Galileo in clay, painted in imitation of marble.

Vincenzio Viviani, determined to do public homage *Viviani's determina- tion to baffle the Inquisi- tion.* to his master's memory, and at the same time baffle the Inquisition, devised the plan of covering the façade of his own house in Via dell' Amore with laudatory inscriptions to the memory of Galileo. This, however, he did not venture to carry into effect till 1693. The bronze bust of the philosopher, which was placed at the same time as the inscriptions, was cast from a model in terra cotta, taken in 1611 by Caccini the sculptor, by desire of Cosmo II. when Galileo was in his prime.

Viviani died in 1703. By his will his property descended to his nephew Panzanini and his successors, charged with the condition of erecting a proper monument to Galileo in Santa Croce as soon as permission could be obtained to do so. Panzanini died in 1733, and the property passed to Nelli, then a *Erection of the monument in Santa Croce, 1737.* very young man, who, in 1737, carried out Viviani's pious intention, during the pontificate of Clement XII. (Lorenzo Corsini), a Florentine.

Viviani says of Galileo that he was of cheerful and pleasant countenance, especially in his old *Galileo's personal appearance.* age; square built, well proportioned, and rather above the middle height. His eyes were brilliant, and his hair was of a reddish hue. His constitution was naturally robust, but fatigue of mind and body occasioned various complaints by which he was often greatly reduced. He was subject to attacks of hypochondria, and was molested by many acute and dangerous illnesses, occasioned in great measure by his sleepless nights spent in celestial observations. For more than forty years of his life he was subject to severe attacks of rheumatism, and latterly to gout. Yet notwithstanding such a multitude of complaints as would have made a miserable valetudinarian of any other man, Galileo's industry was as remarkable as his genius : it was said that none had ever seen him idle.

There is evidence of the importance he attached to constant occupation, in his daughter's letters. Though his to her are lost, we can often guess the context by her answers. She frequently mentions all her different duties, adding that she knows he will be pleased to hear, that she has not an idle moment throughout the day, and that she daily finds the truth of his saying, that occupation is the best medicine for mind and body.

Galileo was fond of a country residence ; he was *His love of the country.* of opinion that the city was in a manner the prison of speculative genius ; that in the country alone was the book of Nature open to him who cared to read and learn from it ; he declared that the characters in which that book was written were those of geometry, and that, when once they were revealed, we might hope to penetrate Nature's deepest mysteries. His library was small, but such books as were in it were of the best : though he recommended the study of the ancient philosophers, he was wont to say that the principal doors into the garden of natural philosophy were observation and experiment, which could be opened with the keys of our senses.

Though he loved the quiet of a country residence, *Galileo's sociable disposition.* he was not the less fond of having the society of his friends, to whom he dispensed a hospitality equally removed from parsimoniousness and from extravagance. He never took a meal alone if he could have company. He was considered to be a great connoisseur in wines, and was diligent in tending and pruning his own vineyard ; gardening in all its branches was his favorite and almost sole relaxation from the severe studies which consumed his days and nights.　His demeanor was modest and unassuming: he neither depreciated nor envied the talent of other men, but gave to all their due, and more than their due.　Of self-praise so much is recorded of him by Gherardini, that, when his eyesight was decaying day by day, he endeavored to take comfort by saying that of all the sons of Adam none had seen *His only boast.* so much as he.　He never spoke of Aristotle in terms of contempt, as was the custom with some of his followers; but contented himself by saying that he did not find his method of reasoning satisfactory.　Of Kepler, whose extravagance was evident, he said, on being pressed for his opinion, that he was undoubtedly a great philosopher, but that his mode of philosophizing was vastly different to his own.　He exalted Plato to the skies, calling his eloquence "golden."　He also praised Pythagoras as unequaled among philosophers, but Archimedes was the only one of the ancients whom he called "master."　He was extremely fond of the writings of Ariosto, and was accustomed to say that reading Tasso after Ariosto was like eating cucumbers after melons.　Endowed with great tenacity of memory, he could repeat by heart a great *His great tenacity of memory.* part of the works of Virgil, Ovid, Horace, and Seneca; the sonnets of Petrarch, the *rime* of Berni, and the heroic stanzas of Ariosto, in whose " Gerusalemme Liberata " he found new beauties each time he read it.　Not to make the list of his attainments too long, we may say that there was no art, sci- *His versatility.* ence nor handicraft in which he was not superior to the generality of men professing them.　He protested that he had never met with a man so ignorant but that something might be learnt from him.　He was wont to say that it was the privilege of the sad not to be envied by the merry, and of the wicked not to be envied by the good. He was easily moved to *His temper and ready wit.* anger, but more easily pacified. His company was much desired and sought after, for his ready wit and pleasant discourse adorned even the most trifling subject brought forward. As a professor he was no less loved and valued than as a friend. However clear a subject might be to his own mind, he was not satisfied till he had made it as clear to the minds of his pupils. "From Signor Galileo," wrote Marsili, professor at Pisa in 1637, "I learnt more in three months than I did in as many years from other men." Such grateful testimony as the above is not wanting. "I thank God," said Paolo Aproino, "for having given me for a master the greatest man the world has ever seen." "When," wrote Ciampoli, after his retirement in disgrace to Montalto in 1634, "when shall I embrace you as a father, and listen to you as to an oracle !"

Pages might be filled with expressions of gratitude *His pupils' attachment and gratitude.* and affection such as these, culled from the correspondence of Galileo's disciples. And truly the great master himself might adjudge them to be of higher value as a testimony to his merit, than the marble monument under which his body now lies in Santa Croce.

APPENDIX.

I.

Sentence of the Tribunal of the Supreme Inquisition against Galileo Galilei, given the 22d day of June, of the year 1633.

We, Gasparo of Santa Croce in Gerusalemme, Borgia ;

Fra Felice Centino of S. Anastasia, called Ascoli ;

Guido of Santa Maria del Popolo, Bentivoglio ;

Fra Desiderio Scaglia of S. Carlo, called di Cremona ;

Fra Antonio Barberino, called di S. Onofrio ; [1]

Laudivio Zacchia of S. Pietro in Vincoli, called di San Sisto ;

Berlingero of S. Agostino, Gessi ;

Fabricio of S. Vincenzo *in pane e perna*, Verospi ;

Francesco di S. Lorenzo in Damaso, Barberino ; [2]

Marzio di Santa Maria Nuova, Ginetti ;

By the mercy of God Cardinals of the Holy Roman Church, Inquisitors of the Holy Apostolic See, in the whole Christian Republic specially deputed against heretical depravity :

It being the case that thou, Galileo, son of the late Vincenzio Galilei, a Florentine, now aged seventy, wast denounced in this Holy Office in 1615 :

That thou heldest as true the false doctrine taught by many, that the Sun was the centre of the universe and immovable, and that the Earth moved, and had also a diurnal motion : That on this same matter thou didst hold a correspondence with certain German mathematicians : [3] That thou hadst caused to be printed certain letters entitled " On the Solar Spots," in the which thou didst explain the said doctrine to be true : And that, to the

[1] Antonio Barberino, the Pope's brother.   He was a Capuchin.

[2] Francesco Barberino, the Pope's nephew.

[3] Welser and Kepler are alluded to.

objections put forth to thee at various times, based on and drawn from Holy Scripture, thou didst answer, commenting upon and explaining the said Scripture after thy own fashion : And thereupon following was presented (to this tribunal) a copy of a writing in form of a letter,[1] which was said to have been written by thee to such an one, at one time thy disciple, in which, following the position of Copernicus, are contained various propositions contrary to the true sense and authority of the Holy Scripture :

This Holy Tribunal desiring to obviate the disorder and mischief which had resulted from this, and which was constantly increasing to the prejudice of the Holy Faith ; by order of our Lord (Pope) and of the most Eminent Lords Cardinals of this supreme and universal Inquisition, the two propositions of the stability of the Sun and of the motion of the Earth were by the qualified theologians thus adjudged :

That the Sun is the centre of the universe and doth not move from his place is a proposition absurd and false in philosophy, and formally heretical ; being expressly contrary to Holy Writ : That the Earth is not the centre of the universe nor immovable, but that it moves, even with a diurnal motion, is likewise a proposition absurd and false in philosophy, and considered in theology *ad minus* erroneous in faith.

But being willing at that time to proceed with leniency towards thee, it was decreed in the Sacred Congregation held before Our Lord (Pope) on the 25th of February, 1616, that the most Eminent Lord Cardinal Bellarmine should order thee, that thou shouldst entirely leave and reject the said doctrine ; and thou refusing to do this, that the Commissary of the Holy Office should admonish thee to abandon the said doctrine, and that thou wast neither to teach it to others, nor to hold or defend it, to which precept, if thou didst not give heed, thou wast to be imprisoned : and in execution of the said decree, the following day in the palace and in the presence of the said most Eminent Lord Cardinal Bellarmine, after having been advised and admonished benignantly by the said Lord Cardinal, thou didst receive a precept from the then Father Commissary of the Holy Office in the presence of a notary and witnesses, that thou shouldst entirely abandon the said false opinion, and for the future neither uphold nor teach it in any manner whatever, either orally or in writing : and having promised obedience, thou wast dismissed.

[1] Galileo's letter to Benedetto Castelli.

And to the end that this pernicious doctrine might be rooted out and prevented from spreading, to the grave prejudice of Catholic truth, a decree was issued by the Sacred Congregation of the Index, prohibiting books which treated of the said doctrine, which was declared to be false and entirely contrary to Holy Scripture.

And there having lately appeared here a book printed in Florence this past year, whose superscription showeth thyself to be the author, the title being : "Dialogue of Galileo Galilei on the Two Great Systems of the World, the Ptolemaic and the Copernican :" and the Sacred Congregation having been informed that in consequence of the said book the false opinion of the mobility of the Earth and the stability of the Sun was daily gaining ground ; the said book was diligently examined, and was found openly to transgress the precept which had been made to thee, for that thou in the said book hadst defended the said already condemned opinion, which had been declared false before thy face : whereas thou in the said book by means of various subterfuges dost endeavor to persuade thyself that thou dost leave it undecided and merely probable. The which however is a most grave error, since in no way can an opinion be probable which has been declared and defined to be contrary to Holy Scripture.

Wherefore by Our order thou wast cited before this Holy Office, in which being examined upon oath, thou didst acknowledge thyself to have written and caused to be printed the said book. Thou didst confess that, ten or twelve years previously, after having received the precept above mentioned, thou didst begin to write the said book ; that thou didst ask for a license to print it, without signifying to those from whom thou didst receive such license, that thou hadst a precept forbidding thee to hold, defend, or teach in any way whatever such doctrine.

Thou didst likewise confess, that the said book is in more places than one so written that the reader might form an idea that the arguments brought forward in favor of the false opinion were pronounced in such guise that by their efficacy they were more apt to convince than easy to be overturned ; excusing thyself for having fallen into an error so alien, sayest thou, to thy intention, for that thou hadst written in form of a dialogue, and for the natural complacence with which each one doth view his own subtlety in showing himself more acute than the common herd of men in finding even for false propositions ingenious discourse to make them apparently probable.

And a convenient period having been assigned thee for thy defense, thou didst produce a certificate written by the hand of the most Eminent Lord Cardinal Bellarmine, procured by thee, as thou saidst, for the purpose of defending thyself from the calumnies of thy enemies, who had said that thou hadst abjured and hadst been punished by the Holy Office. In the which certificate it is written that thou hadst not abjured, neither hadst thou been subjected to punishment, but that only the declaration made by Our Lord (Pope) and published by the Sacred Congregation of the Index had been made known to thee, the which contains that the doctrine of the Earth's motion and of the stability of the Sun is contrary to Holy Scripture, and may therefore neither be defended nor held : and that whereas in the said certificate no mention was made of two particulars of the precept, to wit, *docere* and *quovis modo*, it was to be thought that in the course of fourteen or sixteen years thou hadst lost all remembrance of it ; and that for this same reason thou hadst been silent respecting the precept when thou didst ask for license to print the said book. And all this thou saidst not to excuse thy error, but that it might be attributed to a vain ambition rather than to malicious intent. But from the said precept produced in thy defense, thou hast aggravated thy fault ; whereas, the said opinion being therein declared contrary to Holy Writ, thou hast nevertheless dared to treat of it, to defend it, and to persuade that it was probable ; nor doth justify thee the license which thou didst extort with craft and cunning, not having notified the precept which had been given thee.

And, as it appeared to Us that thou hadst not said the whole truth concerning thy intention, We judged it to be necessary to proceed to the rigorous examination of thee, in which (without prejudice to any of the things confessed by thee, or deduced against thee, as above, respecting thy said intention) thou answeredst like a good Catholic. Therefore, having seen and maturely considered the merits of thy case, with thy above-mentioned confessions and excuses, We have adjudged against thee the herein-written definite sentence.

Invoking then the Most Holy Name of Our Lord Jesus Christ, and of His most glorious Mother Mary, ever Virgin, for this Our definite sentence, the which sitting *pro tribunali*, by the counsel and opinion of the Reverend Masters of theology and doctors of both laws, Our Counselors, we present in these writings, in the cause and causes currently before Us, between the magnificent Carlo Sinceri, doctor of both laws, procurator fiscal of this Holy Office on the one part, and thou Galileo Galilei, guilty, here present, confessed and judged, on the other part :

We say, pronounce, sentence, and declare, that thou, the said Galileo, by the things deduced during this trial, and by thee confessed as above, hast rendered thyself vehemently suspected of heresy by this Holy Office, that is, of having believed and held a doctrine which is false, and contrary to the Holy Scriptures, to wit : that the Sun is the centre of the universe, and that it does not move from east to west, and that the Earth moves and is not the centre of the universe : and that an opinion may be held and defended as probable after having been declared and defined as contrary to Holy Scripture ; and in consequence thou hast incurred all the censures and penalties of the Sacred Canons, and other Decrees both general and particular, against such offenders imposed and promulgated. From the which We are content that thou shouldst be absolved, if, first of all, with a sincere heart and unfeigned faith, thou dost before Us abjure, curse, and detest the above-mentioned errors and heresies, and any other error and heresy contrary to the Catholic and Apostolic Roman Church, after the manner that We shall require of thee.

And to the end that this thy grave error and transgression remain not entirely unpunished, and that thou mayst be more cautious for the future, and an example to others to abstain from and avoid similar offenses, We order that by a public edict the book of " Dialogues of Galileo Galilei " be prohibited, and We condemn thee to the prison of this Holy Office during Our will and pleasure ; and as a salutary penance We enjoin on thee that for the space of three years thou shalt recite once a week the Seven Penitential Psalms, reserving to Ourselves the faculty of moderating, changing, or taking from, all or part of the above-mentioned pains and penalties.

And thus We say, pronounce, declare, order, condemn, and

reserve in this and in any other better way and form which by right We can and ought.

Ita pronunciamus nos Cardinalis infrascripti.

F. CARDINALIS DE ASCULO.

G. CARDINALIS BENTIVOLIUS.

D. CARDINALIS DE CREMONA.

A. CARDINALIS S. HONUPHRI.

B. CARDINALIS GYPSIUS.

F. CARDINALIS VEROSPIUS.

M. CARDINALIS GINETTUS.

II.

GALILEO'S ABJURATION.

I, Galileo Galilei, son of the late Vincenzio Galilei of Florence, aged seventy years, tried personally by this court, and kneeling before You, the most Eminent and Reverend Lords Cardinals, Inquisitors-General throughout the Christian Republic against heretical depravity, having before my eyes the Most Holy Gospels, and laying on them my own hands ; I swear that I have always believed, I believe now, and with God's help I will in future believe all which the Holy Catholic and Apostolic Church doth hold, preach, and teach. But since I, after having been admonished by this Holy Office entirely to abandon the false opinion that the Sun was the centre of the universe and immovable, and that the Earth was not the centre of the same and that it moved, and that I was neither to hold, defend, nor teach in any manner whatever, either orally or in writing, the said false doctrine ; and after having received a notification that the said doctrine is contrary to Holy Writ, I did write and cause to be printed a book in which I treat of the said already condemned doctrine, and bring forward arguments of much efficacy in its favor, without arriving at any solution : I have been judged vehemently suspected of heresy, that is, of having held and believed that the Sun is the centre of the universe and immovable, and that the Earth is not the centre of the same, and that it does move.

Nevertheless, wishing to remove from the minds of your Eminences and all faithful Christians this vehement suspicion reasonably conceived against me, I abjure with a sincere heart and unfeigned faith, I curse and detest the said errors and heresies, and generally all and every error and sect contrary to the Holy Catholic Church. And I swear that for the future I will neither say nor assert in speaking or writing such things as may bring upon me similar suspicion ; and if I know any heretic, or one suspected of heresy, I will denounce him to this Holy Office, or to the Inquisitor and Ordinary of the place in which I may be. I also swear and promise to adopt and observe entirely all the penances which have been or may be by this Holy Office imposed on me. And if I contravene any of these said promises, protests, or oaths, (which God forbid !) I submit myself to all the pains and penalties which by the Sacred Canons and other Decrees general and particular are against such offenders imposed and promulgated. So help me God and the Holy Gospels, which I touch with my own hands. I, Galileo Galilei aforesaid, have abjured, sworn, and promised, and hold myself bound as above ; and in token of the truth, with my own hand have subscribed the present schedule of my abjuration, and have recited it word by word. In Rome, at the Convent della Minerva, this 22d day of June, 1633.

I, GALILEO GALILEI, have abjured as
above, with my own hand.